Pboro 4|13   2 4 AUG

1 3 AUG 2015

D0539518

PETERBOROUGH LIBRARIES

24 Hour renewal line 08458 505606

This book is to be returned on or before the latest date shown above, but may be renewed up to three times if the book is not in demand. Ask at your local library for details.

Please note that charges are made on overdue books

KNIGHT
CRUSADER

Ronald Welch

ILLUSTRATED BY

William Stobbs

OXFORD
UNIVERSITY PRESS

OXFORD
UNIVERSITY PRESS

Great Clarendon Street, Oxford OX2 6DP

Oxford University Press is a department of the University of Oxford.
It furthers the University's objective of excellence in research, scholarship,
and education by publishing worldwide in

Oxford New York

Auckland Cape Town Dar es Salaam Hong Kong Karachi
Kuala Lumpur Madrid Melbourne Mexico City Nairobi
New Delhi Shanghai Taipei Toronto

With offices in

Argentina Austria Brazil Chile Czech Republic France Greece
Guatemala Hungary Italy Japan Poland Portugal Singapore
South Korea Switzerland Thailand Turkey Ukraine Vietnam

Oxford is a registered trade mark of Oxford University Press
in the UK and in certain other countries

British Library Cataloguing in Publication Data
Data available

ISBN: 978-0-19-279357-7

Contents

Foreword   ix

PART ONE

1.   Jusuf Al-Hafiz   3
2.   Jerusalem   29
3.   The Fight By the Pool of Siloam   48
4.   The High Court   71
5.   War   94
6.   The Wells of Saffaria   110
7.   The March to Tiberias   124
8.   The Battle of Hattin   145
9.   Saladin   166

PART TWO

10. Damascus   175
11. The Assassins   202
12. Krak des Chevaliers   226
13. Richard of England   239
14. Peter de Chaworth   255
15. The Battle of Arsuf   266

PART THREE

16. The Joust at Cardiff Castle   283
17. Kidwelly Castle   307
18. The Storming of Llanstephan Castle   328
19. The Fight on the Dais   345

Historical Note   354

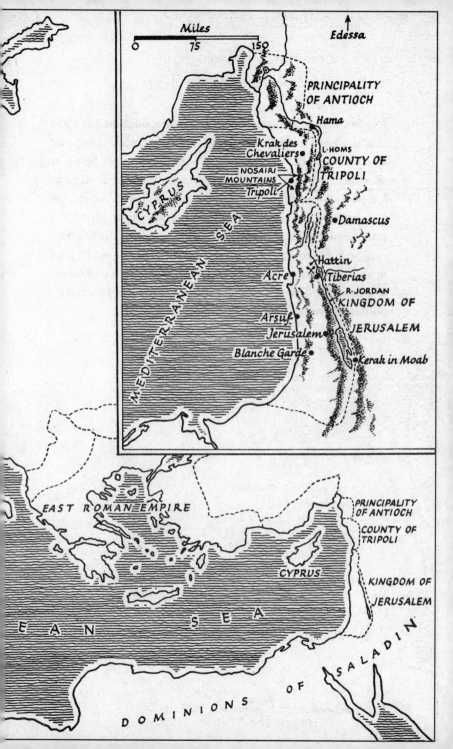

A Note on the Text

Knight Crusader by Ronald Welch was first published in 1954 and has been a much-loved and highly-regarded novel ever since, winning the prestigious Carnegie Medal in its first year of publication. The book is set during a very specific time in history and Ronald Welch has portrayed the battles, landscape, and language accurately, while at the same time giving the reader a truly great adventure to enjoy. Sometimes the language may be difficult, and some words in the text would not be used in any book written today, but *Knight Crusader* is a true classic and therefore deserves to be published in its original form with nothing altered or omitted.

Foreword

THE Holy Land was reconquered from the Seljuk Turks by the First Crusade at the end of the eleventh century. The Crusaders who remained in the East founded the Latin kingdom of Jerusalem, or *OUTREMER*, the land 'across the sea', as they called it in their medieval French.

A hundred years later the kingdom was still ruled by the Christians, but their hold was a precarious one. Outremer was only a narrow strip of land along the coast, and exposed at many points to counter-attacks by the Turks. To guard against this danger, the Crusaders built a chain of castles to cover the most dangerous positions. These huge fortresses were garrisoned by the descendants of the early Crusaders, or by the fighting monks of the two military orders of the Templars and the Hospitallers. By 1185 the kingdom was in great danger. The Crusaders were very short of men, and the Turks had at last found a leader in Saladin. He united them, and was ready to preach a Holy War against Outremer.

PART ONE

Chapter One
JUSUF AL-HAFIZ

PHILIP D'AUBIGNY rode a few yards ahead of his two men servants. The sun was beginning to set, and the three horses and their riders threw long, dark shadows across the reddish earth. The air was hot and still, and the dust drifted away sluggishly, leaving behind a long trail to mark the way they had come.

Philip was hot. He was damp and sticky with sweat, his lips and throat were dry, and his face and hands, as well as his clothes, were powdered thickly with the reddish colour of the dust that never left them. But the discomfort did not cause him much concern. He had been born in Outremer, and was accustomed to the great heat of the summer, though he still disliked it intensely. Instead, he was thinking of the pleasant week he had just spent at the castle of Montgizard, with his cousins, the Grandmesnils.

Sir Fulk, his uncle, had been as kind and amusing as usual; his cousin, Joscelin, had dazzled them all with his new clothes, for he fancied himself as one of the most fashionable young knights, and not even the most blistering of criticisms from Sir Fulk prevented Joscelin from trying some new design of shoe or cloak. They had ridden out with their hawks, hunted in the hills around Montgizard, and practised with sword and horse in the great courtyard of the castle.

And in the evening, up on the high dais in the hall, Sir Fulk had aired his pessimistic views about the likelihood of war again with the Infidels, and the dangerous position of the Latin kingdom of Jerusalem. The new leader of the Infidels, the Emir Saladin, so Philip gathered, was preparing for war. If his uncle was right, Philip thought, he might not have very long to wait now before he took part in his first real battle.

The road dropped abruptly into a narrow valley. Philip twitched his reins, and brought his horse to a walking pace. The road had been like this all day, a switchback winding through a tangle of bare, sun-baked hills and rocky valleys. Ahead, at a distance of several miles, he could pick out the odd, dome-shaped pinnacle of rock that looked down to his father's castle of Blanche Garde. They would be home in less than two hours, and in good time for the evening meal. It would be pleasant to bathe and change his clothes,

Philip decided, as he wriggled himself into a more comfortable position in his high saddle.

'Two horsemen ahead, my lord,' Llewellyn said from behind.

'Where? Oh, I can see them.'

Two black specks disappeared in a turn of the road about a mile ahead. They must be moving slowly, Philip thought. He would catch up with them in a short time.

'Venetian traders, I expect,' he said idly.

'Or robbers,' Llewellyn said. 'I heard there were some on this part of the road.'

'Yes, I remember now,' Philip said. 'Better keep closed up. Michael, see to your bow.'

Michael, the Syrian archer, nodded, and his white teeth showed in a smile against the swarthy brown of his face. There was no need to give any warning or advice to Llewellyn, Philip thought, as he glanced at his servant. For Llewellyn was a veteran soldier, tough, reliable, and imperturbable; his equipment immaculate and shining. Like his master, he had been born in Outremer, a mixture of Welsh, Norman, and Saxon blood. His face was burnt to a deep brown, nearly as dark as Michael's, and a sword cut had left a long, whitish-grey scar down his left cheek, reaching to the corner of his mouth, and giving him a queer, lop-sided kind of smile.

For Philip he had a great affection, and he treated his young master with an odd mixture of respect and reproof. One moment he would address him politely as 'my lord', and the next minute, with almost the same breath, roar at him in the tones of a sergeant major rebuking a raw recruit; for he had taught Philip to handle a horse and sword, and accompanied him on all his journeys.

Philip could not see the two travellers ahead now. He felt the hilt of his sword. The long blade slid easily in the well greased leather of the scabbard. He was in plain riding clothes, without armour of any kind, though Llewellyn and Michael wore helmets and thick leather coats. He supposed he should be making a careful plan to deal with the robbers, if robbers they were, in front. That was what his father would have done, of course, and Philip sighed. He would never reach Sir Hugo's standard, he thought regretfully; and then he grinned at the memory of the last withering rebuke he had received from his father. 'Excitable, impulsive, scatter-brained young squire' had been part of the reproof that had descended upon his head. Well, he would try to be more careful this time. But he had a suspicion that at the first sign of danger he would charge off like an arrow from Michael's bow, and heaven alone knew what trap he would run into.

The track narrowed at this point, and then swung sharply to the right, winding, as Philip knew, like a snake for the next half mile through a tumbled mass of rocks that rose to a considerable height on either side. There could not be a better spot for an ambush by robbers on the whole road.

Philip heard the faint 'whirr' as Llewellyn drew his sword. The little party rode on slowly, their eyes flickering warily from right to left.

'Listen!' Philip cried. He pulled his horse to a sudden halt, and they all cocked their heads, listening.

The faint cry that Philip had heard was repeated. Then it was followed by a louder scream; that of a man in agony or overwhelming fear. It had hardly died away before Philip acted. He ripped out his sword and urged his horse forward with a vigorous kick from his sharply pointed spurs.

'Wait, my lord!' Llewellyn bellowed. 'It may be a trap!'

But he was too late. Philip was already out of sight around the bend. Llewellyn cursed fluently, and added a few phrases about the stupidity of foolhardy young squires. But he, too, wasted no time. With a curt order over his shoulder to Michael, he dashed after Philip.

Philip was enjoying himself. The sudden change of pace after the leisurely ride had filled him with a feeling of exhilaration. The wind of his charge fanned his cheeks as he bent low in the saddle, one hand on the reins, and the other swinging his sword gently, feeling the weight and balance of the long blade.

Then the track straightened, and he was in the midst of the ambush before he had time to pick out more than a fleeting impression of what was happening.

Two horses were rearing immediately ahead. One was riderless, with a limp figure on the ground by its side. Another man was swinging a sword from the saddle of the second horse, while two white-robed men were hacking at him from both sides with long, curved knives.

Philip had seen similar incidents before. One of the

robbers was trying to work his way behind, where he could hamstring the horse. Once the rider was down, his throat would be cut, and his baggage rifled.

The other robber heard the drumming of hooves, and leapt round. He saw Philip racing towards him, a long, gleaming blade swinging up in the air. He tried to jump to one side, clear of the sweep of the sword. He was a repulsive figure, filthy, pockmarked, his robes stained with dust and dirt, and his head swathed in a grimy turban.

Philip took the turban as his target. His horse was galloping at full speed now, and it was no easy task to hit such a small, moving object as a man's head. It demanded superb control of the horse and perfect timing of the blow.

But Philip had not practised for many weary hours in the courtyard at Blanche Garde for nothing. He let his well-trained horse have its head. His arm came up and back in a leisurely sweep of arm and wrist, while he kept his eyes rigidly fixed on the top of the turban. Then he brought the sword down with the instinctive sense of timing that not even years of tuition can teach. The robber flung up his arm helplessly, his face a mask of fear and snarling fury. But there was nothing he could do to ward off this thunderbolt of sudden death that had swept upon him. He went down with a strangled scream as Philip's sword caught him full across his turban, and split his skull with a sound like that of a hammer smashing down on a length of thin planking.

Philip tugged hard on his reins. His horse reared up on

its forelegs, swinging round under the steady guidance of the bridle. The scene had changed in those few seconds since Philip had burst into view. The second rider was falling back from his saddle as his horse went down under the knife of the second robber.

The thief glanced round, saw Philip on top of him, and raced for the shelter of the rocks where no horse could follow. He was half-way to safety when a deep *twang* came from behind Philip. The feathered shaft of an arrow appeared as if by magic in the fellow's back. He flung up his arms, yelled like a fiend in torment, and fell forward on his face, suddenly transformed from a swiftly moving man into an untidy bundle of dirty white robes that lay across the track.

'Good shot, Michael!' Philip shouted, and jumped down from his horse. He sheathed his sword, and bent over the rider who had first gone down.

A second's glance was enough. Philip had seen dead men before in his short life. He shrugged his shoulders, and went across to the second man.

'Still alive,' Philip muttered, as he turned over the limp figure.

Then he stiffened, and ran his eyes over the man with sudden interest. This was no Christian or Venetian merchant. And equally certain, he was no Syrian native, or even one of the numerous half-breeds who had grown up in Outremer from the mingling of Western and Syrian blood.

This was a Seljuk Turk, and a nobleman, too, to judge by the richness of his clothes; a leader of the people against whom the Crusaders had fought for over a century.

'Llewellyn!' Philip said sharply.

There was no reply. Philip looked up impatiently. Llewellyn and Michael were bending over the two dead robbers, methodically running their hands through the men's clothes in search of money or jewellery.

'Leave them alone, Llewellyn,' Philip said curtly. 'And bring me a wineskin—no, a waterskin—from my horse. This fellow's still alive.'

Reluctantly Llewellyn stood up, and went towards Philip's horse, while his master dragged the unconscious man to the side of the track, and pillowed his head against a convenient rock.

Philip was thinking that it might be wiser to give him water. Not all the Infidels obeyed the strict rule of their religion about drinking no wine, but this was a nobleman.

As he waited for Llewellyn, Philip wiped away a trickle of blood from the Turk's forehead. He was wondering what had brought the man so close to the coast. A few years ago there would have been nothing unusual in such a visit. Christians and Turks moved freely in time of truce through each other's territories, and many Seljuks had stayed at Blanche Garde as guests of Sir Hugo. But since Saladin had begun his career of conquest in Egypt, and had welded the Turks into one formidable nation, few Infidels had been seen inland, not even to the east of Jerusalem where the vague and undefined frontiers of Outremer merged into the great belt of the desert.

Llewellyn handed him a waterskin, and Philip splashed water over the Turk's face, and then tried to force some between his lips. His rough and ready doctoring seemed to be effective, for the man's eyelids flickered, and then opened.

'You are quite safe,' Philip said hastily in his fluent Arabic. 'We are friends. Better drink this. You have had a nasty blow on the head.'

The Turk nodded. With one hand on Philip's shoulder, he pulled himself up to a sitting position, and then gulped down the water. Philip watched him with interest, noting the high brow under the silk turban, the thin arched nose above the neatly trimmed and pointed beard, and the long slender fingers that held the waterskin.

The Turk sighed, and looked up again. Some colour had returned to his dark cheeks, and he smiled.

'I will repay you for that drink one day, if Allah wills,' he said. His brown eyes inspected the scene on the track, the two bodies of the thieves, and the still figure of his servant. 'I owe you my life, too, sir Frank,' he said. 'I am Jusuf Al-Hafiz, and my father is the Emir Usamah Ibn-Menquidh, a friend of the great Emir Saladin.'

Philip put out his hand impulsively, as was his habit. He liked the look of the Turk.

'Oh, that's nothing, Sir Jusuf,' he exclaimed in his hurried and jerky way of speaking, as if he were afraid that he might not have time to finish a sentence. 'I am Philip d'Aubigny. My father is Sir Hugo d'Aubigny of Blanche

Garde, a Baron of the High Court of the Kingdom of Jerusalem. Are you feeling better now?'

Jusuf stood up, swaying slightly, with one hand to his forehead.

'You'd better ride to Blanche Garde with us,' Philip said. 'It's only a few miles from here, and my father will gladly entertain you until you are well enough to travel again.'

Despite his aching head, the Turk bowed gracefully. 'I shall be honoured, Sir Philip,' he said, his full red lips parting in a friendly smile.

'Oh, I'm not a knight yet!' Philip exclaimed. 'Only a squire. I expect father will ask the King to knight me in about two or three years' time. When I am twenty.'

He chatted away busily as they rode towards Blanche Garde. Jusuf Al-Hafiz said little. But he listened attentively, watching Philip's expressive face, smiling and nodding gravely when necessary, his long brown fingers stroking his beard, or flicking away the dust that settled on his clothes, with all the dainty neatness of some sleek cat.

Although he did not know it, Philip was being sized up by a shrewd and experienced observer. Perhaps if he had known, he would not have behaved otherwise, for Philip had no illusions about his appearance. 'No beauty' was Joscelin's description; but there were few who could cut much of a figure compared to that elegant young knight.

What the Turk saw was a thickset young man, wide of shoulder, and unusually long in the arm, with a determined and obstinate chin, a pair of very steady grey eyes, and a big curving nose that dominated his face. The astute and cultured Turkish nobleman felt that this young squire might well develop into a leader of men one day.

'Blanche Garde!' Philip cried.

A wide valley lay below them, a strip of green running through the monotonous brown of the surrounding hills. A broad stream meandered lazily down the length of the valley with the scattered houses of the little township on either side, whitewashed buildings with flat roofs, and in the centre the mosque-like church.

Through the town went the main highway from the coast to Jerusalem. Philip's grandfather had built his castle here to protect this favourite route of pilgrims and merchants moving inland from the busy port of Ascalon, and had sited the fortress with care. On one side the high curtain walls rose sheer from the stream, and a natural fall of the rocky ground covered another flank which would have given any attacking force a difficult approach, for the stream widened there and sprawled out over a wide marsh.

The walls of Blanche Garde had been white once, but a hundred years had toned them now to a light grey. Indeed, from the direction in which Philip and Jusuf were approaching, straight into the setting sun, the castle was a mass of sharp black lines silhouetted against the glare.

Sentries sprang to attention as Philip led Jusuf through the huge gatehouse and across the wide inner ward to the foot of the old keep, which was now the main residential part of the castle. Syrian servants ran out to hold the horses, and to unload the baggage.

The great hall was cool and shady after the glare and heat of the sun. More servants were laying the tables for the evening meal, and Philip told the steward to lay an additional place on the high table for Jusuf.

'We're late, Sir Jusuf,' Philip said anxiously. 'Father is very particular about punctuality at meals. Do you mind changing quickly?'

Jusuf smiled as he saw the expression on Philip's worried face, and the smile almost developed into a grin, if such a dignified man could have given way to such a weakness.

'Of course not, Philip,' he said. 'If you will show me to my room ...'

Philip swept him across the hall, up a spiral staircase, and shouting to Llewellyn, bustled his guest into a room in the tower.

Once in his own room, Philip pulled off his dusty clothes, and hurled them carelessly on chair or bed, while Llewellyn poured hot water into a metal bath.

'How much did you find on the robbers?' Philip asked as he splashed luxuriously in the warm water.

Llewellyn grunted with disgust. 'Two bezants only, my lord. And Michael has those now.'

'Why? What about your share?'

'We diced for them, my lord.' Llewellyn's scarred cheek lifted in a grimace of annoyance. 'And Michael won. He always does.'

Philip grinned, and dripped water all over the floor as he clambered out of the bath. He dried himself hurriedly on the rough towel, snatched at the long stockings that Llewellyn gave him, ducked his head into the silk cotte, or loose coat that fell to his ankles, and then put his arms into a wide sur-coat with huge sleeves. Llewellyn buckled a narrow belt around his waist, while Philip dabbed at his hair with a comb, trying to reduce his dark and unruly hair to some reasonable state of tidiness, otherwise Sir Hugo would have something to say about scruffy young squires.

Jusuf was ready, bathed and changed, his beard freshly combed, his clothes well fitting and immaculate, as if he had spent several hours over his toilet.

'Father will be in the solar,' Philip said, and darted down the narrow stairs.

The solar was the private apartment of the lord of the castle, and at Blanche Garde was built immediately behind the hall, with a door leading on to the dais and the high table. There was little of the bleak discomfort of the West about Sir Hugo d'Aubigny's solar, for he had adopted the luxurious and more highly civilized habits of the East.

The large room was bright with silken hangings, the floors covered with rugs, and the chairs filled with coloured cushions. A painted ceiling gave the whole apartment a feeling of coolness and space, and as Blanche Garde was no longer in the front line of the fortresses of Outremer, the windows were wider than usual, and let in some of the evening sun and the cool breeze that sprang up at night.

As Philip ushered his guest into the room, the group of men by the big, empty fireplace broke off their conversation, and turned their heads towards the door. There were the usual guests and passing knights and barons of Outremer, and among them two knights of the Military Order of the Hospitallers, Sir Miles de Plancy, and Sir Amaury de Bethsan, both in their black cloaks with the white crosses on the shoulder.

Philip saw them with dismay. Like the other great Crusading Order of the Templars, the Hospitallers were fighting monks, recruited for a life of warfare against the Infidel. They had no patience with the friendly attitude of many Barons of Outremer for the Turks; their feelings were those of fanatical hatred. Neither de Plancy nor de Bethsan, as Philip knew too well, would be pleased to find themselves sitting down to dinner with a Seljuk Turk.

Jusuf advanced slowly across the room behind Philip. He may have been conscious of the disdainful attitude of some of the men there, but he showed no sign of it as he bowed gracefully to the tall silent man standing in front of the fireplace.

Philip had a great admiration and affection for his father, perhaps because Sir Hugo possessed all those qualities which he was so anxious to acquire himself. The Lord of Blanche Garde was a fine and imposing figure in his rich Eastern robes and sandals, his face burnt a dark brown by a lifetime in Outremer. But for his name, there was little to show that he was a pure-blooded Norman nobleman, and he seemed to have acquired some of the impassiveness of the East in his manners too, as he greeted Jusuf in perfect Arabic, and with a quiet courtesy.

Philip plunged into a hurried and excitable account of what had happened on the road from Montgizard. Sir Hugo listened gravely. He was a man of few words, though he could be forceful enough when he wished.

'You have done well, Philip,' he said. 'But you rushed in as recklessly as usual, it seems. Ah, the trumpets are sounding for dinner. Sir Jusuf?' He waved a hand towards the door, and swept into the hall.

The Hospitallers drew their long cloaks aside as Jusuf Al-Hafiz followed Sir Hugo, and their brick-red faces flushed with anger. But the Turk was their fellow guest, and they swallowed their feelings with some difficulty. Philip grinned, and fell in at the end of the small procession.

Sir Hugo dined in considerable state in his castle, with a silken canopy above his head, and his table covered with silver and glassware, the finest that the craftsmen of the East could produce. Each course of the elaborate meal was preceded by a trumpet call and a procession up the floor of the hall from the kitchen at the far end.

Philip, as a squire, listened to the conversation in silence. The guests would obviously have liked to discuss the changing military position, for the news from the frontiers was depressing. But they could hardly do so with Jusuf present. Fortunately both Christian and Turk had much in common, and they all talked readily enough about hunting, falconry, horses, and weapons, while Jusuf spoke of his experiences in Egypt. He pleaded an aching head towards the end of the meal, and begged to be excused. A servant led him to his room, and silence fell on the high table. It was broken by Miles de Plancy. He was a corpulent and red-faced man, with an expression of obstinate stupidity, and he leant forward excitedly towards his host.

'What's that fellow doing so close to the coast, Sir Hugo?' he barked angrily. 'Up to no good, you know, up to no good!'

Amaury de Bethsan wagged his grizzled head in agreement. Sir Hugo was peeling fruit with great care, and did not even look up.

'I don't suppose he is,' he said placidly.

'But what's he doing here?' repeated Sir Miles wrathfully.

Sir Hugo laid down his knife, and wiped his fingers fastidiously on a napkin that Llewellyn held out for him.

'Spying, very probably,' he said calmly.

The Hospitallers gobbled like turkeys, their faces purple with irritation. Philip stared at his father in amazement.

'Spying?' he exclaimed. 'But why, father? We've had Turks staying at Blanche Garde before this.'

'Of course, Philip. But not for some time. They've been too busy lately, fighting with Saladin to unite Islam. Now they are ready.'

'Of course they are!' snapped Sir Miles. 'And we sit

about waiting for them!' He drained a glass of wine and banged the stem down on the table with almost enough force to break the slender glass.

Sir Hugo watched the fate of his precious Damascus glass with some anxiety before resuming his meal. He reached for a dish of figs and dates, and went on eating quietly while the argument raged around him. Philip had a shrewd suspicion that his father had his own very definite opinions on the subject, but could not be bothered to argue with his guests. Sir Hugo, he knew, did not suffer fools gladly.

'What would Jusuf be looking for, sir?' Philip asked. 'I mean, what sort of information does he want?' he added nervously, wondering if his father would treat him as a fool too.

But Sir Hugo seldom did that to Philip; he might tell his son how stupidly rash he was, or how talkative, or how much he had to learn, but he always answered his questions seriously.

'Oh, he might want to know something about the strength of the various castles, the number of their garrisons, the state of the roads; a hundred items useful to a good general like Saladin.'

The other guests, now that Jusuf's restraining presence had gone, were discussing the latest news. One of them was on his way to the coast from Jerusalem, and had a good deal to say about opinion in the capital.

'The news is bad,' he said gloomily.

'Bad!' snorted Sir Miles. 'It's time we fought the cursed

Infidels again. This truce has lasted long enough. We didn't come to Outremer to live at peace with the fellows.'

'But they will put a huge army in the field, Sir Miles,' ventured the other knight.

'Pooh!' Sir Miles waved away the Infidel hordes with a pudgy hand. 'Why worry about that? We shall beat the Infidels. We always have before!'

Sir Hugo looked at his guest with barely suppressed irritation.

'What are we going to beat them with, Miles?' he asked.

Sir Amaury turned in surprise, his blue eyes popping. 'What with? With our knights, of course, Sir Hugo.'

'How many have you in the garrison at Ascalon?' Sir Hugo asked.

'Oh, about twenty.'

'And at Ibelin?'

'Fifteen. Below strength, of course,' Sir Miles admitted.

'Exactly. And you will find the same story all over Outremer. What can we put in the field?' Sir Hugo demanded, pushing aside the bowl of fruit. 'A thousand knights? Certainly not more.'

The guests nodded gloomily. It was the old story, the continual weakness of Outremer, this frightening shortage of men. Recruits from the West came in a thin trickle, even to the two great Military Orders.

'You can't have it both ways,' Sir Hugo said. 'Either we garrison the castles, and have no army in the field, or else we strip the castles for a campaign, and have no garrisons.'

The argument continued, while Philip nodded in his seat, for he was tired after his ride. He had heard this all before, too, and there seemed to be no solution. The heavily armoured knights were the main striking force of any army at that time, though, of course, infantry and archers were essential. But infantry was not the problem in Outremer; a large enough force could be raised fairly easily; the shortage of knights was the nightmare hanging over the Christians.

'What shall I do with Jusuf tomorrow, father?' Philip asked after dinner.

'Take him out hawking. I shall probably come with you.'

Philip nodded, though there must have been some doubt in his face, for his father smiled.

'Afraid of what he will see? I shouldn't worry. We have nothing to hide, and if we had, I expect Jusuf would soon find it out. He seems an intelligent fellow.'

The other guests had left when Sir Hugo and Philip rode out with Jusuf, hawks on their wrists, and falconers behind them. The main road was crowded with traffic, long trains of horses and mules moving in both directions, for there was a brisk and thriving trade now between East and West. There were the usual pilgrims, too, for this was the shortest route from the coast to the Holy City. Some of the richer pilgrims rode, but the majority were on foot. Philip admired these men of all nationalities and ages, trudging steadily along under the hot sun, haversack on back, staff in hand, with their grey cloaks and round, felt hats. The hats were his chief interest, for he had learned to recognize the different badges worn by the pilgrims, which showed the different shrines they had visited.

One venerable old man stopped Philip. His long white hair flowed from under his hat, for pilgrims often took a vow not to shave or cut their hair until they had accomplished their pilgrimage.

'Can you tell me the nearest place I can spend the night, my lord?' he asked. 'My feet are badly swollen, and I can walk no farther today.'

'You can stay at my father's castle of Blanche Garde,' Philip said. 'Over the brow of the hill. The steward will give you some ointment for your feet, too.'

He ran his eyes over the old man's hat. This was no ordinary pilgrim, he thought, for the hat band was nearly covered with the little badges of the famous shrines he had visited. There was the image of the miraculous handkerchief with the face of Christ on it, which was given to those who had been to Rome; the more unusual emblems of the cockle-shell of Compostella, and the head of John the Baptist from Amiens, and several others. But there was one that was strange to Philip.

'What pilgrimage is that?' he asked, pointing. 'Is it the figure of some saint?'

'That is the shrine of St David, my lord.'

'St David?' Philip was puzzled. 'Where is that?'

'His shrine is in Wales, my lord. But you will not have heard of that country, I expect. It is a small land in the far corner of England.'

Philip leant forward eagerly. 'Wales!' he exclaimed excitedly. 'But I have heard of it! My grandfather came from there when he rode on the First Crusade. Do you know a castle called Llanstephan?'

The old pilgrim looked up at the eager face bending down from the Arab horse. He smiled, and his face broke into a network of fine wrinkles.

'I spent a night at Llanstephan on the way to St David's, my lord,' he said. 'It is the home of the d'Aubigny family.'

Philip was tremendously excited. He was on the point of pouring out a flood of questions when he heard a shout. He looked impatiently over his shoulder. Sir Hugo was waving to him from the distance.

'Oh, I must go!' Philip said. 'But I will speak with you tonight. Ask at Blanche Garde for Ivo the Steward. Say I sent you. I am Philip d'Aubigny.'

He turned his horse and galloped up the road to join his father and Jusuf.

'Father!' he cried. 'That pilgrim has been to Wales! He spent a night at Llanstephan. I asked him to wait for me at Blanche Garde. Think of it! He's actually been to Llanstephan, and I meet him here on this road!'

'Indeed,' Sir Hugo said indifferently. 'He must have come a long way. I will make him a present.'

Philip was not surprised or particularly downcast by his father's lack of interest. After all, why should Sir Hugo be at all curious about Wales or Llanstephan? He had never seen them, and he probably never would. His whole life had been spent in Outremer; he was the lord of a rich fief and a strong castle; his future was bound up with the East, not with the distant country where his father had once lived as a boy.

Sir Hugo beckoned to Philip and Jusuf, and they turned off the main road to follow a track that would lead them to the marshes. The falconers, with the hawks gripping fast to their wrists, trotted on ahead, while Sir Hugo paused at the crest of the hill.

'You can see Ascalon from here, Sir Jusuf,' he said. 'It is a fine view.'

The port was a faint blur in the distance, with the harder line of the coast to mark the boundary of Outremer. Tumbled hills and ravines, brown and bare, with hardly a tree to break the monotony of the savage landscape, marched steadily towards the coast in endless succession, shimmering in a blinding haze of heat.

'We can signal to Ascalon from the gatehouse of Blanche Garde,' Sir Hugo continued. 'And to Montgizard and Beth Gibelin as well. But that is nothing unusual, of course. Krak des Chevaliers, in Lebanon, can signal to Safita and Castel Rouge, just as the castles of Tiberias, Saphet, Subeiba and Toron are all within sight of one another.'

Jusuf's long fingers played with his beard, while for a

moment his brown eyes met and caught Sir Hugo's steady glance. The two men half smiled.

'Interesting,' Jusuf said. 'But then I believe the Lord Reynaud de Chatillon can signal by fires from his castle of Kerak to King David's tower at Jerusalem?'

'Oh yes,' Sir Hugo said. 'Very useful in an emergency, you see.'

'Very useful,' agreed Jusuf gravely.

He shook his reins, and fell in beside Sir Hugo as they cantered after the falconers. The two had understood each other well, thought Philip. But it was just as well to remind the Seljuks how skilfully the great chain of castles had been sited for the protection of the Kingdom.

Philip sent for the old pilgrim after they returned to Blanche Garde. The steward had reported the arrival of the old fellow, and said that he had been treated well, and his feet attended to.

Philip waved the pilgrim to a stool when Llewellyn brought him up to the circular room in the tower.

'What is your name?' Philip asked.

'Walter, my lord. I am sometimes called Walter of the Mill, or Walter of York.'

'York? Where is that?'

'In the north of England, my lord. It is an important city, and has a great cathedral.'

Philip handed the old man a slate. 'Draw a map of England for me, Walter,' he said. 'Mark in York, and then Llanstephan.'

Walter scratched a crude drawing of England on the slate, while Philip leant forward to begin his first lesson in the geography of his native country.

'And Wales?' he asked, when the old man had shown him the position of York and some of the more important cities of England. 'Tell me what the country is like. It is very different to this, isn't it?'

Walter's face crinkled with amusement. 'Yes, my lord, there is a great difference.' He paused to collect his thoughts. How could he give this pleasant young nobleman even the most fleeting and vague conception of England in a few words? He looked through the narrow slit-window let into the thick walls of the lofty tower.

There was a superb view from that height, across the valley of Blanche Garde, over the cluster of flat-topped houses, the dull green of the marsh, and then to the rolling succession of bare hills, brown and treeless, sweltering under the fierce sun that beat down from a steely blue sky.

Philip watched the old man's placid expression, the faded blue eyes, and the general air of contentment. Walter must have led a hard and dangerous life, tramping through Christendom, passing from one country to another, with no settled home, no family, and no ties. But his experiences seemed to have left nothing save this air of tranquillity.

Walter turned back from the window. 'England is a green country, my lord,' he said. 'Grey mists, soft rain, even in the summer. The trees are everywhere, heavy with leaf, and the valleys are deep and moist. Even the hillsides themselves are green. I wish you could see an English wood as I have, my lord, on a summer's day, when the wild flowers are in bloom, and you can hear the bees at their work.'

Philip nodded. His imagination was filled with the vision of green forests that Walter had painted so vividly.

'But the winters?' he asked. 'Aren't they horribly cold? I don't know how you can live in such a climate.'

'Oh, they are not so unbearable, my lord,' Walter said. 'Have you ever seen a frost?'

Philip shook his head and shivered.

'Many times when I have been scorched by the sun on my travels,' Walter said, 'I have longed for a winter's morning in England, when your cheeks tingle with the bite of the air, and you can feel the frost crackle under your feet. And the frost makes patterns, my lord, on everything it touches; the leaves and the trees and all the plants are covered with it. I have seen many wonderful cities and buildings, but I tell you, my lord, that a single tiny pattern of frost is more beautiful than the loveliest stone carving in all Christendom.'

Philip sat motionless in his seat. He was afraid to say anything for fear the old man would stop.

'And there is the snow,' Walter went on. 'All is still, my lord, and white and spotless. It is as if the good Lord is showing us how clean we should keep the earth.'

'Yes, it must be very beautiful,' Philip muttered.

'Would you like to go to England?' Walter asked curiously.

Philip laughed. 'When you speak like that about England, Walter,' he said, 'I wish I could visit it. But my home is here. Now, tell me about Llanstephan. Is it a large castle?'

'No, quite small. Much smaller than this, my lord.' Walter waved a hand around the room. 'It is on the coast, above the mouth of a river. I remember hearing the low roar of the sea when I tried to sleep that night.'

'And the lord of the castle?' Philip asked eagerly. 'Did you speak to him, Walter?'

'That would be Sir Henry d'Aubigny. But it was many years ago, and I expect he is dead now, my lord.'

Philip was vaguely disappointed. He had hoped to hear more about his unknown cousins. The old man stood up to go.

'I must sleep well tonight,' he said. 'In two days I may see the Holy City itself and the Church of the Sepulchre.'

'What pilgrimage will you make after this one?' Philip asked.

Walter shrugged his bowed shoulders. 'Who knows, my lord? This is the greatest of all the pilgrimages. I may never return.'

'Return where? Have you a home, then?'

Walter shook his head. 'York, perhaps. But it is many years since I was there. I think I will return to York. This is the last pilgrimage I shall make.'

He bowed with his simple dignity to Philip and left the room.

Chapter Two

JERUSALEM

Jusuf al-Hafiz left Blanche Garde two days later, and both Sir Hugo and Philip went to the gatehouse to say good-bye. They were sorry to see him go, particularly Philip, for underneath Jusuf's unruffled and almost frigid air of politeness there was great charm. From Sir Hugo's point of view, Jusuf was an experienced soldier and a man of considerable courage, and not even the yawning gulf of religion and race could quite destroy the respect one knight might have for another.

Jusuf paused on the farther side of the gatehouse, and looked down at his hosts. He thanked Sir Hugo gravely for his hospitality, and then turned towards Philip. His face broke into a smile of real affection.

'And don't forget I owe you a cup of water, Philip,' he said. 'I may be able to repay you one day, you know.' He glanced at Sir Hugo, smiled again, and cantered over the drawbridge.

'What did he mean exactly, father?' Philip asked as they strolled across the courtyard. It was too hot to hurry.

'Who knows?' Sir Hugo said gloomily. 'Perhaps we may learn something in Jerusalem. I must attend the next meeting of the High Court.'

They set off for Jerusalem at dawn, for Sir Hugo had no intention of riding through the heat of the day, and planned to spend two days on the journey. It was chilly as the little party climbed out of the valley, with a white mist drifting across the road from the marshes, and Philip huddled gratefully under the warmth of his heavy cloak.

Behind him he could hear Llewellyn cursing the cold, and grumbling with his usual fluency of strange oaths in Arabic, Welsh, and Saxon. Philip chuckled. He had never known Llewellyn do anything but grumble, even when the world was treating him well. In fact, he seemed happiest when he could find some excuse for a grumble.

The rest of the party consisted of Sir Hugo's servant, and half a dozen mounted men-at-arms from the castle garrison. Ivo the Steward and several other servants had ridden for Jerusalem on the previous day, for Sir Hugo, like all the richer barons of Outremer, owned a house in the Holy City, and by the time he arrived, everything would be ready. There would certainly be trouble if it was not, for although Sir Hugo was far from being a harsh or overbearing master, he had no patience with slackness or inefficiency.

As the sun rose, so it swallowed up the freshness of the morning. The air grew sultry and oppressive, and the white dust hung in slowly drifting clouds over the horses and the clothes of the riders. Philip tried to resist the temptation to wipe his face. He knew from bitter experience that his hands only left long gritty smears across his cheeks, and so he rode on in patient discomfort. He should be used to the heat, he thought. But his mind was dwelling yearningly on visions of green fields and cool streams, with the deep shady valleys that old Walter of York had talked about with such eloquence.

They halted at midday, and spent the hottest part of the day in one of the many rest-houses that had been built on the main road to the capital. Sir Hugo was in no hurry to continue his journey. He could face any discomfort or move at a pace that left many behind, if need be, as Philip knew. But only a fool, as he once said, was uncomfortable when there was no necessity for it.

Another stage of the leisurely journey was covered in the cool of the evening, and the night itself was spent at a *maisondieu*, or hostel for pilgrims, set up and supervised by the Templars, for both they and the great order of the Hospitallers had originally been founded to protect and help pilgrims on their way to the Holy Land.

The traffic thickened as they approached the capital.

There were the usual pilgrims, some on foot, some mounted on donkeys, and often travelling in groups. Those who were making for the coast were proudly wearing the palm leaf, or carrying a little flask filled with water from the River Jordan to show that they had completed the greatest pilgrimage in Christendom. Just outside Jerusalem they passed a troop of Templars, grim, purposeful knights in full armour, wearing the long white cloak of the order, the flaming red cross on their shoulders. Their huge helms were slung from the saddle, and on their heads were close-fitting red hats with a small white cap underneath. Their commander recognized Sir Hugo, and saluted as they clattered past.

The sun was setting as Sir Hugo's party followed the winding road through the hills and olive groves. Philip had visited the Holy City on many occasions, but the first sight of the old city from the Jaffa road never failed to arouse his emotions. For one came upon it with dramatic suddeness; the road swung to the left, climbed a steep slope, and there, in the distance, frowning down upon the deep ravines, lay Jerusalem. The long walls and towers, grey and sombre, seemed to grow out of the precipitous hillside. Beyond, in sharp contrast to the grim, encircling curtain of defences, lay the crowded streets, the huddled mass of white buildings, church towers, and rounded mosques.

Every great city, as Philip was to learn, possessed some curious atmosphere of its own, or gave the visiting stranger some instinctive and inexplicable sense of emotion. To him, Jerusalem had always seemed a mournful city. Perhaps it was the site, or the melancholy shades of the vast circle of walls and towers, or the great age of the city, or, most likely of all, the history of this extraordinary place, and the dreadful event that had once taken place just outside the walls.

The road climbed steadily up towards the walls, and brought them to the Jaffa gate, lying in the shadow of the great Tower of David. They rode inside, and pushed their way slowly through the narrow and crowded streets. Sir Hugo's house was not a large one, and from the street there was little to see. For, like most houses in the East, the architect had concentrated on the interior, grouping the chief rooms around a large central apartment. Sir Hugo and Philip reclined at their ease in this room after supper, washed and changed into long silk robes, lying luxuriously on coloured divans and cushions, sipping sherbert and dipping their hands idly into baskets of fruit and sweetmeats. It was a strange setting for two Norman noblemen, though they would not have thought so themselves. The floor was paved with mosaic; hundreds of tiny coloured stones arranged in an intricate and delightful pattern. Above their heads was a vaulted ceiling painted blue to resemble the sky; a small fountain in the centre of the room poured out a continuous stream of tinkling water from the mouth of a stone dragon.

The meeting of the High Court was not until the following afternoon, and Sir Hugo announced his intention of visiting the Royal Palace to meet his friends and pick up the latest rumours and news from the frontiers. Philip decided to spend the morning shopping. Jusuf had given him a superb little dagger in a scarlet sheath of the finest leather. Now he wanted a thin leather belt, the best he could find, to match the colour of the sheath. He promised himself a pleasant morning. Blessed with ample supplies of money from Sir Hugo, he could spend several hours inspecting the stalls of the merchants, and haggling energetically with the Jewish owners.

The streets were very full that morning. Philip found it hot and tiring work to push his way through the jostling crowds. But he was in no hurry, and the extraordinary variety of races and types which thronged Jerusalem always filled him with delight. He saw Jews shuffling by in long drab clothes of grey, Greek priests with unkempt hair and fluttering skirts of black, and bearded Armenians in tall, pointed hats, chatting in groups at the corners of the narrow alleyways. Eager pilgrims pushed their way through to see the famous buildings and shrines of the city, while strings of camels padded silently over the cobbles, dark-skinned Negroes from Egypt perched on their backs, guiding the patient brutes with taps from short sticks on their swaying necks.

Philip stood aside as men-at-arms swept a space clear for a nobleman. It was John de Belleme of Toron, an important castle in the north, covering the ports of Tyre and Acre. He was the owner of a famous Norman name, brick-red in the face from the tropical sun, and was followed by his swarthy Syrian wife and dark-skinned children—Pullani, as those of mixed Norman and Eastern blood were called. Sir John, who had stayed at Blanche Garde, recognized Philip, and raised his hand in a stately greeting, for he was a pompous man. Philip bowed politely, and pushed on to the corner of the street, towards the main shopping centre of the city.

He passed the Fowl Market, filled with a dense crowd of buyers and merchants, haggling and shouting in a babel of different tongues. Behind the market sprawled the great hospital of St John, built and kept up by the Hospitallers for the accommodation of pilgrims visiting the Holy City. This brought Philip to the Money Exchange, a busy crossroads. He remembered that there were some leather merchants in Mount Sion Street, to the right, and he dived across the road.

Outside a merchant's stall he paused, and ran his eyes over the display of goods. There were several belts there which might match his new sheath. But it would be fatal, he knew, to show any enthusiasm for an article. The price would be doubled immediately.

'My lord requires something?' The old Jewish shopkeeper came waddling out, rubbing his hands together expectantly, his shrewd eyes making a rapid and experienced inspection of his customer and his clothes. The price would vary with the apparent wealth or otherwise of the buyer.

Philip braced himself for the contest. He began by pointing to a set of stirrup leathers, and a pleasant five minutes passed in an argument about the price. Philip pushed away the leathers at last, and picked up a bridle. The process was repeated. After fifteen minutes or so he had toyed with half the articles on display. The Jew was still full of fight; he was beginning to realize the calibre of his customer. This was no newcomer or pilgrim to Outremer, but an experienced haggler.

Philip half turned to leave the stall. He hesitated, and casually fingered a red belt. It was exactly the shade and design he wanted.

'Four bezants, my lord,' the Jew said instantly, his beady eyes fixed on Philip's face to see the reaction.

'What!' gasped Philip, his voice rising in realistic horror. '*Four* bezants? Who do you take me for, man? The Grand Master of the Templars? Do you really imagine a poor squire like myself can pay that price for a third-rate belt worth a dozen dinars?'

'A dozen dinars!' screeched the Jew, his grimy hands flying to his head. 'But look at the workmanship, my lord. Feel it for yourself. No better belt ever came out of Damascus.'

'Damascus!' Philip retorted with scorn and disbelief. 'Made by the hundred in a back street in Jaffa more like. Anyway, I have but two bezants to spend, and a poor squire is lucky to have that much.'

'Oh, yes, my lord,' the Jew said, dropping his eyes to

Philip's rich surcoat and sandals of superfine red leather. His eyes began to twinkle. 'Three bezants then, my lord. It is worth every dinar of it.'

'Two bezants.'

'But I would be ruined if I sold this belt at that price, my lord.'

Philip shrugged his shoulders and turned away.

'Two bezants,' he said firmly, and took a tentative step towards the street.

The Jew raised his hands palm upwards in a gesture of defeat.

'Two bezants then, my lord,' he said mournfully. 'I paid four for that belt. But I would not grudge you the loss you are causing me. The belt is yours. Two bezants it is.'

Philip opened his purse and handed over the two heavy gold coins. He reckoned that he was paying exactly the right price, and he walked away chuckling to himself.

There was still some time to waste before the midday meal, and he decided to visit the Palace.

To reach the Palace, Philip had to return to the Money Exchange, and take the road running to the right and in the general direction of the old Temple Area, a walled enclosure on high ground, with the tall round Dome of the Rock in the centre and the Turkish mosque of El Aqsa on its right. This the Franks had converted into a palace, and behind it was the city headquarters of the Templars.

Philip disliked the atmosphere of the court. Sir Hugo was probably responsible for this dislike, for he seldom

returned from Jerusalem without some scathing remarks about the continual intrigue and conspiracy that were the curse of Outremer. The King himself could not set his subjects a good example, for the throne had become an object of bargaining. The pathetic and courageous King Baldwin had died quite recently, a hopeless leper from his youth, and with him had ended the male line of the royal family. Two great barons of Outremer had squabbled over the vacant throne; Raymond of Tripoli, who had acted as regent for the King, and Guy of Lusignan, who had married Sibylla, the King's sister. Sir Hugo had held aloof from the bitter disputes that followed. It was Guy who had won, thanks to the support of the Military Orders, and since then Count Raymond had flirted with the Turks, and was suspected of treason by many barons of the kingdom.

Philip was thinking about this as he passed the sentries and entered the main reception hall of the Palace, filled with men waiting to see the king or one of the Officers of the Kingdom. There was a large ante-room on the left of the hall where barons and knights met and talked while waiting for some court function to begin. It was crowded with a chattering throng, for the meeting of the High Court had brought many barons and knights into the city. Newly arrived from outlying castles and fiefs of the kingdom, they were exchanging greetings, issuing invitations for hunting parties, and gossiping generally.

Philip paused by the door. Some young Pullani noblemen nodded to him. He bowed slightly, and went on. He disliked the half-breeds. They were the worst intriguers in Outremer, and he distrusted them.

He had no difficulty in finding his cousin Joscelin. At the far end of the room was a knot of richly dressed young knights, conspicuous even in that brightly coloured crowd for the magnificence of their clothes. Joscelin saw Philip and shouted across the room. Philip grinned, and went over to join the other men. He was constantly amused by Joscelin, but had a considerable admiration for him at the same time.

For Joscelin de Grandmesnil was a decorative young man. Tall and exquisite, flaunting some new fashion every month, he talked in a high-pitched, drawling voice, as if his one object in life was to give the world the impression that he was a fool and an effeminate fop. He would hardly have been so popular if that had really been the case. For there was only one yardstick by which men were measured in Outremer: their courage, and their ability to handle horse, lance and sword. And by that grim standard Joscelin was rated highly, for he was a fine horseman, and noted for his reckless courage.

'When did you arrive, Philip?' he asked in a languid tone of voice.

'Last night. Is Sir Fulk here, Joscelin?'

'Oh, yes. He wandered off with Sir Hugo,' Joscelin said. 'They were having a good grumble together.' He sniffed delicately at a wisp of coloured silk which he was carrying.

'What were they grumbling about?' Philip asked,

eyeing the silk handkerchief curiously, and wondering what crazy new fashion Joscelin was launching now.

'The usual topics,' drawled Joscelin. 'The growing decadence of Outremer, the danger from the Infidels, and the difficulty of making Syrian peasants work hard enough.' He raised the silk to his nose and sniffed loudly with an expression of sublime contentment.

'What in the name of Saladin have you got there?' Philip demanded.

Joscelin flicked the handkerchief under his cousin's nose. There was a strong smell of some pleasant scent, and Philip recoiled in astonishment.

'Scent!' he exclaimed. 'Joscelin, you really can't . . .'

'Why not?' Joscelin said calmly. 'I find it very refreshing in this hot weather. Don't you like it?'

'Well, it's better than the frightful stink in the streets, I suppose,' Philip admitted doubtfully. 'But you'll be the laughing stock of the Palace, Joscelin.'

'Oh, no I won't. Look at us here. Peter d'Avalon, Jacques de Vitry, John de Brienne . . .'

The three young knights were all flaunting the same coloured handkerchiefs, sniffing incessantly, and obviously highly delighted with their new fashion.

'No wonder Sir Fulk and father were talking about the growing decadence of Outremer,' Philip said.

Joscelin chuckled, raised his hand as if to hit his cousin, and then drew aside hurriedly to allow a group of men to pass.

They were Templars. In front strode a spare, ascetic man, erect and picturesque in his long white cloak. His grey hair, escaping from beneath the red cap of his order, framed the face of a fanatic, vividly alive and filled with a furious and burning energy. He swept past swiftly, his cloak fluttering in his haste, and his deep-set, restless eyes shooting swift side glances at the men around him.

'Gerard de Ridefort,' Joscelin muttered, and bowed with a great deal more respect than he normally displayed towards his elders.

They watched the Grand Master of the Templars as he walked quickly through the gangway of knights and squires who drew aside politely to allow the great man to pass.

'Looks annoyed,' remarked Jacques de Vitry. 'I wonder what's upset him now.'

'Oh, he's always in a state about something,' Joscelin said. 'Have you ever known the Templars or the Hospitallers to be otherwise? And you should know, Jacques. Your brother John is a Hospitaller.'

'Yes, he takes life very seriously,' Jacques said; and Philip was to discover one day how much that would mean to him.

A worried-looking knight came up to them at that moment. He was John de Durus, the son of the Marshal of the Kingdom, who acted as second-in-command of the feudal army of Outremer, and carried the Royal Standard in battle.

'Joscelin, just the man I want!' he said, rushing up in a

fussy and self-important manner. 'Come over and meet these new arrivals. You too, de Vitry, and you, d'Aubigny.'

There was no difficulty in picking out the men to whom he referred. Their complexion alone would have stamped the recruits as newcomers to Outremer, for they were almost pallid in comparison with the dark and sunburnt faces of the other men in the room.

'Must we?' Joscelin asked plaintively. 'They don't look a very pleasant lot, John.'

'Oh, yes, I know,' de Durus said, trying to push Joscelin across the floor. 'But we must give them some sort of welcome, you know. My father was most insistent about it. After all; we don't get many recruits from the West.'

'Well, you mustn't look a gift horse in the teeth, I suppose,' Joscelin drawled. 'Come on, Philip, and you, Jacques. Give me some support. I shall need it, to judge by the look of this lot. Have you ever seen a scruffier crowd? Their clothes!' He held up his scented handkerchief in horror, and then looked complacently at his own gorgeous outfit.

Philip grinned. But Joscelin was not far wrong about these men, for they were only too typical of the type of recruit coming to Outremer; doubtful characters who had made Europe too warm to hold them, and who thought that the East might be a good place in which to retrieve their tattered fortunes.

De Durus hurriedly introduced the newcomers, who stared in growing astonishment at the gaudily dressed young men who surrounded them. The West was far behind the East in its pursuit of luxuries, and the clothes of these newly landed Normans and Frenchmen were drab and colourless.

The conversation was very one-sided. The Normans were obviously men of some experience in the constant little wars and skirmishes of the West, and perhaps they felt they must assert themselves in their new and strange surroundings. They expressed themselves bluntly about the lack of fighting spirit in Outremer, and the need for aggressive action against the Infidels.

The knights of Outremer listened in polite silence. They had heard all this before, and with some of it they were in agreement. For the Pullani noblemen, probably because of their mixed blood, were far too tolerant in their views towards the Turks. But it was one thing to criticize one's own colleagues and acquaintances, and quite another to hear strangers hold forth in such blunt and downright terms.

Philip gathered that the loudest spokesman of the Normans was called Walter de Nogent. He was a rough looking individual, fairly young, but already running to fat, though he was clearly a man of considerable strength. He was tall and broad-shouldered, with muscular arms, and a thick neck; deep lines ran from the corners of his nose, and his heavy chin and thick lips gave him an appearance of truculence and brutality.

De Nogent clearly did not know what to make of the gorgeous young peacocks who surrounded him. At home his acquaintances were accustomed to expressing themselves in forthright terms; they called a spade a spade, as a later century would have put it, and they wasted no time in reaching the point of their argument. But the East had taught the Christians a different lesson. You approached your point after a round or so of polite conversation about nothing in particular. And even then it was customary to put forward one's views in a slightly deferential manner, wrapping up the arguments in polished and courtly phrases.

So de Nogent could make nothing of the polite faces in front of him. Except for Philip, of course, who had not yet learnt to conceal his feelings. He was staring at the Norman with an expression of surprise and disapproval, and de Nogent caught his glance.

'And what do you think, young sir?' he demanded truculently. 'Or are you one who likes the Infidels?' He spat out the word *likes*.

'I have met many Turks,' Philip said quietly, though he could feel his unruly temper rising. 'I expect you will do the same before very long.'

De Nogent's thick eyebrows came down and he scowled at Philip as he caught the note of sarcasm.

'I suppose you entertain the scum in your castle,' he said. His light blue eyes ran contemptuously over Philip's rich Eastern dress and sandals, and the deep brown of his face. He jumped to a conclusion that he was going to regret. 'But then you Pullani are all like that, I'm told.'

Philip clenched his fingers by his side. But he kept his temper. He could see Joscelin shaking his head.

'We do entertain the Turks,' he said, thinking of Jusuf with his exquisite and polished manners, and comparing him unfavourably with this oaf. 'I prefer them to some Franks I have met.'

The group of listeners stirred and then fell silent. Only Joscelin moved, and he raised a hand, but he was too late.

'Meaning me, I suppose!' de Nogent said. He was on surer ground now, and knew how to deal with a quarrel.

'Of course,' Philip said.

De Nogent's thick neck seemed to swell as the veins there bulged out with his rising temper.

'You snivelling little Syrian!' he said. 'I've a good mind to take a whip to you, and teach you how to address a Norman nobleman.'

Philip had restrained himself with surprising success until this moment. The d'Aubignys were noted for their temper, and he knew that he was no exception. He could feel a warm tide of boiling fury surge up into his head; the veneer of Eastern politeness that he had acquired so painfully for one of his temperament dropped away, leaving him with the one thought that he must batter this fat oaf to the ground, and go on smashing at his face . . .

'Philip!' he heard Joscelin's high-pitched voice cry, and strong hands held him back as he sprang forward.

'Keep out of this,' de Nogent said. 'This little Pullani needs a lesson.'

'Don't be a fool, de Nogent,' de Durus said icily. 'Philip d'Aubigny is a pure-blooded Norman from one of the oldest families in the Duchy. His grandfather rode on the First Crusade with the household knights of Robert of Normandy himself, and was knighted by the Duke after the storming of Antioch.'

De Nogent was a trifle nonplussed for the moment by this information. He wiped his streaming face, for he was feeling the heat badly, and shook his head.

'Well, he still needs a lesson,' he growled.

'Philip is only a boy, of course,' Joscelin drawled, hand-kerchief to nostrils, and inspecting de Nogent with the same indifferent and aloof expression with which he might have flung a coin to one of the filthy and leprous beggars in the streets of Jerusalem.

'Keep out of this, Joscelin,' Philip said, a little calmer now, but still clenching and unclenching his fists.

Joscelin looked at him, and sighed. There was nothing he could do. Philip must carry this quarrel to the end now.

'Outside the Gate of Siloam,' Philip said. 'An hour before the sun goes down.'

'Where's that?' de Nogent said. He was soon told, and the simple arrangements for the fight were made. The bout would be on foot with sword and shield until one or the other had had enough.

Philip turned on his heel, and with Joscelin by his side, walked out of the Palace.

Chapter Three

THE FIGHT BY THE POOL OF SILOAM

'You are a young fool!' Joscelin said forcibly as they emerged into the glare of the sun. 'De Nogent is a grown man, and a murderous ruffian if I ever saw one. He's out to break your neck, Philip!'

'Oh, I can take care of myself,' Philip said confidently.

'Of course you can't!' Joscelin said, forgetting his drawl and his affected air of indifference, for he was fond of his cousin. 'You've never had a proper fight yet, and you're too finicky with your sword. That old Greek didn't do your training any good, you know. Too many fancy tricks!'

Philip smiled and shook his head. It was too hot to argue. But Joscelin, he thought, would have a shock before the sun went down. For the old Greek, a veteran of the famous Varangian Guard, the personal bodyguard of the Emperor at Constantinople, had some odd and advanced ideas about the use of the sword.

Swordsmanship then was a crude business, a matter of brute force, and the eternal cut-and-hack with the edge of the blade. But to the Greek it was an art, a beautiful and graceful combination of footwork, of timing, of shrewd thrusts with the point—and the skilful use of all one's weight behind the cut when one's opponent was out-manoeuvred, and his weaknesses discovered. He had found a willing pupil in Philip, who had gulped down the old man's ideas with enthusiasm, and was ready to practise for days and months with a whole-hearted determination that made his tutor smile and twist his grey moustaches and beard with pleasure.

And Philip was unusually strong for his years. He had often practised with Joscelin, but lately he had become conscious of his strength and the added effect that perfect timing gave to his blows. So he had never dared to hit his cousin with his full force.

There were, too, other factors about this particular fight that Joscelin had overlooked in his anxiety. The heat would be Philip's chief ally. Fighting in full armour, covered in gambeson and hauberk, was warm enough at any time.

In the tropical sun of Outremer, there were few who could keep it up for long, unless they were in the strictest training, and accustomed to the climate. De Nogent was a newcomer, and a long voyage would have done him no good. Philip had noticed his tendency to put on weight, and his streaming face in the Palace. Ten minutes' fighting would reduce de Nogent to a quivering jelly, drenched in sweat, and drained of all his strength.

They had arranged to have the midday meal at Sir Fulk's house. Sir Hugo was there when they arrived, chatting to his brother-in-law, or rather, listening with amused detachment to Sir Fulk. For Sir Fulk was a man who liked to air his opinions. He was red-faced and a trifle portly. His hair had long since disappeared, and from his forehead upwards there was a vast expanse of shining scalp which Sir Fulk delighted to stroke as he talked. He held decided views on every subject, and as he suffered from the heat of Outremer, he tended to talk in a series of irritable explosions that gave strangers the impression that he was a bad tempered and fretful old man. In reality, as Philip knew, Sir Fulk was a kindly and charming person who found it difficult to accustom himself to new ideas or changing events, and so trumpeted forth his regret that the old customs and manners of his youth had given way to new-fangled notions.

'Where have you two been?' he barked as the two cousins came in. 'You're late, Joscelin!'

Joscelin had recovered his fashionable airs, and he

raised his brows in polite surprise. 'I've never heard you complain about lateness at meals before, father,' he said. 'We often have to remind you at Montgizard.'

'Well, I've changed!' Sir Fulk snapped irritably. 'Taking a lesson from Hugo here. He's always so devilish punctual about everything. Very sound practice!'

He inspected Joscelin's clothes. Privately he was proud of his son, but he would not have shown his feelings for the world.

'What's that you have there?' he demanded, pointing to the scented handkerchief.

Joscelin handed over the piece of silk, and winked at Philip. He delighted in teasing his father, and Sir Fulk never failed to rise to the bait.

Sir Fulk sniffed at the handkerchief, glared at Joscelin, and then sniffed again, this time with tremendous violence.

'Phew!' he gasped. 'Scent! Smell that, Hugo, if it doesn't turn your stomach. *Scent!* I told you so. Decadence! The country's going to the dogs! That's the youth of Outremer for you. Walking about smelling like a polecat, or a dainty girl. Why, my father would have put his foot behind me and kicked me out of the room if I had come in stinking like this!'

Sir Hugo gravely applied his aristocratic nose to the offending silk, and then smiled at Joscelin.

'Very pleasant,' he said, and they all waited for the explosion.

'What!' roared Sir Fulk. 'Hugo, you must be off your head!'

'But it is a pleasant scent, Fulk. Much more preferable than the frightful stench outside in the streets.'

'Yes, uncle,' Philip said, 'don't you think that most of the disease in Jerusalem, and the plagues, are caused by the filth and the smells?'

'Nonsense, boy! Smells never do anyone any harm,' retorted Sir Fulk. 'Useful too. When the worst smells start you know the hot weather's coming.'

'But that Arab physician who came to Blanche Garde last year said they caused all the plagues,' Philip persisted.

'Rubbish! These Arab doctors have the most ridiculous ideas. I heard one of them. Do you know what he had the infernal impudence to tell me?' Sir Fulk waved his hand in Philip's face. 'Told me that the best treatment for sword wounds was clean bandages and fresh air. To me, who've been wounded scores of times! Everyone knows the only thing to do is to tie the wound up, keep the air out, and let the blood and pus sort themselves out. If they don't, then it shows your blood is unhealthy, and that's the end of you.'

Sir Fulk stood up, and roared to his steward to know if the meal was ready. He beckoned to his guests, and waddled out of the room.

The news of Philip's quarrel was broken to the older men in the middle of the meal. Sir Hugo heard the story calmly, as might have been expected. Sir Fulk, of course, exploded with excitement and indignation.

'De Nogent?' he said. 'Never heard of the fellow!'

'You wouldn't have, father,' Joscelin said. 'He's just landed in Outremer. From Normandy.'

'I guessed as much!' Sir Fulk cried triumphantly. 'Just what I was telling you, Hugo, this morning. Typical of the riff-raff we're getting from the West. Good-for-nothing scoundrels, most of 'em. You must put a stop to this business. Can't have boys like Philip knocked about by these cut-throats.'

Sir Hugo shook his head. 'I expect Philip can take good care of himself, Fulk.'

'Oh, I don't say the boy is helpless,' Sir Fulk said handsomely. 'But a real fight is a very different affair to a practice bout, you know.'

'He's got to make a start sometime. Where and when, Philip?'

'By the Pool of Siloam. An hour before sunset.'

'I know the place. Well, we'll be there.'

Philip tried to sleep during the hottest part of the day. But he felt too restless and excited to keep still, though he did lie down, tossing about on his bed for a couple of hours. Joscelin arrived then to watch him dress for the fight.

Llewellyn supervised the details. His stolid and matter-of-fact attitude to the whole business helped to calm Philip, and Joscelin too, who was fidgeting about the room, picking up articles of equipment, and making pessimistic comments.

Philip stripped completely from his ordinary day

clothes, and Llewellyn helped him on with the gambeson, a thickly quilted undergarment. No more unsuitable dress could have been devised for such a hot climate, but no knight of that time could afford to fight without it. Otherwise the bare skin would be chafed by the steel rings of the hauberk and chausses, and it possessed the additional advantage of protecting one's skin from the shock of a blow. The chausses came next, long stockings of steel rings sewn together, reaching to the waist, and fastened securely by a belt.

When he was satisfied with their fit, Llewellyn held out the most important and expensive item of a knight's equipment. This was the hauberk, a closely fitting and very thin leather shirt on which hundreds of steel rings were sewn. This particular hauberk was of the latest type, and known as banded mail, for the lines of rings overlapped each other, falling to the right and then to the left in alternate rows. In turn, each row was separated from the one below by a narrow tuck in the leather, a device that made the links lie flat. The rings themselves were riveted together—an expensive refinement that few squires or knights could afford. But Sir Hugo had poured out considerable wealth when he had equipped Philip. The hauberk dropped down from Philip's shoulders to his knees, while the sleeves reached over his wrists and hands, fitting loosely there and cut open like mittens along the palm, so as to ensure a firm grip on sword hilt and reins.

Neck and throat were covered by a coif or hood of mail,

but before putting this on, Llewellyn carefully fitted a padded leather skull cap on Philip's head, to act as a buffer against a sword stroke. Then, after adjusting the coif with the greatest care, and when Philip nodded to show that he was satisfied, Llewellyn fastened it in place with a narrow strap that buckled at the back of the head. He went over to the chest on which he had laid out his neat piles of equipment, and then came back with some small straps. Kneeling down, he drew two of them around the chausses by the knee, and another pair around the wrists, not drawing the buckle tight until Philip had flexed his arms and stretched out his legs to make certain that he had full freedom for his limbs.

'Right, Llewellyn! Now the surcoat.'

Philip's face was framed now in the mail hood, and he was completely covered from head to foot in the banded mail. But the Crusaders had soon discovered that mail was unbearably hot in the eastern sun, and they had copied the Turkish habit of wearing some thin, white covering. This helped to ward off the worst of the burning sun, and the linen covering was known as the surcoat. It was a sleeveless garment, light and thin, and fell to the knees in ample folds. Over the surcoat, and around the waist, went the thick, strong sword belt, and this, too, was buckled with great care.

'Sword now, Llewellyn,' Philip said.

Joscelin was holding Philip's sword. 'Sharpened it lately?' he asked.

Llewellyn sucked in his breath crossly. Was he likely to send his master into a fight without spending several hours on the blade of his sword?

But Joscelin seemed to think he was the only person there who knew anything about preparing for a fight. He ripped out the long blade, and the bright sunlight flashed on three feet of highly polished steel, thick and broad near the plain cruciform hilt, and tapering gradually to the sharpened tip about which Philip, with his own type of sword play, was so particular.

Joscelin ran his finger gingerly along the razor-sharp edge.

'Sharp enough,' he admitted.

'Of course it is!' Philip snapped irritably. 'Don't fuss so much, Joscelin.' He could feel the gathering tension boil up inside.

Joscelin shot him a swift glance, and wisely said nothing. Instead, he helped Llewellyn to fasten the heavy, leather sheath to the sword belt on the left side, while Philip buckled on the knife that Jusuf had given him, resplendent in its new scarlet sheath. A dagger could be useful in hand-to-hand fighting, and might be invaluable for cutting loose any leather work that broke or became tangled.

'I'll carry the helm for you, my lord,' Llewellyn said; for no knight put on the ponderous steel helmet that covered his head until the last possible moment.

'I'll have the shield now,' Philip said.

Shields, like hauberks, had changed lately. They were

smaller and more triangular in shape, made from well-seasoned wood, and covered with tough leather. A strap was passed over Philip's shoulder, and then clipped to the inside of the shield. There were grips, too, for the left hand, but the shoulder strap gave a man an additional safeguard if his arm grew tired, or if he was in danger of dropping his guard and exposing himself to attack.

Philip was ready now, except for the helm. On the face of his shield and the breast of the surcoat was painted the device of a black hawk. Like so many knights in Outremer, Sir Hugo had adopted some means of identification, for no one could be recognized under a helm. These simple badges were the beginning of the complicated system of heraldry, but the rules then were few. The most important regulation in Outremer was that a knight must not adopt a device already taken by another man.

The horses were ready in the street, and Sir Hugo and Sir Fulk were already mounted when Joscelin and Philip came out.

'Feeling all right, boy?' shouted Sir Fulk.

'Of course . . . Philip bit off the hasty answer. 'Yes, uncle, quite all right, thank you.'

He saw his father eye him, and he thought there was a flicker of a smile on that impassive face. Then they were riding through the cobbled alleys of the old city, with the white walls of the houses rising high above them on either side.

The Gate of Siloam was in the southern wall of the city,

just below the Temple Area and the Royal Palace. To reach it, Philip's little party took the same route as he had followed that morning. The streets were not so crowded now; the country people who had come in for the various markets had left, or were on the point of doing so, for all the gates in the great walls of Jerusalem were shut at sunset, and no one could leave or enter without special permission.

The cattle market by the Siloam Gate was half empty as they rode up. A few farmers were sitting about discussing the day's business, and there were still hundreds of animals in the long lines of pens. The sentries saluted as Philip rode past with his father, and they clattered down the road that followed the stream through the Vale of Gehenna.

The pool of Siloam was about half a mile from the city, and just above it was a smooth piece of ground, well shaded from the sun. This was a favourite spot for private disputes, and Philip had been there as a spectator before now. He spurred his horse down the hill, more as a safety-valve for his feelings than any real need for haste, for he knew he was in good time. Then he pulled up to allow the rest to catch up with him, and in a few minutes they reached the small group of trees beside the Pool.

'Hullo, there's a crowd here!' Sir Fulk remarked as they rode up and dismounted.

He was right. There must have been several hundred men already pushing forward to gain a good view of the fighting ground. Jerusalem was unusually full of knights and barons of the kingdom as a result of the meeting of the High Court, and Philip's quarrel with de Nogent had taken place in a crowded room.

Philip watched Llewellyn tether his horse. Joscelin waved to some of his friends, and was soon making bets on the result of the fight. Once more the tight sensation returned to Philip's stomach, and he shifted his feet uneasily in the dust.

'You know what to do, Philip?' his father asked quietly. 'Let de Nogent carry the fight to you. He'll tire himself quickly enough in this heat.'

'That's what I thought,' Philip said. 'Is he here?'

'Over there.'

'Why, he's not wearing a surcoat!' Philip exclaimed in surprise.

'Not all the knights in the West do. He'll soon pick up the habit here, though.'

Llewellyn tapped his master on the shoulder. 'Your helm, my lord.'

He raised the helm, and Philip ducked his head. The helm of that date was a clumsy and ponderous affair, flat-topped, and covering a man's head completely. There were narrow slits for the eyes, and smaller breathing holes. As Llewellyn dropped the heavy weight on to his shoulders, Philip blinked. For the sunlit scene, with the shifting and chattering crowd, the bright colours and the blue of the sky, suddenly vanished, and he was in a small world of darkness, warm and stifling. Even the sounds around him died away to a muffled hum.

Then he shifted the helm until the eye slits were in place, and nodded as a signal to Llewellyn to strap the buckles that held the helm in place. There were three layers of protection over his head now, the padded skull cap, the mail hood, and the helm with its strong, tempered steel.

Joscelin shouted in his right ear. 'Ready, Philip?'

Philip nodded, and drew his sword. As he did so, Llewellyn pulled off the sheath. There was no point in wearing it, and the long strip of leather might catch his legs and make him stumble.

For a moment Philip stood there, hitching up the shield, while Llewellyn made a last-minute adjustment of the shoulder strap. Then he stepped forward, and from the other side of the ring de Nogent stalked towards him, and the crowd fell silent, weighing up with expert eyes the two armed men in their jingling mail, with blank, expression-less faces of steel.

Now that the moment had come, Philip lost some of his tension. He knew that once he had made the first move, he would forget even the slight remnant of nervousness. He knew, too, that all the advantages were on his side; his greater fitness, his experience of the heat, and his finer equipment. He could feel the perfect balance of his sword in his hand. Only the most skilled of smiths could make such a weapon. For the art of sword-making lay in the balance—that subtle craftsmanship which made the heavy blade swing up and back with a feeling of airy lightness, and yet brought it down with all the weight swinging through with the blow.

Both men met in the centre of the circle. They eyed each other through their narrow slits, shields covering their left sides and much of the helm, knees slightly bent, both bodies tense and rigid.

Then de Nogent stepped forward. His right arm swung up, and the sun flashed on his sword as he brought it down with a vicious grunt in a whirring circle of steel.

Philip shifted his feet deftly. His lithe body twisted to the right, and the sword whistled past his shoulder and shield. A shout went up from the crowd. They had not expected that swift move. Nor did de Nogent expect the equally swift counter-attack.

Philip slid his right foot forward in a smooth shuffle, a continuation of his side-step. His sword flickered out and towards de Nogent's throat. Up went the shield. But it was too late. The pointed tip caught him full on the throat against the coif, and he staggered back.

Another shout went up. This was swordsmanship, and there were many there who could appreciate the skill.

De Nogent recovered quickly. After all, he was an experienced fighter, and he was full of confidence. He could break through this boy's guard, and batter him into insensibility in a few minutes. He had done the same against much stronger opponents in far-off Normandy. For three minutes he rained upon the boy a series of tremendous cuts. He could not hope to penetrate that magnificent hauberk of Philip's, but a heavy blow on the shoulder might break a bone, and a full hit on the helm could stun the wearer.

Philip weathered the storm easily. He side-stepped and made his opponent miss, or he took the blows coolly on shield or sword. And for each cut he sent in a swift stab or a full-length lunge. Not all of them got home, for de Nogent had learnt to expect the swift reply, but they were sufficient to upset the rhythm of his attack, and slow up his advance. He was infuriated, too, by these lightning thrusts that caught him off his balance, and seemed to spring at him from all angles.

Then he stood back. Philip kept his distance. He could hear the panting breath from his opponent, and he had a shrewd idea of de Nogent's position. He himself was hot now; he could feel the prickle of perspiration under his gambeson, and streams were running down his cheeks and nose under the helm. De Nogent must be bathed in sweat, his body one burning mass of heat. And he must be tired, too.

For the hauberk was a heavy weight, dragging down the shoulders and arms. Great strength was required to hold up a shield, or swing a sword with that constant weight on the arms. Only a man in the fittest condition could keep up a steady pace for long. And de Nogent was slack and flabby after his long voyage.

But the man had courage and determination. He

paused for a few moments, and came on again. He slashed down, saw the stroke finish on Philip's shield, stepped to the left, and cut again. A third time he slipped away, and Philip obediently slewed round to face his opponent. He had the fight well in hand. In a few minutes he would be able to take the initiative.

For the fourth time he brought his shield up, and took a glancing blow with ease and confidence. Then in a flash he realized his mistake. The slanting rays of the sun caught him full on the face of his helm. He blinked, tried to move, and shook his head to clear his vision. A tremendous blow caught him full on the top of his helm. He heard the screech of tortured metal grating in his ears. With a crash his helm was driven down with shattering force on to the top of his head. A reddish mist floated in front of his eyes, and his knees buckled.

Instinctively his feet took him out of danger, and he brought his sword and shield up to guard against the next blow. He had a brief vision of de Nogent's sword whizzing down at his head. The blade caught the tip of his shield; the shoulder straps dragged down his body, but his strong legs resisted the pressure, and he staggered back, still upright.

Desperately he flung out his sword. He felt the jar as it hit de Nogent's shield. There was no force behind the jab, but it slowed down the other's advance, and gave Philip the momentary breathing space he needed. He swung to the left. The sun was out of his eyes now. His head was throbbing as if several hammers were pounding away at him, but he was unhurt.

There was a pause. That last violent onslaught had drained away the last of de Nogent's energy. He had staked everything on that furious attack; he was dripping with perspiration, and his arms and legs were heavy and leaden. He was panting loudly; harsh, rasping gasps of sheer exhaustion that Philip heard and acted upon.

He was hardly tired yet. Hot, yes, but not unduly so, and he was used to the feeling. He wanted to brush away the sweat pouring down his nose, and the realization that this was impossible with a huge helm over his face made him grin.

As if from a distance he heard the roar of the crowd. There was little love lost between the newcomers to Outremer and the long established barons. Philip was a member of one of the original Crusading families, his father a rich and respected baron of the kingdom, and there were few in the crowd who supported de Nogent.

As Philip stepped forward, taking the initiative for the first time, the shouts of encouragement rose to a bellow of excitement. Philip lunged. Up went de Nogent's guard. The long blade slid over his shield, and grated against the top of his helm. It was a harmless enough blow, but Philip had delivered it deliberately. As his opponent covered up, he brought his sword back in a sweep, the first time he had really used the edge of his blade in a cut.

It was a beautiful blow, perfectly timed and aimed,

struck with an apparently effortless ease, but all Philip's weight and strength were behind the stroke. De Nogent's shield caught the full force, his left arm was dragged down under the impact, and he staggered back, desperately throwing up his sword to parry the next attack.

Philip leapt forward. He slashed down again. This time de Nogent was not so well prepared, for he had been given little time to recover. His shield was beaten down, and with a screech of metal, Philip's sword caught him full on the helm.

To a tired and exhausted man, the crushing impact must have been stunning. De Nogent swayed on his feet, his shield down, and his helm exposed. Philip rose on his toes, and swung down with all his strength. He felt the jar of the blow upon his arm, heard the clang of the blade on his man's helm, and saw the sparks fly up.

But still de Nogent stayed on his feet, though he must have been barely conscious after the hammering of those two tremendous cracks on his head. He was helpless now, his knees buckling, shield and sword drooping, completely at Philip's mercy.

But Outremer was a hard school. Life there, despite the luxury and gaiety that impressed newcomers from the West, was a crude and harsh existence beneath the thin layer of chivalry and bright colours. Kill or be killed was the savage code that had been drummed into Philip's ears. You respected a beaten enemy if he had fought bravely. But only when you had beaten him.

So Philip jumped forward, swinging back his sword, and coolly selecting his next target. He could hit his man where he chose now, and he dropped his own guard to give himself all the additional power for the decisive blow.

He brought his sword down on de Nogent's left shoulder, just where the neck joins the collar bone. Not even the finest hauberk could have saved a man from that terrific blow. De Nogent's collar bone snapped like a twig. He reeled to one side, dazed, staggering and barely conscious of what was happening to him. Only his training and strong legs kept him upright.

Philip swung back with a speed and precision that brought appreciative cheers from his critical audience. He slashed sideways at de Nogent's neck, and caught him a sweeping blow under the ear, a deadly stroke at a vital spot. De Nogent was bowled off his feet, the last faint shreds of consciousness hammered out of him. His sword dropped from his fingers, and he crashed to the ground, rolled over on his back, and lay there, his helm staring up blankly at the blue sky and the setting sun.

Hands pounded Philip on the back. Eager fingers unstrapped his helm, and the cool air soothed his streaming face as he blinked in the strong light. The practical Llewellyn pushed a wineskin under his nose. Philip clutched the skin and gulped down the cool wine. Now that the fight was over he realized how hot he was; his whole body seemed on fire under his gambeson, so dripping with perspiration that he might have stepped out of a bath.

'Twenty bezants!' yelled a voice in Philip's ear, and he caught a whiff of scent as a silk handkerchief was flourished in his face. It was Joscelin, of course, waving a purse that jingled with the weight of the gold coins that he had won.

'Well done, boy,' cried Sir Fulk. 'Should have finished the fellow off long ago, though. Too many of these newfangled lunges for my liking.'

Philip smiled and nodded at the shouted comments, some from men who had never before bothered to speak to him, a young and unproved squire. He was far more anxious, though, to hear what Sir Hugo had to say, and he looked around the circle of sunburnt faces.

Sir Hugo was standing a few feet away, composed and aloof as usual, listening calmly to the excited chatter. He caught Philip's eye and nodded.

'You fought well, Philip,' he said. 'I am proud of you.'

Philip flushed. This was the first time his father had said that. But there was more to come. There was a sudden swirl in the crowd, and a narrow gangway opened up to allow two men to approach. Philip caught the muttered remarks.

'The King! The King! Make way, seigneurs.'

Guy of Lusignan, King of Jerusalem and Protector of the Holy Sepulchre, made his way through the ranks of his barons and knights with an easy grace and dignity. In the prime of life, tall and athletic, with fair hair and beard, blessed with a face of exceptional beauty, a deep voice, and a charming manner, he was a most impressive and striking figure. No man could have looked more like a king and a leader than Guy.

He nodded at Philip, and turned to Sir Hugo. 'You have trained the boy well, Sir Hugo,' he said. 'Are you knighted yet, Philip?' he asked, though he must have known the answer.

'No, my lord,' Philip said.

'Time enough,' Sir Hugo said. 'He is just seventeen.'

'As young as that!' The King examined Philip, and then smiled the charming and irresistible smile that had made him so many friends and helped him to his present position. 'But not too young, I think. Bring him to me before the meeting of the High Court, Hugo. Tomorrow.'

He swung round, and the crowd gave way for him again. But the man who had been with him stayed for a moment. He stood with his hands on his hips, staring at Philip, eyeing him from head to foot as a merchant might inspect some piece of goods he intended to buy.

There could not have been a greater contrast between two men as between the King and this baron. Where Guy of Lusignan was all grace and charm, this man was aggressively brutal and forthright, with a hooked nose that sprang from the centre of his dark face, blue eyes that blazed under shaggy brows, and a pointed beard that jutted out belligerently, jerking up and down as he spoke. Even his voice was in keeping with his appearance, hoarse and rasping, throwing out curt, impatient sentences, as if he had no time for the courteous and polished phrases of the East.

'Promising, Hugo,' he said, his hard eyes swinging away from Philip's bowing figure. 'We could do with more of his kind. An improvement on these snivelling Pullani,' he added, careless of the feelings of any Pullani noblemen who might have overheard. He nodded brusquely, turned on his heels and stalked away after the King.

'Tactful fellow, Reynaud, isn't he?' remarked Sir Fulk.

'Who?' exclaimed Philip, hearing the name.

'Don't you know, boy? Well, you're not likely to forget him, now that you have met him. That's one thing I will say for Reynaud de Chatillon.'

'Reynaud de Chatillon!' Philip muttered.

You could not live for long in Outremer without hearing of the Lord of Oultrejourdain, the holder of Kerak in Moab, one of the strongest castles in the kingdom. Reynaud had landed in Outremer as a penniless adventurer, but he possessed the qualities most needed in the East; he was a brilliant soldier, recklessly brave, a man who thrived on danger and difficulties. Even a long imprisonment at the hands of the Turks had failed to damp his burning energy and ambition. He had married one of the greatest heiresses in the kingdom, and now from his rich fief of Kerak, standing on the exposed southern frontier, he commanded the vital caravan route from Egypt to the north, the lifeline of the Turks, and the chief communication between north and south.

Philip rode back to the city, still receiving compliments as he passed other riders. Sir Fulk was throwing out invitations to a dinner-party that night to celebrate his nephew's victory. It would be a noisy and tiring evening, Philip felt, but he was in the mood to enjoy himself.

Chapter Four

THE HIGH COURT

SIR FULK'S long dining-room was crowded when Philip and his father, bathed and changed, were shown in by a Syrian manservant. Sir Fulk, red faced and excited, shouted greetings to his guests, talking ceaselessly, barely pausing to listen to the replies, and pushing people into their seats, bellowing orders to his servants, and clearly in the highest of spirits.

Philip sat at the lower end of the room, with Joscelin and the younger men. Joscelin, resplendent in a silken cotte and surcoat, was still waving his handkerchief, and there were several other knights who displayed the same fashion.

Philip was introduced to a young knight he had not met before. As the man was an obvious newcomer to Outremer, Philip was surprised to see him there, for Sir Fulk held strong views. But this man was of a different calibre from de Nogent and his ruffianly friends.

'Sir Gilbert d'Assailly,' Joscelin said, and Philip bowed.

'D'Assailly?' he repeated. The name seemed familiar.

'Yes, he's a nephew of the late Grand Master of the Hospitallers,' Joscelin said.

Philip nodded. That would explain the newcomer's presence. And he liked the look of his new acquaintance, too. Gilbert could not have been much older than himself, a tall, thin, awkward young man, with long shambling legs, and a bony, high-cheeked face. He was shabbily dressed in comparison with the brightly coloured clothes of the other knights.

Not much money, Philip guessed, looking at the drab colours of Gilbert's cotte. It was easy to see that he had just arrived from Normandy. His red face was beginning to peel under the hot sun. His neck and hands, Philip was distressed to see, were far from clean. Western knights took some time to adopt the habits of the East.

'You are going to join the Hospitallers, Sir Gilbert?' Philip asked.

'Oh, no, I don't think so. At least, I may, if I do not find some baron who wishes to enrol another knight in his garrison,' Gilbert said, shuffling his feet, and speaking with some nervousness.

The servants were pressing the guests to take their seats, and Philip found himself sitting by d'Assailly. The Norman was gazing round the room with awestruck eyes, looking up from the array of gold and silver spread before him to the long line of gorgeously arrayed men and women in their Eastern robes, matching so perfectly the graceful beauty of the room with its silken hangings and profusion of bright colours.

'And what do you think of Outremer?' Philip asked, smiling a little, for he had seen this expression on the faces of newcomers before.

Gilbert stammered and waved his hand helplessly. The fingers were long and dirty, with blackened nails.

'I am just amazed,' Gilbert said, struggling for words. 'But I suppose you are used to all this. You were born in Outremer?'

Philip nodded, and a servant laid the first course before him. Gilbert glanced at his neighbour to see how these strange dishes should be eaten, before he started his dinner.

'But what amazes you, Gilbert?' Philip asked.

'Well, you don't really imagine we live like this in Normandy?' Gilbert said.

'I don't know anything about Normandy,' Philip confessed. 'But this is only my uncle's town house, you know. At Montgizard . . .'

'Only his town house!' echoed Gilbert. 'You should see Assailly. My father has a rich fief, but his castle is a hovel

73

compared to this! The floors are covered with smelly rushes, and the servants sleep there with the dogs. There's only one carpet in the whole castle, and that's in the solar. It's quite a small one, too. My mother and sisters wove it themselves.'

'Rushes?' Philip said in surprise, wrinkling up his nose.

'Yes, and they smell,' Gilbert said feelingly. 'I never realized how much they did smell until I came to Outremer. But you wouldn't know.'

'Oh, yes, I do,' Philip said ruefully. 'You wait until you ride through the streets of Jerusalem or Ascalon on a really hot day. You'll soon know what smells can be like then!'

'Oh, the streets,' and Gilbert waved his hand again, until he suddenly noticed Philip's carefully scrubbed fingers and nails. He flushed and stammered again. 'You make me feel as though I'm a dirty barbarian,' he muttered, trying to conceal his hands under the table.

'Don't be silly,' Philip said hastily. 'You must come and stay with us at Blanche Garde. You'll soon get used to it all.' He liked d'Assailly more each moment he listened to him. 'Tell me more about your home.'

'I hardly know where to begin.' Gilbert looked across the room. 'We have bare walls, no lovely hangings like those over there. In the winter they stream with damp.'

'But you have fires?'

'Yes, and the smoke blows all over the hall. Your eyes smart all winter, and the draughts blow down your neck and freeze your feet. If you sit near the fire, you're roasted on one side, and chilled on the other. And your clothes stink from the smoke as if you'd been pushed into the middle of a bonfire.'

'It can't be as bad as that!' Philip said.

'Worse!' Gilbert said emphatically. 'As for the furniture'—he laughed and fingered the soft cushion on his chair—'there isn't a comfortable chair in the whole of Assailly. Or a decent bed, either. No, you stay in Outremer, Philip.'

'I shall,' Philip said. 'But why did you leave Normandy?'

'Oh, I'm a younger son. There was nothing for me at Assailly. And my uncle made a career for himself out here. My father fitted me out as best he could, but it's an expensive journey here.'

'Yes, the Venetians charge a lot for a sea passage,' Philip said. 'But we can't do without them and their trade.'

'Do you know any barons who want extra knights in their fiefs?' Gilbert asked.

'Plenty,' Philip said. 'We're terribly short of knights. I'll think about it, though.' A sudden thought struck him, and he looked quickly at Gilbert's open face and air of pleasant honesty.

They started to talk about the fight by the Pool of Siloam. De Nogent, so Philip had learnt, was not seriously hurt. His collar bone was smashed, and he would suffer a stiff and aching neck for many days. They were soon interrupted by a bellow from the top of the table. Sir Fulk was on his feet, his face flushed with heat and wine. He mopped his streaming forehead with a gaudy handkerchief, and banged on the table.

'My ladies and seigneurs,' he shouted, waving a full glass in the air. 'I give you the toast of my young nephew, Philip d'Aubigny.'

To Philip's intense embarrassment, everyone stood up and turned in his direction, smiling at him with approval. Deep voices echoed the toast.

But Sir Fulk had not finished. He launched himself into a wandering harangue about Outremer, about noble Norman families, the ideals of chivalry, the villainy of the Infidels, until he fell back into his seat, and shouted to the servants to refill the glasses and tankards.

Despite the late hour at which the feast ended, Philip was up early the next morning, and joined his father at breakfast. They ate in silence for a while, until Philip decided to broach the subject on which his mind had been working since the previous evening. He must be tactful, he thought, and talk his father round skilfully.

'I met another new arrival last night, father,' he said.

'Oh, who was that?'

'Gilbert d'Assailly. His uncle was the Grand Master of the Hospitallers once.'

'Yes, I knew him,' Sir Hugo said. 'He was drowned in the West, when he went home to raise recruits for Outremer.'

'He's a very nice fellow, Gilbert,' Philip said, sticking manfully to his plan. 'Can I ask him to stay at Blanche Garde, father?'

'Why not? But isn't he joining the Hospitallers? I expect he will be sent to Krak, or one of the great northern castles.'

'Oh, he doesn't want to join them,' Philip said. 'He wants to become a knight in some baron's garrison.' He paused and waited anxiously. But, not for the first time, he had underestimated the quickness of Sir Hugo's brain.

'And we are one knight short of our quota for the feudal levy.'

'Two, father.'

'Not after this morning. You are going to be knighted, you know, Philip.'

'I hadn't thought of that,' Philip said, forgetting Gilbert for the moment as he visualized the scene in the Palace. But his father broke into his dream.

'And you think this Gilbert d'Assailly will do for the third, eh?'

'I didn't say that, father!' Philip exclaimed hastily, a little put out that Sir Hugo had read his thoughts so uncannily.

'But you had it in mind?'

'Well, yes, I had,' Philip confessed ruefully. 'He's quite nice, you know. But he's got no money, and . . .'

'And you want me to fit him out?' Sir Hugo's dark eyes twinkled with amusement.

Philip fidgeted uneasily with a dish of figs. His careful plan was finished before he had really begun.

'Bring him to dinner tonight,' Sir Hugo said. 'If I like the look of him, I'll give him to you as a present for being knighted. With a horse, a hauberk, and an outfit of clothes.'

'What!' The silver dish clattered to the stone floor, and the figs cascaded in a stream across the room to Sir Hugo's feet.

'But not if you dent one of my best dishes,' Sir Hugo said. 'You must learn to control your feelings, Philip.'

'Yes, father,' Philip said. 'And thank you very much, father. I'll see Gilbert at the Palace, I expect. I can ask him then.'

He was gone with a rush from the room in search of his horse. Sir Hugo chuckled, and bent down to pick up the figs and the silver dish.

The main entrance hall of the Palace was crowded when Philip and his father arrived. The meetings of the High Court were open to all the barons and knights of the Kingdom who owned land, but few attended the routine meetings. Today it was known that the threatening military position would be discussed, and decisions reached that might affect the future of Outremer, and many barons had ridden into Jerusalem from distant fiefs and castles.

Philip found Gilbert after several minutes' search, and gave him the invitation to dinner, and the news that Sir Hugo might take him as a knight and fit him out. Gilbert was delighted. This was more than he had expected, and he thanked Philip in his grave way.

'Tell me about this High Court,' he went on. 'We have nothing like it in Normandy.'

'It's the highest court in the Kingdom,' Philip explained. 'The King must have its consent for anything important he wishes to do.'

'What, anything?'

'Oh, yes. If he wants to declare war, for instance, or raise a new tax.'

The hall was clearing now, for the knights were drifting gradually into the large audience chamber beyond. Two other knights were to be made in addition to Philip, and Sir Hugo came across to lead Philip to the foot of the dais at the far end of the great room.

'You know what to do?' he asked in a low tone.

Philip nodded. He was feeling excited again, the tense and nerve tingling sensation he had experienced just before the fight by the Pool of Siloam.

He had seen many men knighted. The ceremony was a simple one at that time, and there was little for him to do except listen. The dais was filled with the high officers of the Kingdom, the Marshal, the Chamberlain, the Constable, and the Chancellor, all waiting for the King, who walked through a side door as Philip reached the foot of the dais.

The two other squires were unbuckling their belts and swords, and Philip did the same. The Marshal signed to Sir

Hugo, who took Philip's belt and led him to the platform, where they both bowed to Guy.

The King smiled pleasantly at Philip, and then, with his own hands, buckled the belt around his waist, while the Marshal, John de Durus, bent down and fastened spurs to his heels.

'Kneel,' Sir Hugo whispered.

Philip went down on one knee. He felt the light tap of a sword blade on his shoulder, and the deep voice of the King above his bent head.

'Rise, Sir Philip.'

Philip stood up again, his eyes fixed rigidly in front. He could see the dark, bearded face of Joscelin de Courtney, the Seneschal, and the grave, pallid features of the aged Bishop of Tripoli, who acted as Chancellor of the Kingdom.

The King was still speaking, giving Philip the advice bestowed upon newly created knights.

'Keep before you the example of that pattern of all knights, Duke Godfrey of Bouillon. Defend the Christian Church and the True Faith. Fight to the death against the Infidel; be true to your lord, speak the truth, keep your word, and at all times be the champion of right against evil and injustice.'

Guy patted Philip on the shoulder and spoke a few charming phrases that made Philip his friend and admirer for life. Then he signed to him to stand at his side, and went through the same short ceremony with the other two squires.

'Now, seigneurs,' he said briskly. 'To the High Court. Philip, you will attend behind my chair.'

Philip flushed and bowed. This was an honour, and he walked into the Council Chamber behind Guy's tall and stately figure.

The barons of Outremer ranged themselves on either side of long tables running down the centre of the room. Near the King, at the head of the table, were the chief officers, who spread out piles of parchments and heavily sealed documents in front of them.

Philip had not, of course, been present at a meeting of the High Court before, and at first he listened with interest to the proceedings, though there was nothing particularly exciting in the first half hour's business.

The officers dealt with the routine matters first; taxation and receipts from the customs; disputes about a coat of arms, for two knights had adopted a similar design; long and learned arguments about titles to property, and an animated discussion about the trading rights in the kingdom of the Venetians and the Genoese.

All this was of great importance, no doubt, but Philip soon found it extremely boring. He fidgeted on his hard stool, and shifted it slightly so as to avoid the hot sun streaming in through the tall windows. He was not the only person there whose attention was wandering. Several men were dozing, while others whispered to each other.

Then there was a pause, and the King pushed back his chair and rose to his feet. This was the moment the barons had been waiting for. Silence fell on the whole assembly, and all heads were turned to the handsome man at the head of the table.

Guy of Lusignan reviewed the military position. He added details about the latest moves of the Turks. The least imaginative man there could not fail to judge the position for himself. Outremer was in deadly peril; at any moment invasion and total destruction might descend upon the Christian states. The King's face was drawn and anxious as he came to the end of his speech. 'We must decide on our future plans, seigneurs,' he said. 'Are we to wait until Saladin attacks us? He may not do so, of course. For we are not completely helpless. Our castles are strong, and guard the passes through the mountains. The Infidels may fear the risk of an invasion with a long and vulnerable line of communications. But they may decide to attack. Should we wait, or attack first?'

He sat down, and waited for the others to speak. The arguments were numerous and heated. For there were two distinct sides in the High Court. There were those like Reynaud de Chatillon and the two Grand Masters, who urged swift action immediately against the Turks. Reynaud delivered a forcible speech, shouting and banging the table; immediate action was what he wanted; attack, attack: anything that would hurt the Infidel.

But the opposition was equally strong. The Pullani noblemen led this side. They had mixed blood; they held rich fiefs, and regarded the Turks with none of the fanatical hatred of the Military Orders or the more recent arrivals from the West. And they were determined not to risk their lands in a war.

Philip listened to all this attentively. He knew the two arguments well. Many times the same phrases and points had been hurled across the high table at Blanche Garde by visitors.

Guy of Lusignan listened too, with strained attention, nodding his head at each fresh speech. But the barons knew only too well that they would get no lead from him. For behind Guy's noble appearance, his charming manner and majestic dignity, there was a mind that could never come to a decision. He would always agree with the last speaker, and would reach a different decision six times during the day.

Sir Hugo had said nothing up to this point. He fingered his black, pointed beard, and listened impassively to each speaker. Philip noticed, though, that his father was watching the King with some anxiety. For Sir Hugo held strong and decided views, and he was afraid that Guy would be stampeded into a fatal course of action.

The room was hot, despite the high ceiling and the tall open windows. The barons were tired and restless. Sir Hugo timed his intervention in the dispute with practised skill. As he stood up, tall, dignified and aloof, all eyes turned to him hopefully. He was respected by every man there. They were all intriguers, ambitious, greedy, and intensely jealous of one another's possessions or power, constantly plotting and scheming, and fatally weakening Outremer in the process. Sir Hugo was well known as a man who held aloof from these squabbles, and a schemer has always a sneaking respect for the man who refuses to dirty his fingers in his own disreputable game.

Sir Hugo was in no hurry to begin. He swept his eyes around the waiting faces and then turned in the direction of the King. This was the man he was talking to, the person who could make the final decision.

'I cannot wholly agree with any seigneur here,' he said. 'We must fight the Infidel, of course. Otherwise there is no point in the existence of Outremer. And some day we must destroy him, or else he will destroy us.'

Reynaud de Chatillon thumped the table vigorously, and the two Grand Masters nodded their agreement. From many of the others came a hum, but Sir Hugo held up a hand. There was instant silence. He held them all effortlessly by the sheer force of his personality.

'But this is not the right time to attack,' he said. 'We have neither the men nor the money. Nor do I think the Emir Saladin will attack us. His position is not entirely secure. One setback, and the Turks will split into groups once more. But if he is provoked by people like Sir Reynaud here, then he will preach a Holy War immediately.'

Many nodded. This was sound common sense. Even Reynaud was watching Sir Hugo with respectful attention.

'We need a breathing space,' Sir Hugo said. 'We must

appeal to the Pope for help. He must preach another Crusade. We want men and money. Then we can attack. And Damascus must be our aim. With Damascus in our hands we shall cut the lifeline of the Infidels, and split them in two. We shall be safe for generations.'

He sat down with the same unhurried dignity with which he had risen, his face showing no sign of any emotion. Philip watched his father and sighed. Why couldn't he behave like that, instead of blurting out the first things that came into his head, and giving the game away by every changing mood and expression on his face.

Sir Hugo had done his work. The King was convinced. No one else wished to speak. They were all tired; the meeting had lasted long enough and the vote was taken. No war would be declared. Immediate appeals were to be made to the Christian states of the West for men and money.

On the way home, Sir Fulk, who had said little at the High Court, gave a running commentary to Sir Hugo.

'You're quite right, of course, Hugo,' he trumpeted. 'But you'll never keep de Chatillon quiet. I know the fellow well. Always waiting to get his own back on the Infidels for keeping him a prisoner for so long.'

'Yes, I know,' Sir Hugo said.

'There he is at Kerak,' Sir Fulk went on. 'Like a hawk waiting for a heron on passage. Right on top of the caravan routes. Do you think he'll keep off that?' Sir Fulk laughed scornfully. 'I'll bet you the best horse in my stables at Montgizard against that new hauberk of yours.'

'I won't take you, Fulk,' Sir Hugo said. 'You're quite right, too. Still, Reynaud might hold off for a time, and give us a chance.'

Gilbert d'Assailly came to dinner that night, and was duly inspected by Sir Hugo. To Philip's relief he passed the test, and at the end of the evening, he took the oath of allegiance to Sir Hugo as his new lord.

Gilbert was eager to see the most famous sights and buildings of the Holy City, so Philip acted as his guide. They went to the Church of the Holy Sepulchre, rebuilt by the Crusaders after the capture of Jerusalem eight years before, and Gilbert was shown the tiny chapel of the tomb of Christ.

Near the church lay the huge Hospital of St John, where the Hospitallers daily handed out alms on a lavish scale to pilgrims, and Gilbert watched the ceremony with interest, astonished at the obvious wealth displayed by the Military Order.

After that Philip took him through the narrow alleys with their high, blank walls and overhanging arches, to the old Temple Area. He told how this had once been covered with the wonderful buildings of the old Jewish Temple, one of the sights of the ancient world, and totally destroyed by the Romans. The vast enclosure was bare now, except for the Dome of the Rock, a mosque built by the Turks.

Early the next morning, before the sun was directly overhead, they rode out through the Gate of Jehosaphat, down into the Vale of Kedron, splashed across the little brook, and mounted the slope to a small garden on a ridge overlooking the city walls.

'What is this?' Gilbert asked as Philip dismounted.

'The Garden of Gethsemane,' Philip said.

Wide-eyed with reverence and awe, Gilbert walked around, touching the gnarled elms which, tradition said, had stood there since that fatal night of the Passover so long ago.

'Where next?' he asked as they rode away.

'Up to the Mount of Olives. There's a wonderful view from there.'

Philip was right. Gilbert was to say afterwards that it was the most amazing prospect he had ever seen. For probably from no other spot could he have gained such a revealing aspect of the land to which he had come.

Below them lay the ancient city, spread out like a map, sprawling slantways across the hills of Judaea, encircled by its grim walls and towers, set amidst the savage and relentless mountains and valleys. From a cloudless sky the sun burnt down on the parched earth, bare of any vegetation, the yellowish soil and outcrops of rock shimmering in the terrible heat.

'Look over there,' Philip said, and they turned their backs on Jerusalem, and gazed out over the panorama to the east.

The tangle of gulleys and hills fell gradually towards the Jordan, until in the far distance Philip pointed out the tiny blue patch of the Dead Sea, and the sun shining on the pinkish mountains of Moab beyond.

'Yes, it's beautiful in a way,' muttered Gilbert. 'But I think it must be the cruellest country I have ever seen.'

'Cruel!' Philip glanced at his friend in startled surprise.

'You were born here, so you wouldn't notice that. But there's no softness about this.' He waved his hand over the tawny yellow hills baking in the sun. 'And Jerusalem frightens me, Philip. It's like some savage beast waiting to jump.'

Philip looked at the city, and then at Gilbert. He suddenly remembered what the old pilgrim had told him about England. A soft, kindly countryside. Perhaps Gilbert was right. There was certainly no softness about Jerusalem.

Philip grunted, and rode down the steep slope towards the Brook Kedron. He was still thinking about Gilbert's remarks when they skirted the lofty walls to the north, and entered the city by the Gate of the Flowers. Well, there was nothing he could do about it all, he decided. Outremer was his home. It might be pleasant to live in a land of green fields and woods like England, but there was no future there for him.

The beggars were already out in the streets as Sir Hugo and his party left Jerusalem four days later on their way back to Blanche Garde. One of them ran up to Philip's horse, and held up his skinny arms. His clothes were tattered rags, his skin was filthy, and his face covered with sores. Philip shuddered in instinctive disgust, but he threw the man a coin from his purse. The action was seen by another beggar. He rushed across the street and pawed at Philip's feet with his claw-like hands.

'Something for the love of God, my lord,' he whined. 'Something for the love of God!'

Philip recoiled in disgust, and tried to push past. The man's entreaties changed in a flash to a string of wild curses and foul abuse. Llewellyn, who was riding just behind Philip, leant down from his saddle. He brought his whip across the beggar's face with a back-handed slash that cut the skin like a knife. The wretched man recoiled with a scream of agony.

'Leave the poor devil alone!' Philip shouted in a sudden flash of anger. 'You may be snivelling about the streets yourself one day!' He hurled another coin at the writhing figure on the cobbles, and with a sigh of relief passed by the Tower of David and out into the open country.

They made the usual leisurely journey, for Sir Hugo was in no particular hurry. The hottest part of the day was spent in the shade, and the night at a rest-house. It was not until the following afternoon that the moment came for which Philip had been waiting. The party climbed a hill, and as they topped the crest, the ground fell to the wide valley of Blanche Garde. Philip gestured to Gilbert with his whip. For there was the white, flat-roofed town, the winding stream, the green splash of the marsh, and the tall grey walls of the great castle.

A single banner was fluttering over the gatehouse, and

as Philip watched, he caught the flash of the sun on the steel helmet of a sentry. Through the still air came the sweet call of a trumpet, and tiny, black figures ran across the wide courtyard. The approaching party had been seen and recognized. The Lord of Blanche Garde must be received with all ceremony, for Sir Hugo had a sharp eye and tongue for slackness.

Gilbert was inspecting his new home with grave interest. 'It's a vast place,' he muttered respectfully.

'Not compared to some of the castles in the north,' Philip said. 'I've never seen Krak of the Knights, the big Hospitaller castle in the Lebanon mountains, but father has been there. You could put Blanche Garde down inside it, and lose it!'

Gilbert shook his head and laughed.

'No, Philip is right,' Sir Hugo said. 'There are some enormous fortresses in the Kingdom. Blanche Garde is out of date now, and quite small compared with Safita, or Beaufort, or Reynaud's keep at Kerak in Moab. But I expect you will see them for yourself.'

That was the start of a new existence for Gilbert. He soon learnt to copy the habits of the others, in clothes, food, and daily customs. He took baths regularly, lounged on soft cushions, appreciated the delicious fruits of the East, and wondered what his family in far-away Assailly would have said if they could have seen even one glimpse of the luxury and comfort in which he lived.

But that was only one side of his life. He soon learnt

that the main life of a knight in Outremer was spent in fighting, or preparing for the next campaign. The Kingdom had been at peace for a few years now, but he listened to Philip's account of the last invasion by the Turks, when a huge army had marched up from Egypt, and Blanche Garde had closed its great gates, and waited for the attack that never came. For the Christians took the Infidels by surprise near Montgizard, and smashed their army into a rabble of fleeing soldiers.

That year was a pleasant one; looking back, Philip thought afterwards that it was the happiest he ever spent in Outremer. For the first time he had company, for Gilbert was always with him, practising with sword and lance in the courtyard under Sir Hugo's critical eye, riding out with their hawks on the hills around the castle, visiting neighbours, and entertaining the constant flow of guests.

Philip came to have a great affection for Gilbert. He often fretted impatiently over his friend's slowness, but he soon learnt that Gilbert was no fool, and invariably arrived at the correct solution. He was a stolid and dependable friend, rather apt to look on the gloomy side of things, perhaps, but as Philip was always much too optimistic, that was no great fault. On foot, Gilbert, despite the Eastern clothes which he soon grew to like, was still the thin and shambling figure, all hands and feet, that Philip had first met; but on horseback he was a different man. There he was all ease and grace, an instinctive horseman and a magnificent rider.

But Gilbert would have been the first to admit that he was not in the same class as Philip. For that year changed Philip from a promising young squire into a finished knight; a man who was recognized by the experts as one of the most formidable swordsmen and jousters in the Kingdom. He would not reach his prime, perhaps, for a few years, but he won the tournament at Ascalon in the winter, and at Christmas was only beaten in the final bout of the great jousts of Jerusalem.

The short, bitter winter of Outremer came and went. With the spring the bare hills were covered with a carpet of flowers, the air was fresh and fragrant, and for a short time they enjoyed the loveliest season of the Holy Land.

But the long, sweltering months of the eastern summer lay ahead. A burning sun scorched the flowers on their green slopes. The countryside lost its deceptive air of softness, and was transformed into an expanse of tumbled hills and deep valleys, of bare, brown, sun-baked earth, and rocks that shimmered in the sun. Swirling dust clouds blew up from the south, fanned by the sultry wind of the Khamsan, irritating the skin and pricking the eyes, until riding and any movement became a grim discomfort of heat, dust, and flies.

There seemed, even to Philip, an added gaiety and frenzy to that last year. Gilbert was still bewildered by the luxury of the life he led, by the continual round of feasts and entertainments. But slowly he began to take for granted the spotless bed linen, the baths, the array of gold and silver ornaments, the strange and exotic fruits and dishes, and the magnificent surroundings of mosaic floors, of bright wall hangings, and comfortable furniture. He learnt the names of the frequent visitors to Blanche Garde, the swarthy, sunburnt men in turbans and silk burnous, and their gorgeous ladies, dazzling in tunics of gold embroidered thread, their faces lavishly painted with cosmetics, chattering gaily in shrill tones, and moving with mincing step and manner.

Long afterwards, Philip realized that the Crusaders must have been conscious of the brooding disaster that hung over their heads, and so plunged feverishly into an even more frenzied round of gaiety. For in the cities of the East, beyond the frontiers of the Kingdom, Saladin was steadily building up his strength, crouching like some great cat for his leap upon the Christians. He was ready now, and was waiting only for some excuse to send his Infidel hordes streaming through the mountain passes and down into the plains of Outremer, by-passing the great castles, and penetrating into the heart of the Christian lands.

Chapter Five

WAR

DINNER at Blanche Garde was almost finished. Sir Hugo sat under his canopy with Philip and Gilbert on either side, for there were no guests at the castle that night. Philip was describing the day's sport; he and Gilbert had been out with their falcons.

From the direction of the gatehouse came the raucous peal of a trumpet. The chattering servants and soldiers around the tables in the body of the hall fell silent. Sir Hugo put down his glass of wine, and turned his head, his eyebrows rising in silent inquiry.

'Some late traveller?' Gilbert said, filling the uneasy silence.

Sir Hugo shook his head. Philip felt a sudden chill, and under the table his feet moved uneasily. For some reason he thought he could detect a note of urgency in that trumpet call, the peal of a tired man bringing bad news. A ridiculous fancy, he decided, but all trumpet sounds had their own meaning for him. It was as if the feelings and emotions of the blower were instinctively blended with the formal notes of the call.

Voices could be heard beyond the screens at the far end of the hall, and then the curtains were thrust aside. The steward stepped back, and a man in the royal livery strode towards the dais. He walked stiffly, as a man who had ridden hard through the heat of the day. His dress was white with dust, and his face streaked with smears of dirt where he had tried to brush away the gritty perspiration.

Sir Hugo stood up quickly, his heavy chair grating in the silence as he pushed it back. In silence he held out his hand for the thick parchment the messenger bore.

'From the King, my lord,' the man said, and stepped back, his shoulders drooping with fatigue, and relaxing now that his duty was ended.

Sir Hugo glanced at the large, red seals on the letter, and waved a peremptory hand to the servants. 'Wine and food for this man,' he said curtly, and broke the seals.

Ivo the Steward moved to Sir Hugo's side. He acted as his master's secretary, for Sir Hugo's Latin was weak.

Together they ran their eyes over the thick black lettering on the paper.

'A meeting of the High Court, my lord. The Emir Saladin has broken the truce, and is marching on Galilee and Tiberias.'

Sir Hugo grunted and sat down, staring at the letter. With a tremendous effort Philip restrained himself from a flood of excited questions, while Gilbert rubbed his large, beaked nose, and stared curiously at Sir Hugo.

Sir Hugo drained his glass, grunted once more, and turned to the two young knights.

'I will ride for Jerusalem at dawn,' he said. 'I expect the High Court will declare the *arrière ban*.'

They both knew what that meant; the calling out of all able-bodied men in Outremer to join the feudal levy of the King.

'I shall probably be back here in four days,' Sir Hugo went on. 'I want to find everything ready. Leave a small holding garrison for the castle. Cut it to half the usual number.'

'Half!' Philip echoed in surprise. This was taking a risk he would never have imagined his father capable of running.

'Yes, half. The mobile force must be ready to move with fodder and food for two weeks, if you can raise enough carts from the town. And the usual reserve ammunition of arrows and spares, of course. Collect all the waterskins you can find. We shall probably need water more than food in this heat. Gilbert, you will supervise the equipment with Llewellyn. Philip, you concentrate on the horses. I want them in perfect condition.'

He poured out a rapid stream of instructions, precise and detailed, covering all possible emergencies suggested by his long experience of past campaigns in the East.

'If you have time,' he added at the end, 'you'd better have that fall in the ditch on the southern curtain wall seen to, Philip. Get hold of the rais from the town, and tell him to send up a working party. In fact, you might start them on that in the morning. It might be safer if things go wrong.'

They moved from the dais into the solar. Sir Hugo went on with his instructions, and Llewellyn was summoned to join the discussion, for he was the most experienced of the men-at-arms, or sergeants, as they were called.

Gilbert asked questions about the *arrière ban*, for the system in Outremer differed from that of his native Normandy.

'In time of war, every baron and knight must take the field,' Sir Hugo said. 'The only excuse is sickness or old age. The King must pay each knight five hundred bezants, and the knight must produce four horses for himself. And heaven knows where the King will find the money for this war. The kings of Jerusalem have always been short of funds.'

'What about replacement of horses?' Gilbert asked, for a knight's chief possession was his mount. Without that he dropped to the humiliating status of the foot soldier.

'Oh, the Marshal of the Kingdom sees to that,' Sir Hugo said. 'By the system called Restor. He collects all captured horses, and those of any men killed, and you claim a fresh horse from him.'

It was still dark when Sir Hugo rode through the gate-house the next morning. There was a chill breeze from the direction of the coast as Philip watched the little party clatter away into the darkness. He shivered, and pulled his cloak over his shoulders.

But the dawn came quickly and suddenly, as it did in Outremer. He could see a reddish glow spreading over the hills to the east, and then the sun was up, eating into the white mist hanging over the marsh below the castle, and bathing the wide valley in a hard light. The grey slopes of the mountains took on their familiar shade of tawny yellow, and another day of sweltering heat had begun.

Up above Philip's head the trumpets sounded. Raucous orders turned out the old guard, heavy feet clattered on the stone steps and the hard-packed surface of the courtyard. From the stables came the whinny of horses, and the great castle hummed with life.

Philip turned to Gilbert, and they planned their busy day.

'I'll ride down to the town and collect a party for the ditch,' Philip said. 'By the time I'm back, Llewellyn will have the garrison fallen in for inspection, and we can start.'

Down in the town Philip found the rais, or head man, and gave him his instructions for a working party at the castle. The men would grumble, for they disliked work that took them away from their fields and crops, but they were bound by the feudal laws to obey their lord, and Philip knew he could leave the rest to the rais.

Back at the castle, Llewellyn was calling the roll of the garrison. Every available man was on parade, and as soon as they had been checked, Philip and Gilbert started their first task. They divided the men into two groups, one small—dangerously small—for the defence of Blanche Garde, and the other, consisting of the bulk of the garrison, for the mobile force that would ride out behind Sir Hugo to the *arrière ban*.

But, as Philip knew, there was little point in leaving a large force behind. The danger was not from the south, where the last attack had come. Saladin was striking at the narrow waist of the Kingdom this time, far to the north. If the Infidel came as far south as Blanche Garde, then the Kingdom would indeed be lost, and it would matter little how long the castle could hold out.

Once the division of the garrison had been made, Gilbert began the slow and detailed check of the men's equipment. Philip went off to the stables, and saw to the horses.

Half Sir Hugo's force would be mounted, for he was a wealthy baron, and reserve chargers would be needed for the knights at least. Philip had soon galvanized the stables into a state of frenzied activity. The smiths were busy at their anvils, waves of hot air belched out from the furnaces, horses stamped and whinnied, and the scene was one of total confusion—or so it might have appeared to an outsider. But every man knew his job, and Philip was well satisfied.

He could have wished that the horses were bigger, though. The chargers of the West were far stronger than those of the East, and the early Crusaders had won their battles by sheer advantage of weight and speed. But the Western horse degenerated in the East, and Sir Hugo had been forced to import fresh chargers at great expense to provide suitable mounts for himself and the two knights.

Satisfied with the work of the smiths, Philip went back to the courtyard. Gilbert and Llewellyn were moving slowly down the line of men, bending down and inspecting each item of equipment, ordering repairs or replacements here and there. They would spend most of the day at that task alone.

In the ditch, thirty men from the town were already at work, stripped to the waist in the burning sun, digging away at the fall of earth, while others carried away the soil in baskets. Philip gave the rais some further instructions, pointed out the part that needed the most urgent attention, and then rejoined Gilbert.

They worked hard for the next three days. On the fourth they held a final inspection. Everything was ready. The men were fully equipped and armed. Wagons were drawn up with reserve supplies of arrows, bows, articles of armour, fodder for the horses, waterskins, food, tents, and the hundreds of things that might be needed on a long campaign.

'Well, father ought to be satisfied,' Philip said, though there was a faint note of doubt in his voice. Little escaped Sir Hugo's eye, as his son knew by bitter experience. But he really did think this time that the task had been well done.

Sir Hugo arrived on the evening of the fifth day. Philip heard the trumpets and the shouted orders from the gate-house, and he ran to the steps of the hall to welcome his father.

It was obvious that Sir Hugo had not made one of his leisurely journeys on this occasion. He was covered with dust, hot and grimy, and thankfully gulped down the wine that Philip had shouted for.

Then he strode across the hall with Philip and Gilbert at his heels.

'What's the news, father?' Philip asked impatiently. 'When do we march?'

'Tomorrow.'

'But where?'

Sir Hugo was half-way through the door that led to his rooms in the tower. He half turned his head.

'Acre,' he said, and disappeared.

At dinner he was more explicit, and after Philip had bombarded him with questions—

'Saladin is besieging the castle of Tiberias,' he said. 'And . . .'

'Tiberias!' Philip exclaimed in surprise. 'But that is in

the Count of Tripoli's dominions, father! Does that mean that Count Raymond has broken his truce with the Turks?'

Count Raymond was the most distrusted and unpredictable baron in the Kingdom since his unsuccessful bid for the throne of Outremer.

'If you had not interrupted me,' Sir Hugo said crushingly, 'I was about to explain that.' Philip blinked, and nodded apologetically. Gilbert grinned at him behind Sir Hugo's back.

'Yes, the count has broken with the Infidels,' Sir Hugo went on. 'And that is one of the best pieces of news we have received so far. Saladin is besieging his own castle at Tiberias, and the Count's family is inside the walls. The Count himself is at Acre now, I believe, and is waiting for the King to join him there with the whole of our army.'

'Is anything known about the size of the Turkish army, sir?' Gilbert asked.

'Not much. But it is supposed to be the largest they have ever put into the field.'

'How many shall we have, sir?'

'The King and the Marshal think about three thousand mounted men. I doubt it! We shall be lucky if we can raise two thousand, plus about fifteen thousand footmen and archers. And that can only be done by stripping all the castle garrisons. But we have no other choice.' Sir Hugo was gloomy.

'But that is a large army, sir,' Gilbert said. 'Bigger than we could find in Normandy from the whole duchy.'

'Perhaps so. But Saladin is said to have sixty thousand men with him.'

'Sixty thousand!' Philip gasped in horror. Gilbert whistled, and rubbed his nose furiously, a sure sign that he was perturbed.

'I expect the number is hopelessly exaggerated,' Sir Hugo said. 'But he will almost certainly outnumber us. The best news is that we can pay for the war. King Henry of England has sent a vast sum as a penance for the murder of his archbishop.'

'Yes, Thomas Becket of Canterbury,' Gilbert said. 'I heard about that before I left Normandy.'

In the solar, Sir Hugo brought out a map of Outremer, and Gilbert bent over it eagerly, for he was not so familiar as the other two with the lie of the ground to the north.

'There's Lake Galilee,' Sir Hugo said, pointing with his forefinger to the centre of the map. 'Tiberias is right on the lake, as you can see.'

'Which way do you think he will march from there, sir?' Gilbert asked.

'If he is wise, he will wait for us to go to him,' Sir Hugo said. 'And if we have any sense, we shall stay at Acre.' He saw the puzzled expression on both the faces listening to him. 'Look,' he said. 'Saladin set out from Damascus. He decided not to march north, because of the chain of castles there. Krak of the Knights, for instance, and then, farther inland, Safita, Castel Rouge, and Tortosa, guarding the routes to the coast. He could march past them, of course, but the farther inland he goes, the longer is his line of communications, and he must bring up food and supplies for his men. The castles can cut that line.'

They bent over the map again.

'He has crossed the Jordan just south of the lake,' Sir Hugo said. 'Castles bar his route inland and to the south. Toron and Subeiba are above him, and they are extremely strong. Blanche Garde is a toy fortress in comparison. And Belvoir and Mount Tabor can stop him to the south.'

Gilbert stroked his nose reflectively. 'What will he do, sir?'

'He can only hope we are fools enough to attack him,' Sir Hugo said. 'In this heat the crops will be parched, and he won't be able to feed his men for long where he is now. Either he will be forced to advance inland, and then we can hit him hard, or else he will retreat, and the danger will be over.'

'That sounds all right,' Gilbert said with a sigh of relief.

Sir Hugo snorted, and folded up the map. 'I wish I could think so,' he said. 'But those fools, the Templars and the Hospitallers, will move heaven and earth to march at the Infidels.'

'But they couldn't be so silly,' Philip said.

Sir Hugo shrugged his shoulders impatiently. 'They've talked us into trouble before this,' he said. 'And they'll do it again. The King is a ditherer, and he'll do whatever the last person to speak to him suggests. And if the last man to get at him is someone like Gerard de Ridefort of the Templars, then the Kingdom is lost!'

Sir Hugo put away the map, and then sent Gilbert off to issue the orders for the march on the following day. Philip was about to go with Gilbert, when his father motioned to him to stay.

'I have something to show you, Philip,' he said. 'Come with me and bring that lamp.'

Philip picked up the oil lamp, and, feeling puzzled, followed his father's tall figure out of the solar, and along to the foot of the great round tower beside the hall.

Lewellyn was standing at the bottom of the winding stairs, and he saluted Sir Hugo as they approached. He seemed to be expecting them, which made Philip stare with surprise.

'Stay here on guard, Llewellyn,' Sir Hugo said. He opened the heavy door that led to the cellars below.

The door opened with a protesting creak of rusty hinges. The lamp flickered in the draught of clammy air that was wafted up from below, and without a word, Sir Hugo took the lamp, bent his head, and ducked down to avoid the low lintel of the door.

Philip followed, more bewildered than before. Perhaps his father was searching in the cellar for some particularly precious wine which they would drink to celebrate the opening of the campaign against the Infidel. There were some wine casks down there, he knew. It was chilly in the cellar, for they were below the level of the ground. Philip disliked the whole business. He found it difficult to see much in the heavy blackness, and his father's tall figure obscured what little light the lamp gave. He stumbled against a wine cask and then put out his hand cautiously. He could hear the sound of another door being opened, and reluctantly he shuffled slowly into a tiny cellar beyond. It was hollowed out of the solid earth, the roof supported by ponderous baulks of timber. The walls, or the little he could see of them, were dripping with moisture; the atmosphere was dank and oppressive, with a peculiarly earthy smell that did not attract Philip in the slightest. He wished he could hurry away from this unpleasant spot.

'Here, Philip,' Sir Hugo said.

Philip went forward. His father was kicking away at the earth on the floor.

'What is this place, father?' he asked. 'A wine cellar?'

'Yes.' Sir Hugo held out the lamp to the full extent of his long arm. Some casks were piled in one corner. 'Pull that first cask away,' he said.

Philip tugged at the heavy cask. But there was not much room, and the shape of the cask made it an awkward business. Impatiently Philip exerted his full strength, and with an effort managed to roll the cask to one side. Sir Hugo grunted with satisfaction, and started to kick again at the hard-packed earth.

Philip was completely baffled by this time. He watched his father in silence. Suddenly he noticed the outline of a square stone appear in the earth. Sir Hugo muttered something, and bent down.

'There should be a ring there,' he said. 'Feel for it.'

Philip was interested now. He knelt down and felt in the loose earth with his fingers. 'Yes, here it is, father,' he said.

'Good! Pull it upwards. Carefully!'

Philip's stocky figure took the strain. For a moment there was no feeling of movement from the ring. Then he felt a slight jerk, and suddenly the whole stone came upwards, so abruptly that Philip nearly toppled on his back.

Sir Hugo bent forward eagerly, holding the lamp down towards the ground. Philip peered from behind with the most intense curiosity.

'What on earth is this, father?' he asked.

Sir Hugo chuckled. 'My secret hoard,' he said.

Philip could see now the lid of a large square chest, with thick bands of iron running from one side to the other. His father made no attempt to unlock the ponderous fastening. He knelt down to examine the lid, and then told Philip to replace the stone with the ring. The earth was carefully swept back and stamped down firmly, and the cask rolled into place once more.

'I expect you are wondering why I have bothered to take such elaborate precautions,' Sir Hugo said as they left the cellar and climbed the stairs to the daylight once more. 'But I have always felt that the Kingdom might collapse one day. If we lost Blanche Garde, we should lose everything. So for years now I have accumulated my ransom money and spare fortune in jewels and coins. They are all in that chest. Even if the Infidels captured Blanche Garde and destroyed it, you or I could still find that cellar.'

'We might not be able to reach Blanche Garde,' Philip said.

'Possibly not. But either of us could pass for an Arab if we took sufficient precautions. Anyway, that is a difficulty that can wait. Climb your mountains when you come to them, Philip.'

They returned to the Great Chamber, and the welcome warmth and light of the evening sun.

'Say nothing of this to Gilbert,' Sir Hugo said. 'No one knows about the chest in Blanche Garde except Llewellyn. He helped me to dig the hole and put the stone over it.'

Two days later the garrison marched out of Blanche Garde. As the long column wound down from the drawbridge, Sir Hugo reined his horse into the side of the road, and with Philip and Gilbert at his side, watched the men pass.

In the van was Llewellyn, carrying the standard with the black hawk on the white background. Behind him rode the sergeants, the mounted men-at-arms, carrying lances and swords, and wearing steel hauberks, for Sir Hugo had fitted them out at great expense. Following this compact little group of highly trained and well equipped cavalry marched the long lines of the footmen and the archers, Syrian natives all of them, but experienced soldiers and reliable men. At the rear rumbled the vital supply train; clumsy wagons, packhorses, spare horses for the cavalry, food, water, reserve ammunition for the archers, and tents for the knights.

Sir Hugo examined it all intently, bending forward in his saddle, hand to his pointed beard, his dark, calm eyes taking in every detail.

'You have done very well, you two,' he said as the last of the wagons rattled past on the uneven surface of the road. 'I have never seen the garrison in such a good state.'

He clapped his pointed spurs into his horse's side and rode on to take up his position in the van. They splashed across the ford outside the town, and then began the steady climb out of the valley. As the head of the column reached the crest of the hill, Philip turned in his saddle and looked back.

The sun was up now, lighting the walls of Blanche Garde. He could see the high tower where he had spent most of his life, the banner waving from the gatehouse, and a few servants walking across the wide courtyard. Then the scene vanished as the road dropped into a fold of the ground, and Philip trotted forward to fall in beside Gilbert. He felt that one chapter of his life had ended. Much would happen before he saw his home again. He would fight in his first pitched battle against the Infidel. He might even be wounded. But he refused to think any further than that now. The future would be exciting and fascinating, and he was too young to worry overmuch.

Chapter Six

THE WELLS OF SAFFARIA

PHILIP had once stirred an ants' nest with a stick. Within a few seconds a patch of lifeless soil had been transformed into a tumbled confusion of ridges and valleys, all covered by thousands of tiny insects hurrying distractedly in every direction.

He was reminded of that incident several times during the next week. Saladin's invasion had convulsed Outremer into a gigantic effort. Over the undulating hills the Christians were now moving in long lines of armed men, their faces to the north, and their feet stirring up great clouds of yellowish dust that drifted sluggishly across the sun-drenched countryside.

The call to arms had brought out detachments from every castle, town, and village of the Kingdom. As each unit reached one of the main roads, it became merged in the endless columns strung out over the network of routes that converged on the port of Acre.

The Blanche Garde force soon joined that from Montgizard. Sir Fulk was there, clearly feeling the terrible heat, but he was full of explosive energy, chattering incessantly about the dust, the flies, and the temperature. With him rode Joscelin, and it was difficult to recognize the exquisite nobleman of Jerusalem in this grim-faced knight in hauberk and surcoat, long sword dangling from his side, spear in socket, small pennon fluttering above his head.

But Joscelin had a good deal to say about the discomfort of a campaign in the middle of the summer, the hardness of his mattress, and the difficulty of washing frequently. They were all in agreement about the heat. Experienced soldiers who had fought in many campaigns in Outremer confessed that they had never found it hotter. Philip thought so, too. He could feel the glowing heat of his body under his gambeson. His fingers were yearning to scratch at his chafed and itching flesh. What it would be like when the time came to wear the great helms, he shuddered to think. But at the moment his helm was still hanging from his saddle.

A day's march south of Acre they joined the main party from the County of Jaffa, in which Sir Hugo was one of the chief barons. The holder of the fief at that time was Sir

Balian d'Ibelin, who had often stayed at Blanche Garde, and was a godfather to Philip.

He welcomed them with a flash of white teeth and an effusive flow of compliments. Sir Balian was descended from one of the Sicilian Normans who had followed Bohemund of Sicily on the First Crusade, and there were still traces of Italian blood in his swarthy face and in the quick, excitable movements of his hands and shoulders.

'Ah, Hugo!' he cried, and waved them to stools scattered around his big tent. 'Philip, how are you, my dear boy?' He shouted for wine, and pushed Sir Fulk and Joscelin on to a bench.

Philip sipped the cool wine and listened to the chatter of the experienced soldiers. They were asking eager questions of Sir Balian. He was one of the most important barons of the Kingdom, and kept his finger on all that went on. An ambitious man, he loved intrigue for the sake of intrigue. Softly spoken, and with charming manners, he could talk round a bitter enemy, and he was never happier than when dabbling in the confused and shifting policies of Outremer.

'Well, Balian,' Sir Hugo said, when he had drained his tankard of wine. 'What's the news?'

'Good and bad, Hugo. We shall have a large army in the field for once. The castles are stripped of their garrisons, and even the trading towns are sending contingents. We shall need them, too,' he added, wiping his lips with the back of his brown, hairy hand.

'What about the Turks?' Sir Fulk demanded.

'Still at Tiberias,' Sir Balian said. 'The castle is holding out well.'

'And the King?' Sir Hugo asked, watching Sir Balian's face with close attention. 'What is the bad side of the news, Balian?'

Sir Balian glanced at Sir Hugo out of the corner of his restless eyes. 'The King has left Acre,' he said, 'and is marching inland.'

'What!' Sir Hugo stiffened on his stool.

'I thought you would say that, Hugo,' Sir Balian remarked with satisfaction. 'But what can you expect from a stupid ditherer like Guy of Lusignan!'

A rather shocked silence fell on the tent. The King was not popular with all his barons, for they distrusted his shifting opinions and lack of decision. But it was another thing to criticize him so openly at this particular time.

'How far is he marching?' Sir Hugo asked, unmoved by Sir Balian's scathing remark.

'He is concentrating the army at the wells of Saffaria,' Sir Balian said. 'Raymond of Tripoli advised against the march, but he was overruled.'

'Saffaria,' Sir Hugo said. 'Well, it might be worse. There is plenty of water there.'

'And none beyond,' snapped Sir Balian. 'The wells on the road to Tiberias will be dry in this heat.'

'Guy won't be such a fool as to try that road!' Sir Fulk said.

'It all depends who talks to him last,' Sir Balian said gloomily.

They broke up for the night, and the march was resumed at dawn. Acre, with its high white walls, came in sight during the late afternoon as the tired and dusty troops plodded steadily along the coastal road from the south. All day messengers had ridden back with the same urgent appeal. 'Haste, haste! The Infidel is at Tiberias!'

The tents were set up under the shadows of the walls of the port, and before the sun was up, the army was on the move once more, striking inland for the Wells of Saffaria.

The country was fertile and green on either side of the road, but the heat was still oppressive. The line of march was marked by the long dust clouds, and through the haze Philip could see where the sun flashed on helmet and hauberk. It seemed as if the whole kingdom was marching on Saffaria.

They reached the Wells in the late afternoon. It was a pleasant spot of green slopes and white houses, covered now by the tents and lines of the Christian army. In the centre lay the great red tent of the King, and here all the members of the High Court assembled on that fateful evening of the second of July in the year 1187.

Philip went with his father, for he was the holder of a small fief near Blanche Garde that Sir Hugo had passed to him, and was now a member of the Court in his own right.

There were seats for the more important barons, while the rest stood or leant against the canvas walls. Guy of

Lusignan was at the head of the table, his handsome face strained and tired as if he felt the appalling weight of his responsibilities upon his shoulders. On his left was his brother, Amaury de Lusignan, the Constable of the Kingdom, and the commander of the feudal levy in the field.

Philip knew the Constable by sight, but the face of the man on the King's right was unfamiliar. He whispered to his father.

'Who? Oh, that's Count Raymond of Tripoli.'

Philip moved to his left to gain a clearer view of the count. He saw a tall, thin-faced man, with an enormous nose. Raymond was looking down at the polished surface of the table, his long fingers tapping out a swift tattoo of impatience and worry. Philip watched him with interest. For the count was reputed to be the ablest man in Outremer, ambitious, unscrupulous, and astute. And yet there was no man in that tent who was so deeply distrusted by the barons of the Kingdom. He had lost the throne to Guy, and then made a truce with the Turks. True, he had broken the truce and Saladin had attacked his own County, but the barons were still uneasy about his motives.

The hum of conversation died away as the last arrivals wedged themselves into the crowded tent. All the men there were armed, clad from head to foot in coif and hauberk, their white surcoats emblazoned with their personal designs, and their dark, sunburnt faces encircled in steel.

Guy rose to his feet. 'Seigneurs,' he said. 'We must

decide on our next move. Saladin is besieging the castle of Tiberias.' He paused, and every eye went to the Count of Tripoli, who held the castle, and whose family was inside the walls. But the count did not look up.

'The Infidel has a great army in the field,' Guy went on. 'Some say he has double our strength.' A murmur of dismay went up. 'Seigneurs, what is your advice?'

He sat down, and waited anxiously. There was a short pause. The barons had expected the count to speak first. By virtue of his County of Tripoli he was an independent Prince, an ally of the Kingdom, just as the Principality of Antioch, far to the north, was the third of the Christian states set up in Outremer.

But Raymond made no move. Philip had a shrewd suspicion that the count wished to speak last, and so exert the most influence on the wavering mind of the King.

There was one man in the tent who could not wait. From the other end of the table came a rasping and familiar voice.

'I say that we should march at dawn, sire,' barked Reynaud de Chatillon. 'The lake is but fifteen miles from here. We shall be there before the late afternoon. We can encircle the Infidel, charge, and drive him into the waters of Galilee!'

A hum of approval went up from many men. This was the aggressive policy so many favoured. The two Grand Masters thumped the table, and shouted their agreement.

The King's face cleared, and his shoulders straightened. The count looked up for a second, and his fingers stopped their flying tattoo on the table. Then he stood up, his long, thin body leaning over the table.

Silence fell. He looked deliberately around at the faces watching him. They were hostile faces, and he knew it. But his expression was one of cold disdain.

'There is an alternative plan, seigneurs,' he said in a quiet and yet oddly compelling voice. 'We can retire upon the walls of Acre.'

Reynaud jumped to his feet, glaring down the table. 'Traitor!' he growled furiously.

The count's thin lips tightened, but he kept his temper. 'I am no traitor,' he said quietly. 'If I were, do you think I should counsel retreat when my wife and children are at the mercy of the Infidels? The castle of Tiberias is mine. It is my land the Infidels are ravaging.'

He paused to allow his words to take their effect. His argument was so simple and crushing that few there could doubt his sincerity at that particular moment. Philip could feel the strength of the count's personality, and he began to realize how correct was the estimate of the man's ability. But then Philip had listened to his father's conversation with Sir Balian, and he had come to the meeting half convinced.

'I beg you to listen to me, seigneurs,' the count said, leaning forward across the table. 'If we fall back, we shall have the strong walls of Acre behind us. The town is well

provisioned and there is ample water there. We can choose our own ground and time to fight. For Saladin must follow us. You see, I know the Infidel.'

'Too well,' rasped a voice from the end of the table.

The count ignored Reynaud's jibe. 'I know the Infidel,' he repeated. 'Saladin's reputation is at stake. He has led a huge army into Outremer. He cannot stand still at Tiberias. His followers will force him to follow us. His lines of communication will be stretched. One check, and his men will melt away. Then we can fall upon him and strike a blow that will make the Kingdom safe for ever!'

He paused again. But there were men in the tent whose hatred of the Infidel was too great to allow them to be convinced by the strongest of arguments. One of these was the Grand Master of the Hospitallers.

'But why not advance to Tiberias, my lord Count?' he asked. 'The Infidels are not so strong that we need fear them. We have beaten them before this. We have a great muster of the Kingdom; our hearts are high. We have the True Cross itself here, brought from the Church of the Holy Sepulchre. Do you really think that God will allow us to go down in defeat against the Infidel, armed as we are in our faith, and with such a holy relic in our midst?'

Philip stirred uneasily. There was something compelling about the fanatical faith of the Grand Master. Other men in the tent felt the same wave of emotion, and muttered their agreement. But the Count of Tripoli was unmoved.

'It would be fatal to march on Tiberias,' he said firmly. 'Fifteen miles in burning heat, and without water.'

'There are wells on the road,' a voice said.

'They are dry. They always are in the summer. And the Turks have probably destroyed them to make certain.'

'But we can carry water!' shouted a baron.

'Only a little,' the count said. 'We must travel light if we are to reach the lake quickly. All the baggage wagons must be left here. And if we are checked, we shall have to fight with fifteen miles of waterless desert at our backs.'

'We shall not be checked,' Reynaud shouted.

'Oh, we may win through, Reynaud. But we are taking a very dangerous risk. Cannot you see that we have the game in our hands if we stay here, or fall back to Acre? Saladin must come to us, or march back to Damascus. Why put the fate of the Kingdom to a gambler's throw? It is sheer madness!'

Other men took up the argument. Guy of Lusignan followed the heated words with strained attention, moving restlessly in his seat, and wiping the sweat from his face with a hand that shook. For although the sun was nearly down, the heat was still oppressive, the air sultry and suffocating.

Count Raymond was a clever man. As well as any there, he knew how the King's mind worked. The final argument would be the decisive one, and he timed his last speech skilfully. He stood up suddenly, and once more his personality dominated and held the attention of the barons. On his cold, impassive face, Philip thought he could see the deep, inner conflict of the man, coolly picking the right moment to speak, and yet utterly and passionately sincere.

'Seigneurs,' he said quietly, his voice rising as he went on. 'Though my wife is within the walls of Tiberias, and my children are there, and all my wealth, and though it is my own castle in my own land, yet I would rather all those were lost than the Kingdom should be thrown away.'

He paused. There was dead silence in the tent. The count gathered himself for his final effort.

'And surely if you march on Tiberias,' he said, half turning to the King, and speaking with studied deliberation, 'you will destroy the realm for ever. I know the Infidel armies. I have seen them for a lifetime. And never was there gathered such an army as this!'

He sat down. No one spoke. Not even Reynaud de Chatillon or the Grand Master of the Hospitallers had the courage to follow that dramatic and crushing speech.

Guy of Lusignan's face cleared, and he rose to his feet. His mind was made up, and once more he looked the leader of men.

'Seigneurs,' he said. 'I thank you for your advice. The army will remain at the Wells of Saffaria. We will send out scouts, and cover the approaches from Tiberias, but there will be no forward advance.'

By his side Philip heard the audible sigh of relief from his father and Sir Balian.

In a few minutes the tent was empty as the barons streamed away to their lines, and issued orders for the night. The sun was down now, but there was no relaxation of the heat. Few could sleep, though many tried to do so in that stifling atmosphere. There was not the slightest semblance of an evening breeze, and everywhere men lay and tossed uneasily in the breathless air.

Philip abandoned the effort after a short time. He stepped over Gilbert's lanky legs, and stumbled out into the night. As he did so, he heard shouts, and the running of feet. Men were moving quickly through the lines of tents, repeating a message, so Philip thought. He heard his father come out of his tent, and join him, both straining their ears to catch the words. Then the bulky figure of Sir Balian loomed out of the darkness. He was muttering hoarsely, mouthing oaths and bitter scorching phrases.

Sir Hugo caught him by the arm. 'What is it, Balian?'

'We march on Tiberias at dawn.'

'March!' Sir Hugo's control deserted him for once. His voice rose in furious anger. 'March! Are you raving, Balian?'

'I wish I was. But someone else has been to the King's tent.'

'Reynaud?'

'No. Gerard de Ridefort of the Hospitallers. He has talked the fool round.'

They stood in silence. For once words failed even Sir Balian, and Sir Hugo had recovered himself. They turned as a group of men approached, the red glare of burning torches lighting up hauberks and emblazoned surcoats. It was the Count of Tripoli's retinue.

'Well, Sir Balian?' the count said, coming to a halt. But he did not wait for an answer. He blundered away into the gloom of the night, walking with the gait of a drunken man. They could hear his voice receding into the distance.

'The Kingdom is lost! The Kingdom is lost!'

Chapter Seven

THE MARCH TO TIBERIAS

PHILIP felt as if he were being grilled slowly in front of a great furnace. From a cloudless sky the sun flayed him with a searing flame, and he drooped in his saddle, half dazed with utter fatigue, every movement of his horse an agony to his aching limbs and body.

The army of the Christians was crawling with painful slowness through the hills towards Galilee. Only the van, led by Reynaud de Chatillon, marched with any semblance of a disciplined formation now, and the tail of the long column, shepherded by the Templars, was a disorganized mob of exhausted footmen trying to find some easier route than the narrow track which was the pretence for a road.

There were few men in the army now who believed that they could reach Tiberias and the Lake of Galilee before nightfall. For they had covered a bare eight miles since dawn.

There had been no enemy to check them, though it was reported that the Infidels were not far away. The sun, the heat, the dust and the frightful country through which they marched were their most dangerous enemies. The low rolling hills provided no shade; the tumbled limestone rocks on every side reflected back the dancing glare of the sun until eyes could no longer bear the pain. Men dropped and died under the thickness of their armour; horses lay down and gasped away their life by the side of the road, until the trail of the army was marked by a horrible litter that stretched back towards Saffaria.

And now the precious water was running short. Enormous quantities had already been consumed in an attempt to quench the raging thirst of men tortured almost beyond endurance by the heat. The horses had been given the greater share. For without their horses the Christians would be lost, a mass of footmen unable to attack or even to defend themselves against the mounted hordes of the Infidels.

But worse than all these horrors was the steady loss of confidence. The well trained army that had left Saffaria was now a mob of dispirited men who realized the trap into which they were marching so painfully. Some had already turned back, under the pretence of sickness, of course, for there was no mercy in Outremer for the deserter. The rest marched on doggedly, because there was no hope now but to advance, and to pray that the True Cross would bring them victory over the heathen.

Philip was riding beside his father, with Gilbert d'Assailly on his left. They had ridden for some time in complete silence. Gilbert was normally a man of few words, but he was unprepared for this appalling furnace of a country, and the sun had battered him into an automaton that sat drunkenly in the high saddle of his horse, his eyes half-closed against the glare, his shoulders bent and his head down, swaying from one side to the other.

Philip and his father were in slightly better condition, for they were both more used to the climate. But Philip felt that he could not ride much farther. He tried to think of gentler things than this bare, sun-baked valley; he conjured up visions of cool running water in his tired brain, the tinkle of the fountain of the house in Jerusalem, or the feel of soft silk against his skin instead of the itching agony of his gambeson and the intolerable weight of his hauberk, that seemed to crush down on his shoulders and arms. He gulped. But there was no moisture in his parched and aching throat. A fly buzzed against his cheek, and he waved it away. But it was no use. Hordes of flies droned around them, settling with a ghastly persistence on face and hands and horse, while the grey dust drifted past and covered them, until not even the scorching sun could raise a sparkle from all that vast expanse of steel that covered the army.

'I must drink,' Gilbert croaked.

Sir Hugo flung up his head. 'No, Gilbert!' he said. 'Keep it for the horses. Else we are lost.'

Gilbert nodded and relapsed into his coma of heat and

exhaustion again. Philip could see the muscles of his friend's throat working convulsively, and his own moved in sympathy. He rubbed his grimy fingers across his mouth and winced as the dry skin broke under the rasping roughness of his hand. For a moment his nerve almost left him. He could endure this no longer, he decided. He must shout, scream, kick his horse into a gallop, do anything but sit there and be grilled into a horrible death in that sun. Better gulp down the last remnants of the brackish and lukewarm water that gurgled and rolled in the waterskin hanging from his saddle than ride on into certain death.

Then he heard his father's quiet voice, and he fought down the mad impulse.

'We must keep on,' Sir Hugo said. 'We must march through the night.'

He was speaking to Sir Balian d'Ibelin, who had dropped back from the van of their detachment of the army.

Sir Balian shook his head, glanced round, and lowered his voice. 'We can never do it, Hugo,' he said. 'The footmen can go no farther. Better to leave them, perhaps.'

'That would be madness,' Sir Hugo said impatiently. The heat and his exhaustion had made him lose his customary calm. 'You know as well as I do, Balian, that we have always lost when we fought the Infidel without footmen.'

'Well, we shall lose unless we reach Tiberias and the shores of the lake tonight,' Sir Balian said grimly. 'It's a pretty coil Gerard de Ridefort has led us into.'

Sir Hugo nodded his head vigorously. It was an effort

to speak, parched as they were. Suddenly the column jolted to a halt; one of many such irritating pauses which had held up the army all during the day.

'Another false alarm,' Sir Balian growled. 'Can't the van keep moving?'

'Infidels! Infidels!' came shouts from the front.

'Yes, on the right; up on the slope,' roared Sir Hugo, finding his voice now that there was a prospect of action after the tedium of the frightful march.

Philip looked up towards the low, rolling hillside on their right. The sun was flashing on steel helmets. A dense mass of horsemen was moving across the shoulder of the ridge, spreading out rapidly, and rolling down towards them. He could see the coloured turbans now, and the white fluttering robes of the riders.

'Helms on!' bellowed Sir Balian. 'Helms on, seigneurs, and close up!'

The trumpets were sounding the alarm; harsh bellows of sound in the hot, still air. Shouts of 'Close up!' 'Close in!' went down the long lines of horsemen. Knights frantically pulled on the ponderous helms which had been hanging from their saddles.

Philip hastily adjusted the straps of his helm; it had not taken him long, for he was used to such a manoeuvre. He gulped with excitement as he did so, and for a few seconds forgot his weariness and heat, though he could not help noticing the almost suffocating feeling now that he was enclosed in the huge helm. He wriggled himself into a firm position in the saddle, heaved his shield across his breast, and lifted his lance out of its socket by his right foot. All the time he was peering through his eye-slits towards the advancing Infidels.

'Watch for the arrows!' yelled Sir Balian and Sir Hugo, their voices flat and muffled through their helms. 'Don't charge until the trumpets sound. Close in, seigneurs, close in, and stand fast!'

There were many knights and squires in the ranks of the Christians who, like Philip, had yet to experience their first fight against the Turks, but they were all well versed and trained in the tactics employed by the enemy. The Turks used few lances. Instead, they relied almost entirely on mounted bowmen, firing from the saddle with great speed and accuracy. They would ride within range, fire a volley, and then wheel off to right and left, hoping to encircle their enemy, and forcing them into a tightly bunched mass of men infuriated and weakened by the incessant arrow fire.

If the Christians tried to charge, the Infidels would retire at high speed on their smaller and faster horses, and then wheel round once more, repeating their tactics over and over again until their enemy were so exhausted and weakened that a charge home would not be shaken off.

But the Christians were fully aware of these tactics. They had their own archers and footmen, and a skilful combination of these footmen with their much greater weight of horse and armour had won all their previous battles whenever they had employed the correct tactics.

Philip could see the Infidels quite clearly now as they rode swiftly down the long, gradual slope towards him. They were small, wiry men on light Arab horses, wearing little armour compared to the Christians, and crouching down in their saddles behind small, round shields. One man in the centre of the line opposite Philip seemed to be the leader of this particular column. His head was swathed in a white turban that sparkled with jewels. A vivid scarlet saddle-cloth fluttered in the breeze as he urged on his horse and waved a curved scimitar to his followers.

Philip felt his fingers tighten on the butt of his spear; he was breathing quickly, and his toes twitched in their steel shoes. This was no tournament, rough and dangerous as such fights were. This was life or death now, kill or be killed, the culmination of his whole short life, the moment for which he had been trained since he was old enough to hold a sword and lance. He was not frightened; he was intensely excited.

Suddenly a flight of arrows shot up from the front ranks of the Turks. They curved up into the air, seemed to hover, and then rushed down with terrific speed towards the Christians. Philip watched them. It was difficult to believe that he was really being fired at.

One arrow was coming straight for him. One second it was twenty feet away and then it was almost in his face. He flung up his shield and crouched down in the saddle. A sudden wave of nausea shot up into his throat as he waited; the sensation of fear was so acute that it hurt, a sickening pang deep down in his stomach and thighs.

Something hissed wickedly past his head. From behind came the terrible scream of a horse in agony and the shout of the rider. Philip peered cautiously over the top of his shield. The Turks had not pressed home their charge; there had been little danger of that. They were wheeling away to the flanks, waving their bows, and shrieking their high-pitched howls of 'Allah il-allahu! Allah il-allah!' From the rear came the clashing of cymbals and then more roars and chants as they swept across the front of the steady Christian line that waited grimly for their chance to strike back.

'Stand fast! Close up!' the voices of the leaders bellowed.

A trumpet pealed farther down the line. Philip heard a roar of Christian cheers and the drumming of hooves. Some excitable fools were charging out from the column. The Turks turned their horses round and galloped away, firing another volley as they went.

The charge was delivered at thin air. The Crusaders lost their impetus riding up the slope, then turned and began to fall back. A shower of arrows fell on them, and horses went down, kicking wildly, with their riders trying to roll clear or stumbling dazedly on the hard ground. The main body of the charging men were back with the column, but a cloud of Turks swept down and around the fallen men, yelling furiously, and waving their curved swords. Philip watched in horror.

One knight broke through, bending low in his saddle,

and urging on his wounded horse. A Turk closed in, took his aim coolly, and the arrow was driven home to the feathers. The horse reared up with a scream, and the rider was flung to the ground. He struggled up to one knee, tugging at the hilt of his sword. Three Turks flung themselves from their horses and ran forward, swinging their scimitars. The first blow smashed the Christian knight to his back, and the Infidels leapt upon him, hacking down at his writhing body with a cold-blooded ferocity that appalled Philip. He wanted to look away, but his eyes watched the scene with a fascinated horror.

At last the knight lay still, an untidy heap of slashed surcoat and torn hauberk. The Turks kicked at him derisively, and rode away with shrill yells of triumph, waving their swords at the Christians.

Philip gulped painfully, fighting down another pang of sickness. For a moment he wondered bitterly if his nerve would give way now that he was faced with the reality of battle and a merciless enemy. He wrenched his eyes away from the pitiful figure of the knight that sprawled limply on the ground in front, and listened to the conversation between his father and Sir Balian d'Ibelin. The two veteran soldiers were discussing the position with their usual calmness. To them, this was a mere skirmish. They could see beyond the immediate outcome of these flank attacks, and visualize the campaign as whole.

'We must keep moving, Balian,' Sir Hugo said.

'I know. The whole advance will be held up,' Sir Balian

said impatiently. 'Heaven knows, we have wasted enough time now.'

There were other men in the Christian army who realized the vital necessity for a steady advance, for at that moment the trumpets sounded again from the van, and the long column set off once more. The Infidels were on either flank now, but the Crusaders had brought up their own mounted archers, and the Turks kept their distance, waiting for the opportunity to make fresh charges.

For half an hour the Crusaders plodded along. Then on the part of the line opposite Sir Balian's section of the army, Philip noticed that the Turks were massing in a dense cluster for a new attack. They swept over a stony ridge of the hills, and as they flowed down towards the road, the trumpets pealed and the Crusaders came to a halt.

But cool and experienced eyes were watching the Turks. Sir Hugo d'Aubigny flung up his arm and pointed, shouting to Sir Balian as he did so.

'Look, Balian, there are two waves of them!'

Sir Balian's helm nodded. He turned to his trumpeter.

'Be ready to sound the charge when I give you the word. Hugo, pass the warning down the line.'

For the Turks had made a mistake. There was a gap of perhaps fifty yards between their two detachments, not a great deal, but enough for skilful soldiers such as Sir Hugo and Sir Balian to turn to their own advantage. As the first Infidel wave fired and wheeled away, their second line would close up, blinded momentarily by their own friends immediately ahead, and unable to watch the moves of the Christians clearly in the thick, swirling dust.

Philip could appreciate the intention of his father and Sir Balian. Many times at Blanche Garde he had listened to lectures on the proper tactics to be employed against the Infidels. In the peaceful security of his home, a battle had assumed the aspect of a game of chess, but out here in this turmoil of noise, dust, and heat, with one's senses dazed and battered by exhaustion and excitement, the fight had become a blurred and shifting nightmare, in which a man's first instincts were to defend his life, and to concentrate on the things closest at hand.

Philip brought his lance down to the level, clamping the butt firmly under his armpit. The fingers of his left hand were twined around the reins; over his arm came the shield, and as he dug his heels firmly into the stirrups, he crouched down, the top of his helm just showing over the rim of the shield.

The first wave of the enemy was within arrow range now. They had fired, and the shafts screamed overhead. The horses kicked up a dense cloud of dust as the Infidels wheeled off to either flank.

And into this empty space, covered now by the blinding dust, Sir Balian flung his heavily armoured knights. His mailed arm shot up stiffly into the air. The trumpets blared raucously, harsh and challenging, filling Philip with a sudden rush of exhilaration. The Crusaders broke into a roar of cheering, and up went their old battle cry:

'*Deus Vult!* God wills it! *Deus Vult!*'

The second wave of the Infidels heard the trumpets and the cheers. They knew what they meant. But if there was any doubt, the drumming of hooves and the clatter of arms and hauberks would have told them. They saw the solid mass of Christian knights burst through the swirling dust, the red nostrils of the big horses, the flat-topped helms, the long shields and the tips of the levelled spears with the fluttering pennons.

But the Infidels were too late. Their pace faltered; they tried vainly to open out and wheel away, and then the Christians smashed into them.

Philip felt the wind of the charge through the eye-slits of his helm. He could see the long shaft of his spear stretching out ahead. But he ignored that. His eyes were searching for a target. Keep your eyes on the mark, and your spear will take care of the rest, he had been taught.

Immediately in front was a richly dressed Turk, dark and bearded, with a white cloak hanging from his shoulders. Philip pressed his knees firmly into his horse's sides, twitched the reins very gently, and fixed his eyes on the Infidel's small, round shield. The spear went home with a jar that he felt right up the full length of his arm. But he was ready for that. There was no semblance of any weakness in his charge as he concentrated all his skill and strength and weight into that slender shaft.

The Turk was hurled from his saddle, the spear transfixing him from breast to spine. His horse, caught in the flank by the full weight of Philip's charger, was bowled over like a toy. Then the brief picture had vanished as Philip wrenched his spear back and down again to the level.

There was barely time to spare before he was on the next man. His blow was not so shrewd this time, nor so well directed. The tip caught the Turk's shoulder with another jarring shock; the man reeled, and then his small Arab horse too was hurled to the ground.

There was open ground beyond. Philip had crashed through the Infidel line. He pulled hard on his reins, swung round, and heard the trumpets sounding the recall. He glanced around. The ground was littered with Arab ponies and Infidels. Christian knights were falling back, waving their spears exultantly and shouting incoherent cries of triumph.

'Philip, Philip!' It was Joscelin de Grandmesnil, sword in hand, for his spear must have splintered. 'I enjoyed that!' he yelled.

Philip could not see his cousin's face under the helm, but he could guess that Joscelin must be grinning.

'Better fall back,' Philip said warningly.

'I suppose so. Wish we could have another go at them, though.'

But the column was on the move again. The Turks had lost heavily in that brief skirmish. The Christian archers had closed in and shot them down as they reeled and scattered from that sudden charge, and the whole flank had been cleared.

For some time the Christians were able to move ahead, unhampered by the pin-pricking attacks, but the pace was still terribly slow. And there was no slackening in the torrid heat of the sun. The exertion of the charge had drained away much of the reserve strength of the Christian knights, and their efforts, short as they were, had made them hotter than ever. It was difficult to regain one's breath under the suffocating closeness of the great helms, and impossible to wipe away the streams of sweat that rolled down cheeks and eyes.

Philip heard horses trot up from behind, and a compact party of knights rode past, making for the van. Leading them was Count Raymond of Tripoli. He saw Sir Hugo and Sir Balian, and closed in to speak to them.

'I am going forward to the van, Sir Balian,' he said. 'Unless we push on we are lost. Keep your men moving.'

'How is it with the centre and the King?' Sir Hugo asked. For it was from there that the leadership, if any, must come.

'He is losing heart,' the count said contemptuously. 'But it is too late to turn back now. The Infidels are behind us, as well as being on either flank.'

He lifted a hand to his helm in salute, and trotted away.

'I don't like the sound of that,' Sir Balian said. He turned in his saddle to look at his column. 'For the love of the saints, Fulk, put back your helm!' he cried sharply.

Sir Fulk de Grandmesnil had lifted his helm from his head, and was mopping his face. He was gasping for breath, and his cheeks were almost purple in colour.

'I must, Balian,' he said. 'I must. This heat is too much for me. I'm finished!' He was clearly at the end of his tether.

Joscelin bent forward with his waterskin, and his father gulped down a mouthful of the precious liquid. Some of the dangerous colour drained away from his cheeks, and he grunted his thanks.

'Stand fast!' Sir Hugo roared. 'Here they are again. Fulk, watch out for the arrows, man, and put on your helm.'

Philip bent down once more behind his shield. The Turks were not attacking in such force this time. They rode up and fired a volley of arrows, turning away with their usual tactics. One shaft whistled past Philip's leg, hit the ground and bounced on the hard, sunbaked surface of the track.

Then the brief attack was over, and Philip looked back to see what damage had been done. He saw a picture of swift and violent tragedy. Sir Fulk was swaying in his high saddle, his hands to his throat. Blood was spouting through his tightly clenched fingers; the feathered shaft of an arrow protruded from his throat.

'Father! Father!' Joscelin cried in an agony of fear and distress.

He pushed his horse alongside his father, but there was nothing he could do. Sir Fulk dropped his hands and crashed to the ground. Sir Hugo and Joscelin leapt down, and bent over the writhing figure, their helmeted faces blank and expressionless, despite the appalling fear that possessed them both. Sir Fulk rolled over in his agony and then lay still.

'Dead!' Joscelin moaned. 'They've killed him. Curse them, curse them!' He ran to his horse, scrambled up into the saddle, and kicked his spurs cruelly into his horse's side. 'Come on, Philip, we must do something, not sit here and make faces at them!'

He was already five yards away as he shouted the last words, sword waving, yelling incoherently, as he rode out towards the Infidels. Philip had instinctively started to follow. But a hand clamped down on his arm, and a spear was held out in front of him.

'Stand fast, you young fool!' Sir Balian shouted. 'You can do nothing.'

'He has chosen his way,' Sir Hugo said quietly. He moved his hand from Philip's wrist. 'Let him go.'

The nearest Infidels saw Joscelin galloping towards them, and three rode in to meet him. But the first went down with a scream as Joscelin slashed madly at his head. The other two flashed past on either side of Joscelin, and one fired at his horse at point blank range.

Philip gave an inarticulate cry of horror as Joscelin went down underneath his madly kicking horse. His leg was trapped as he struggled desperately to free himself.

Then the Infidels dismounted, and Philip turned his eyes away. He could bear the sight no longer. Joscelin would be hacked to death like some piece of meat on a butcher's stall, lying defenceless on the ground, with no Christian there to lift a hand to help him. Joscelin, with his scented handkerchief, his cheerful laugh, and love of fine clothes;

with whom Philip had played as a boy, with whom he had ridden out hawking, against whom he had argued at the high table at Blanche Garde and Montgizard.

'All over,' Sir Hugo said. 'Ride on, Philip. He died well.'

Philip shook his head, while scalding tears ran down his cheeks. What honour or virtue was there in a filthy death like that, he wondered, lying under your horse, squirming like a trapped animal while two men slashed you to the bone, and then bent down and cut your throat in cold blood?

But the Christians advanced slowly. The Infidels still rode on either flank, their numbers increasing at every mile the Crusaders made in that torrid heat.

'I don't envy Gerard de Ridefort in the rear with the infantry,' Sir Balian said.

'If Count Raymond quickens the pace of the van they will never keep up with us,' Sir Hugo said.

'But we must go faster,' Sir Balian said impatiently, with the tone of a man who knew that he was asking the impossible. 'Yet if we go faster, we shall lose the infantry. If we slow down, we die of thirst.'

But the sun was beginning to sink at last. Philip watched it with dull eyes. Perhaps they were near the end of the torture of heat, dust, and thirst. He could not go on much longer, he knew. Even Sir Hugo's iron body was wilting in his saddle. As for Gilbert d'Assailly, only his high pommel and cantle held him in place on the back of his horse.

'Where are we, Balian?' Sir Hugo asked. 'You know this part, don't you?'

'About six miles from Tiberias, I should think. Those hills in front overlook the lake.'

They seemed a formidable barrier to Philip, especially for an army exhausted by a frightful day's march, short of water, and hampered by a long tail of stragglers extending probably for several miles behind.

'We shall have to fight our way through them,' Sir Hugo said. 'The heights are filled with Turks.'

Sir Balian shaded his eyes against the glare of the setting sun.

'There are two passes,' he said. 'The Wady-el-Mullakah, and the Wady-el-Hamman. We should be wise to take the second.'

A horseman came trotting back from the van. He was a knight in the Count of Tripoli's detachment, and he pulled up by Sir Balian.

'Where is the King, my lord?'

'In the centre of the column. How is the van?'

'Within three miles of Tiberias, my lord.'

Sir Balian nodded his satisfaction. 'Better than I had expected,' he said. 'Well, here is the King now.'

Guy of Lusignan was riding forward, accompanied by his chief officers. The harassing attacks of the Infidels had died away, as if the enemy was reserving his efforts for the defence of the hills of Tiberias and the passes to the Lake of Galilee. The Christians pulled off their helms, and a short conference was held by the side of the road.

'You have a message from Count Raymond?' the King asked eagerly.

'Yes, my lord. He is within sight of the lake. Haste, haste, he says. We must reach Tiberias by nightfall!'

The King turned to the others. His face was drawn with fatigue. Once more he was being forced to make a decision.

'We can't possibly march any farther, Guy,' his brother Amaury said. 'The Grand Master has just sent up a rider from the rearguard. The Infidels are on either flank of him. The infantry are exhausted. We shall need them to storm the passes, and they can never reach us tonight.'

'We can do that without the infantry,' Sir Balian said angrily. 'The Count of Tripoli is right, my lord. We must reach Tiberias tonight!'

The King looked anxiously around the circle of faces, appealing dumbly for some stronger spirit to take the lead, and save him from his horrible dilemma.

'We must find water, seigneurs,' he muttered.

'The Count of Tripoli knows where there is water,' the knight from the van said quickly.

'Where?' six voices demanded.

'In the Wady-el-Hamman. Three miles to the north. There is a stream running through the valley.'

All the faces turned to the north. The hills lay there, rising to a height of a thousand feet at least, grim and bleak, sprawling across the line of march to the water for which the whole army craved.

Amaury de Lusignan shook his head doubtfully.

'We shall never force the pass tonight,' he said. 'We are too tired. And if we press on we shall leave the two Grand Masters behind with the rearguard. You cannot do that, Guy.'

The King glanced at Sir Balian and Sir Hugo, who shook their heads decisively. But other important barons of the kingdom had joined the unofficial council of war. Humphry of Toron was there, with Joscelin of Edessa, Hugh of Gibelet; men with great stakes in the future of Outremer. They were all of the same mind: encamp for the night, and force the pass through the hills at dawn.

'By that time the infantry will have come up and be rested, my lord,' Hugh de Gibelet said. 'We have enough water for ourselves and the horses tonight.'

'I doubt it,' Sir Balian said bluntly.

But he was outvoiced in the clamour. The King shrugged his shoulders helplessly, and then gave way to the majority.

'We shall encamp here for the night,' he said. 'Amaury, see that my tent is set up on the knoll over there.'

Sir Hugo and Sir Balian walked away disconsolately. There was nothing more they could do, even though they were both convinced that the campaign was as good as lost. There was another man of the same opinion, and he galloped furiously into the camp an hour later. It was the Count of Tripoli.

'What is this I hear, Balian?' he demanded. 'I could not believe it! Has the King decided to stay here for the night?'

Sir Balian nodded. 'It was not our advice,' he said.

'I cannot conceive that either you or d'Aubigny would give the King such mad advice,' the count said. 'I will go and see him now.'

He strode off towards the King's red tent, but he was back very shortly, his face filled with despair.

'The King will not move,' he said. He paused, and then burst out in the agony of his despair. 'Alas, Lord God, the war is ended! We are delivered over to death, and the realm is ruined.'

He mounted and rode away, leaving behind him a silent and gloomy group of knights standing around the tired horses. There were no tents available, for all the heavy baggage had been left at Saffaria. But they were little loss, for the heat was still appalling, though the sun was now setting over the hills. Long black shadows were moving slowly across the brown earth and stunted grass. But even in the shade there was little relief. The air was very still, the atmosphere sultry, with the dry heat of an oven.

Philip tried to eat some cold meat which he had brought in his saddle-bags. But his throat was too parched to allow him to swallow with any comfort, and the water supply was so minute by this time, that he was reduced to a few mouthfuls of the lukewarm, brackish liquid. Then he curled himself upon the ground, put his head on his saddle, and tried to sleep.

Chapter Eight

THE BATTLE OF HATTIN

PHILIP awoke with a start. A hand was gripping his shoulder, shaking him out of his sleep.

'Wake up, Philip! The Infidels are upon us!'

Philip struggled to his feet, and then rubbed his eyes painfully. They were gummy and sore after the glare of the march from Saffaria. The close darkness around him had a velvety warmth that was overpowering and clinging.

Gilbert was standing by his side, fumbling for his sword. All about them men were shouting and cursing, yelling for their horses, and trying to discover what the alarm was about.

Philip heard arrows whistling through the air, and he crouched down behind his shield. But the fire seemed to be coming from all sides, and he felt horribly exposed.

Some horses must have been hit, for he could hear their high-pitched screams of agony, the most nerve-shaking sound of all to a horse lover like Philip. His own beast was close by, trembling with fear, and Philip forgot his own worries for the moment while he went over and tried to comfort it.

But the Turks did not close in on the camp. They kept their distance, firing spasmodically into the Christian lines for the next hour. Philip's eyes became more used to the darkness. He could distinguish the dark mass of the King's tent, around which the Crusaders had huddled as if for protection during the night.

'Better lie down, Philip,' Sir Hugo said. 'They won't attack. This arrow fire is only meant to keep us awake, and tire us out.'

Philip grunted, and wriggled himself into a more comfortable place on the ground. His short sleep had done him some good, but he was depressed and gloomy.

'Tired?' asked his father.

'I was thinking about Joscelin and Uncle Fulk,' Philip said. 'You shouldn't have stopped me. I let Joscelin go alone.'

Sir Hugo did not reply for a moment. Philip heard him sigh, but he could not see his expression in the darkness.

'What could we have done?' Sir Hugo said harshly. 'Do you think I liked watching Joscelin go to his death? Or

Fulk? I grew up with Fulk. He was your mother's brother. I stood by while Joscelin was christened.'

His voice broke. Philip turned in amazement. He had never known his father to give way to his emotions like this before.

'I shouldn't have said that, father,' he said quickly.

'Never mind, Philip. You will get used to seeing your friends killed before you're much older. I'm hardened to it. At least, I thought I was,' he added bitterly.

They lay there in silence for a time. Philip was thinking of his room in the tower at Blanche Garde. There was always a large jar of water by the side of his bed. On hot nights in the summer, he used to plunge his hands deeply into the cool water and bathe his face. At the mere thought of it, he groaned and shifted uneasily.

'Lights!' Sir Hugo said suddenly. 'Over there!'

Others had seen the lights, too, and a hubbub of shouts and inquiries ran around the uneasy lines of the Christians. Philip stood up. He could pick out a circle of flickering lights around the camp.

'What are they?' he asked.

Sir Hugo raised his head and sniffed. 'They have set fire to the grass,' he said sharply.

Philip caught the smell now, acrid and sharp, as the smoke billowed across their lines. The tang of the burning grass irritated his dry throat, and he coughed, trying not to, for even that simple action caused him acute pain. From every side he heard the Crusaders cough; hard, racking sounds as this fresh and devilish device of the Infidels had its effect.

The night passed slowly, a long-drawn-out agony of heat, of stifling smoke and parched throats, sore eyes, whistling arrows, screams, and shouts of pain or alarm, and the constant fear of an unseen enemy who might rush the camp at any moment.

It was with tremendous relief that the Christians saw the sun come up. There was no gradual dawn in Outremer. The sky lightened slightly, the sun burst over the hills, and it was day; another period of burning heat and dust.

A final council was being held near the King's tent. This time Count Raymond was heard with attention. Everything he had said at the Wells of Saffaria had been borne out by the incidents of the previous day, and now with pathetic but tragically belated hope, the barons of the Kingdom turned to him for advice.

'We must abandon the advance to Tiberias,' he said. 'Water is our first need. There is a stream in the Wady-el-Hamman, about three miles to the north. We must fight our way through the pass at all costs.'

Guy of Lusignan nodded. He was in the mood to accept any advice now, desperate to seize at a gambler's chance to retrieve the position.

'Very well,' he said. 'Are the Grand Masters here?'

Both men stepped forward, Gerard de Ridefort and Roger de Moulins. They had been riding with the rearguard, for it had long been the custom in Outremer for the Military

Orders to lead the van or cover the rear of the army.

'What of the infantry?' Guy asked.

'Bad!' snapped Gerard de Ridefort, wasting no words. 'They have lost their nerve.'

'But they will fight?' the King asked anxiously.

'I don't think so,' de Moulins said. 'Their water is finished, and they are exhausted. Some of them have started to desert already. They're on their way back to Saffaria. They won't get far,' he added grimly. 'The Infidels are behind us now.'

Guy of Lusignan pulled at his fair beard while his barons discussed the news in undertones. Whatever may have been Guy's faults of indecision and vacillation, he was a man of courage and a soldier of experience. He could see his course at last, perilous and possibly hopeless though it looked. But it was one that fitted his temperament, and at this crisis he spoke like a king.

He drew himself erect, tall and imposing in his long hauberk and white surcoat.

'Then we must fight our own way through the Infidels,' he said. There was no trace of hesitation or faltering in his confident voice as he spoke. 'Gerard, you will command the rear. Raymond, you and Reynaud de Chatillon will take the van. My banner will march in the centre with the True Cross. God is with us, seigneurs, and we shall break through to Tiberias, and carry everything before us!'

The barons of Outremer stiffened their tired bodies as they listened. Their dust-streaked faces glowed with animation. As they mounted and fell into their places, the trumpets blared for the advance, each section of the army moved off, and two thousand deep voices raised the defiant battle cry of the Crusaders. *'Deus Vult! Deus Vult!* God wills it!'

And indeed, the position was not completely hopeless. All were weakened by the march from Saffaria, and the infantry could be written off as lost, but the Christian army was still a formidable fighting force, with its solid core of heavily armed and well mounted knights. The Turks, if they were to prevent their enemy from bursting through to the Lake of Galilee and the castle of Tiberias, must stand and fight, and the greater weight of the Crusaders might yet enable them to smash their way through by sheer weight and determination.

But the Infidels rode into battle with high hopes, too. They made no attempt to withdraw in face of the resolute advance of the Christians. As the ground opened out into a wide and fairly level plain, they closed in, prepared to bar the way to the lake and the water which the Crusaders must reach, or die of thirst where they stood.

Philip watched the Infidel host regroup itself until it seemed that the entire plain was covered with the vast army that Saladin had mustered. Everywhere he looked, he could see the jostling mass of mounted men, brightly coloured banners, white and red turbans, gleaming armour, all wheeling and manoeuvring in the hard glare of the sun that beat down on both sides impartially.

But the Christian van rode on steadily, led by Count

Raymond. The air was filled with the clash of the Infidel cymbals, the roll of their drums and their shrill yells to Allah. In reply, the Crusader trumpets sent back their defiant blare, and the knights, enveloped in their hauberks and great helms, crouched down behind triangular shields, advancing with grim determination for the centre of the Infidel host.

Philip settled down into his saddle. There would be no wheeling now or retreat by the Turks. They must stand and fight. His spirits began to rise, and he forgot his tiredness and thirst. He would be charging in a few minutes.

Then the trumpets sounded again from the centre of the Christian army. It was the signal to halt.

Sir Balian d'Ibelin turned in his saddle, and his furious voice boomed through his helm.

'Halt?' he cried incredulously. 'What is this? Treachery?'

The column came to an uneasy halt. Count Raymond arrived from the van, galloping hard, and making for the royal banner in the centre. The reason for the delay soon reached Sir Balian's ears, as Count Raymond returned.

'The whole army must halt, Balian. The infantry will not move a foot.'

'Then we must go on without them! That was what we decided.'

'I know. But it would mean leaving the Templars and the Hospitallers behind. So we must wait.'

Sir Balian and Sir Hugo shook their mailed fists in

despair. But there was no alternative, except to keep closed up, for the Turks would not miss such a chance as this to strike the first blow.

The throb of the drums and the clamour of the cymbals rose to a wild crescendo of sound. Clouds of white dust drifted over the scene as dense masses of mounted bowmen galloped towards the Christian line.

Philip ducked his head behind his shield. He knew that the attacks of yesterday would be mere pin-pricks compared to the storm of arrow fire that was about to descend upon the Crusaders. He heard the twang of many taut bow strings and the whistle of the shafts in the air as they curved gracefully upwards and then rushed down with ever increasing speed.

But the hauberks of the Christians were too strong for arrows shot from short bows. The shots clinked up against shields or bounced harmlessly off steel hauberks. It was otherwise with the unfortunate horses, though, and all down the long line the poor brutes reared and screamed as the arrows went home.

That was the first of many attacks, all delivered at the full range of a short bow, for the Infidels were wise enough not to charge home yet. They knew too well the danger of hand-to-hand fighting with their enemies, and the Christians were still waiting for the Military Orders to come up into line.

There was one man who refused to wait. Count Raymond rode up the right flank where the Jaffa detachment was posted.

'I am going to charge and cut my way through, Balian,' he said.

'But you must stand fast, count,' Sir Balian said.

'Too late for that. Sir Reginald of Sidon and the knights of Nablius are with me. If you and Sir Hugo and his men join, we can break our way through.'

But Sir Balian shook his head. The count did not wait to argue. A few minutes later Philip saw a compact little group of knights charge into the flank of the Turks, and disappear in a flurry of tossing banners and heaving men.

'Are they through, Hugo?' Sir Balian asked.

'I think so. But their horses are tired. They won't get far.'

But, as Philip learnt much later, the count did break through, and made his way to Tripoli, to die there before the end of the year, a sick and heartbroken man.

The Christians waited impatiently for the Templars and Hospitallers to arrive. Fresh messages were sent back in a last attempt to persuade the infantry to advance. But they would not move. Not in the direction of the enemy at any rate, but in a mass of panic-stricken and nerveless men they withdrew to a hill on the flank, and watched the final tragedy of the battle from there.

The knights stood fast and stolidly received the arrow fire of the Infidels. The casualties were surprisingly low, and the horses again took the main brunt. Nearly half the Christian force was on foot now, huddled together with drawn swords, and waiting for the Turks to close in.

But they were all tiring. Few had any water left, and the

sun was directly overhead, scorching the armoured men with its fierce and merciless rays.

It was at this point that the knights of the two Military Orders came up into line. Word was passed to all the detachments. All those who had horses would charge when the trumpets sounded. It was the only hope left for the Christians; they might still smash through.

Philip roused himself from the stupor of heat and exhaustion into which he had fallen. His horse was unwounded, though weak from lack of water. The Blanche Garde party grouped themselves around the erect and indomitable figure of Sir Hugo, with Philip and Gilbert on either side of him, and the mounted sergeants, led by Llewellyn, immediately behind.

The Turks were also making their preparations. For Saladin had seen the banners of the Templars and Hospitallers move up into the Christian line. He knew them to be his most determined and fanatical opponents, and he was too skilful and experienced a general not to realize the possible tactics of his enemy.

So there was a pause in the fighting. Both sides were bracing themselves for a supreme effort. The next half-hour would decide the battle, and with it the future of the East.

Guy of Lusignan was in the centre of the Christian army, near the True Cross. When he was satisfied that his knights were in position, he raised his arm as a signal. The trumpets sounded, and all down the long line the signal was repeated.

There can be few men whose blood is not stirred by the massed call of trumpets, blown as they were at that moment with a desperate sense of urgency and challenge. The Crusaders had been waiting impatiently for the opportunity to charge, and with a concerted bellow of wild cheering, the massed chivalry of Outremer surged forward in one great wave.

The loud jingle of innumerable rings of steel on the hauberks was drowned almost immediately in the deeper roar of the hooves of the horses, a steady drumming rumble that rose to a thunderous din like the sea breaking on a long sandy shore. Dense clouds of yellow dust rose in the hot, still air, but they did not altogether obscure the sight of the charging Crusaders, with their fluttering surcoats, their flat-topped helms, glittering hauberks, and their long lances, each with its tiny pennon stretching out ahead of the riders crouching behind their emblazoned shields.

Philip could see nothing of all this. His vision was limited to the narrow and flickering picture immediately ahead of his narrow eye-slits. But he could hear the tremendous uproar of the charging horses all around him, and, like all his fellow Christians, he was worked up to a high pitch of exhilaration by the raucous voices of the trumpets and the infectious feeling of wild excitement that sweeps over anyone taking part in a great concerted manoeuvre such as a cavalry charge. This was the moment for which he had been trained all his life: to be a part, however small, in a mass attack upon the hereditary and natural enemy of the knights of Outremer.

Then the two armies met in a shattering crash, a blending of many sounds, the splintering of lances, the screams of horses, the clatter of sword on sword, and the gasping shouts of men hacking furiously at each other with all the concentrated bitterness of religious hatred, fear, blood lust, and exultant rage and fury.

Philip saw his lance go home. He felt the familiar jar, and saw a swarthy face under a white turban grimacing in the agony of sudden death. Then his lance had broken, and he hurled the useless butt away, dragging out his sword in a flash of time, so often had he practised the movement.

His horse ploughed its way through the press, bowling over two small Arab ponies, while their unfortunate riders went down screaming beneath the kicking, iron-shod hooves. Philip leant forward in his saddle and cut furiously at every figure within reach, sobbing and cursing, using up in that wild burst of fighting all the reserves of energy in his tired body.

The Christians had cut their way deep into the Turkish line. In the centre Saladin himself was nearly swept off his horse and killed, and for a brief moment the whole battle swayed in the balance. But the Crusaders had shot their bolt. Their horses were exhausted, and for once their superior weight and armour were of no avail.

The impetus of the charge had died away. Like those of all the knights around him, Philip's horse was standing still, while he hacked at the yelling Infidels. A grey-bearded Turk forced himself between Sir Hugo and Philip, and aimed a sweeping blow at him with his curved scimitar. Philip warded off the stroke, but another Turk was at his left elbow.

'Left, Philip, ware left!' Sir Hugo shouted.

Philip saw his father stand up in his stirrups to his full height. Sir Hugo paused coolly, and then brought down his sword in an arc of flashing steel, full on the turbaned head of the Turk.

Philip heard the thud of the terrific blow, saw a figure reel from the saddle out of the corner of his eye, and then he had thrust hard at the exposed throat of the man on his left. The yell of the Infidel turned to a horrible gurgle, and he too vanished from sight.

But the Christians were being forced back by the greater weight of the deep Turkish lines, slowly at first, and then as the trumpets blew the retreat, more quickly, until they were back once more in their original position.

In that desperate encounter the battle had been won and lost. The Turks had rallied their line when it was on the point of being broken, and their fresher horses had pushed the Christians back. But their casualties had been high; far higher than the Crusaders', whose armour had saved them. So the Turks decided to resume their long-range attacks of mounted bowmen, reserving their charge home until they were sure that the Christians were too weak to resist. It was still dangerous to come to hand-to-hand fighting with those determined knights.

The red tent of King Guy had been pitched as a rallying point for his men, and the Christians grouped themselves around their king in a great arc. The majority were on foot now, for the horses had suffered in the arrow fire, and those who were still mounted could do little; their chargers were too weak to raise even a trot.

The infantry who might have saved the battle with their bows were still isolated from the main body. The Turks had surrounded them, and now they charged. That single attack was enough to break through the ranks of the tired and demoralized Crusader footmen. They were butchered where they stood by the merciless Infidels.

There was no hope now for the Crusaders, and they knew it. But for long hours they stood stubbornly on the battlefield while the Turks wheeled round the motionless lines, pouring in their hail of arrows. The sun and the heat completed the disaster. Exhausted, and mad with thirst, the knights of Outremer knew that there was no hope, no chance of retreat, but they refused to give in.

Those who were still mounted grouped themselves together for occasional charges when the Turks came close enough. Philip, Sir Hugo, and Gilbert were among these, but they were almost at the end of their strength. Philip felt that any moment he would roll helplessly from the saddle. His head was throbbing dully under the weight and pressure of his helm, and his body ached under his hauberk. He kept licking his dry, cracked lips with his tongue, and he wondered how long this torture would last.

But he still found some hidden reserve of energy that made him lift his shield and swing his sword. Time had lost all meaning now; how long the battle had lasted he had no idea. He was living in a nightmare of noise and heat, choking dust and a blinding glare from the sun, hissing arrows and wheeling Turks who appeared suddenly through the curtains of dust, and then as quickly disappeared again.

But there were men among the Crusaders whose long experience of war rose above their fatigue. Sir Hugo was one, and Sir Balian another.

'We must charge, Balian,' Sir Hugo said.

'No use, Hugo. The horses are finished.'

'I know. But it would be better to die charging than wait here for the end.'

Sir Balian's helm nodded. 'You're right, Hugo. And there may be a chance. There's always a chance.'

The same plan had occurred to other knights who were mounted and unwounded. They closed in together, and then at a signal from Sir Balian rode out towards a group of Turks.

Philip's head cleared slightly, though he was still in a daze as he rode a few paces behind his father. The advance was hardly a charge, for the horses could not rise to more than a trot, and none of the Crusaders had lances. They had all splintered long ago in the earlier fighting.

Philip picked out his man, a plump little fellow with a silver helmet. As he neared him, Philip wrenched his horse to one side and cut at the silver helmet. The Turk parried the blow and thrust back. Philip was prepared for that. He made no attempt to guard. Instead he brought his sword across in a flat sweep, and caught the Turk just above his bare wrist.

He caught a brief glimpse of the Turk staring incredulously at an arm that no longer possessed a hand, and then he heard a familiar voice shouting urgently.

'To me, Philip, to me!'

Philip swung round. He saw his father kneeling on the ground, staggering away from a kicking horse that had gone down with an arrow driven home at short range. A Turk was bending down to cut at Sir Hugo, who flung up his shield.

Philip pushed his tired horse forward. The Turk never saw him. It is doubtful if he ever knew what hit him. For Philip swung hard at the back of his unprotected neck. It was a blow delivered with all the fury left in Philip's aching arm, but aimed with all the precision of a man who might have just joined in the battle, fresh and unhurt.

The Turk sagged forward, his head almost severed from his body. But Philip did not bother to look, For three other Turks were closing on Sir Hugo.

'Behind me, father!' Philip yelled, and tried to push himself between Sir Hugo and the Turks. He saw Gilbert close in on his right, and then they were surrounded by a circle of yelling Infidels.

Sir Hugo went down again, knocked over by a rushing horse. Philip killed the rider, but he knew the end must be near now. He cursed and shouted, berserk mad, and yet oddly detached, as if he was outside his body and watching and listening to what was going on. He saw two Turks slip from their saddles and bend over Sir Hugo.

Then his own horse suddenly reared up on his forelegs with a scream, and Philip toppled sideways. Even at that moment he remembered his training. 'Let everything go except your sword, and roll clear!' But he hit the ground with a crash that shook the breath out of his body. A dark shape loomed overhead. He thrust blindly upwards. A horse screamed as his sword sank into its belly, and then he was up, gasping for breath.

Sir Hugo was lying on his back. A Turk was bending over him, and Philip ran forward, swinging back his sword as he approached. The jar of the blow hurt his tired muscles, and the Turk staggered sideways, exposing his throat. Philip's point flickered forward and through, and the man collapsed across Sir Hugo's body.

'Father, father!' Philip ignored the other Turks. He jumped astride his father's body and looked down, afraid of what he might see. That one glance was enough. Philip knew death when he saw it.

'Take the pony, Philip, quick! Grab his bridle!'

Gilbert was pushing a riderless Arab horse towards Philip, warding off a charging Turk as he did so. Philip nodded, gripped the bridle and swung himself up. He looked down again. Sir Hugo's helm had been torn from his head, and his eyes were closed. His face seemed very placid, Philip thought. But then Sir Hugo was never excited, he decided. Not even when he was dying.

'Fall back, Philip!' Gilbert bellowed. 'We can do nothing for Sir Hugo.'

Obediently Philip turned his pony towards the Christian lines. Hot tears were running down his cheeks, and he hardly realized what he was doing. If Gilbert had not ridden beside him, and guided him, he would never have reached the safety of the main body of the Crusaders.

Philip never really knew the full details of the rest of the battle, nor even the exact part he played himself in the final stages of the fighting. He was as a man suffering from concussion. Heat, exhaustion, and thirst, and the searing shock of his father's death, had all had their effect on his dazed brain; a series of stunning blows that reduced him to the state of a fighting automaton.

He took part in several more forlorn charges. His new pony was fairly fresh, and he found a waterskin hanging from the saddle. There was only a bare mouthful of water left, but even that small amount, which he swallowed with a gulp of delirious pleasure, gave him sufficient strength to carry on for a little longer.

Few Christians were mounted now. But their casualties were astonishingly low, for the short bow fire of the Turks had little effect on the steel rings of the hauberks. The sun and the lack of water were the best allies of the Turks. The Crusaders still stood in a great circle around the True Cross, but they were incapable of any further resistance.

The Infidels saw that their moment had come. The drums and cymbals crashed out for the last time. Saladin rallied his freshest troops, and flung them at the Christian centre in one overwhelming wave.

Philip was one of the few knights who could fight back. He hurled himself at the flank of the main wedge of the Infidels that was already deep in the Christian line. 'One last effort,' he was muttering to himself. 'The Kingdom is lost, my father is dead, Joscelin is dead, everything has gone. Kill and be killed.'

His pony charged home. A Turkish rider was caught off his balance and went flying. Philip forced himself through the gap and was in the centre of the Turkish wedge. There is always some hidden and unsuspected reserve of strength in a man who is well trained and fit, and Philip drew on these last remaining shreds of his endurance.

He saw through his eye-slits the dark, swarthy faces, the turbans and the white snarling teeth, the blood-red nostrils of frightened horses; swift, flickering pictures that came and went before him. Four men went down before his mad rush, and then he was through to the Cross.

He recognized Guy of Lusignan swinging his sword, just before the King went down before a concerted charge of Infidels. This was the end, Philip thought, and he went mad, a raging fury that cut and hacked with all the fearful strength of a person possessed. A richly dressed Turk swung at him, and Philip swerved aside, crashing his sword down on the other's shield.

Quickly he recovered for the blow that would finish the man, but two Turks pushed back his pony by sheer weight, hacking at him from both sides. Philip warded off the left-hand attack with his shield and sent in a backhanded cut to the right that swept an Infidel from his saddle with his face a smashed ruin.

A stab of red hot pain surged up his leg. His pony toppled sideways, and with a groan Philip felt himself falling. He flung his shield away, crashed to the ground on his face, rolled over, and struggled up.

'Surrender, sir Frank, surrender!' he heard the Infidels shout in the Arabic he spoke so fluently.

But Philip was long past all understanding or reason. On his feet again, he flung himself forward. But as he put his weight on his left leg the damaged tendons gave way, and he lurched sideways. 'Wounded', his brain told him, 'you're finished'. But he refused to accept the message. He swung his sword up for the last time in that battle. A Turk staggered back, but Philip had gone down, this time of his own accord, for his legs would keep him upright no longer.

A heavy foot stamped on his wrist, and his sword fell from his hand. Philip groaned. He drew one knee towards him, and tried to force his head up. But his helm was too heavy now, and a blow sent him back to the ground. This time he made no further attempt to move.

All over now, he thought. With a feeling of utter relief he let his tired body relax. He would not have long, he thought. Someone would pull off his helm, and a Turkish knife would rip his throat.

A rough hand grasped his shoulder, and he was hauled

to his feet. He felt fingers fumbling with the straps of his helm, and then the full glare of the sun on his face made him blink. But it was wonderful to be freed from the stifling darkness and the close heat of the steel prison in which his head had been enclosed all day.

A circle of dark faces was watching him with curiosity, and he heard muttered comments in Arabic on his youth. But no one made any attempt to harm him, much to his surprise.

Then he heard a low remark which he thought he must have misinterpreted. 'The Emir Saladin ordered me to bring him to the tent.'

A hand tapped him on the shoulder, and in a daze Philip turned obediently and followed the other Christian knights who were stumbling over the rough ground, a long column of dispirited and disarmed men.

Philip limped painfully, head down and shoulders drooping under the dragging weight of his hauberk. He was not particularly interested in the future or the present. He was too tired, and his brain seemed numb.

Chapter Nine

SALADIN

PHILIP found himself next to Gilbert, one of a long line of dejected Christian knights, standing with bent shoulders and sagging knees, too dulled by the sense of their defeat and their exhaustion to do more than watch the scene before them.

Ahead was an open space, and just to the left of Philip a party of Arab slaves was busily erecting a small coloured tent. Other men were setting out tables, and bringing silver trays covered with long goblets of Damascus glass. Philip's whole parched and aching body yearned with a dreadful urge for those slender glasses filled with bubbling sherbet, the favourite drink of the Turks.

Perhaps this was the torture of the Infidels, he thought, as he tried to brace himself for the ordeal. But the weight of his hauberk dragged down his shoulders, and his left leg was very painful now. He looked down at it for the first time. The steel rings of his chausses were ripped and torn, and blood was trickling down over his mailed foot.

A stir ran down the line of the Christians, and Philip glanced up quickly. Guy of Lusignan, Reynaud de Chatillon and the two Grand Masters were being led forward towards the tent. With them were the leading barons of the Kingdom. Guy bore himself with dignity at this moment, his handsome face calm and impassive. Reynaud was scowling and defiant, his shoulders back, and his black beard shooting out aggressively.

There was a pause. The slaves completed their tasks and disappeared behind the tent. Four enormous Negroes, stripped to the waist, took up posts on either side of the open flaps of the tent, each man holding a naked scimitar. The circle of Turks facing the Crusaders stiffened, and into the open space in front of the tent walked a small group of very richly dressed Emirs.

A few paces ahead was a slightly-built man with the thin, aristocratic features of the highly bred Seljuk Turk. He was the man with whom Philip had exchanged blows in that last flurry near the True Cross. With a shock of startled surprise, Philip realized that this must be the Emir Saladin himself.

Saladin inspected his prisoners in silence. He stood with

an easy dignity, his face inscrutable, without any trace of triumph or anger in his dark eyes. His dress and armour were no richer than those of his Emirs, but he possessed some indefinable force of character and personality that impressed even Philip, and all the Crusaders standing there.

'So we meet again, Sir Reynaud,' Saladin said quietly.

Reynaud de Chatillon moved forward and stared back into Saladin's face. There could be no mercy for him, he knew, and he expected none. For it was he who had provoked the war, broken the truce with Saladin, and attacked the Turkish caravans. Saladin had sworn openly to have his revenge on Reynaud.

But Reynaud, whatever may have been his faults, was no coward. He drew himself up, his dark face still scowling.

'Infidel and unbeliever,' he growled, and spat contemptuously on the ground in front of Saladin.

Saladin's eyes half closed. He whipped out his scimitar in one swift movement and swung it back in the air. Reynaud stood his ground, his head back, watching the flashing blade with stoical courage. Then he went down, blood gushing from his head. Two of the Negroes leapt forward, and hacked at Reynaud as he lay on the ground.

Philip heard the sound of the blows and the panting breath of the Negroes, and he shut his eyes. When he opened them again, Reynaud's limp and twisted body was being dragged away, his mailed feet leaving a trail in the dust.

A murmur of horror ran down the line of the Christians. Guy of Lusignan turned his head towards the Grand Masters as if to bid them farewell, and then he braced his shoulders back, and waited for his turn to come.

Saladin sheathed his sword leisurely. His face was quite calm again. Indeed, nothing might have happened at all, to judge by his expression.

'Sir Gerard de Ridefort?' he said. 'And Sir Roger de Moulins?'

The Grand Masters were pushed forward, though neither of them made any attempt at resistance. Fanatics both, they welcomed their moment of martyrdom. Saladin had sworn to wipe out the Military Orders, and he would hardly fail to seize his opportunity now.

'Take them away,' Saladin said. 'And all the Christian knights with red or black crosses on their shoulders.'

The Turkish guards went down the lines of prisoners. But the Templars stepped proudly forward of their own account, and they were led away to execution in silence. The rest of the Crusaders closed in, waiting with patient resignation for their fate.

Saladin had turned to King Guy. They eyed each other for a moment, and then Saladin put out his hand and smiled.

'Kings do not kill kings,' he said, and waved to the waiting slaves.

Philip licked his dry, cracked lips as the slaves came forward with the trays of sherbet. He watched Guy and the barons take the goblets, and sip the sherbet, trying vainly to disguise their appalling thirst.

Then a hand touched his shoulder, and he turned to see a dark, smiling face that was oddly familiar. Philip groped in his tired brain for the memory of where he had seen that pointed little beard and the curving nose. Then he remembered.

'Jusuf!' he exclaimed.

'Yes, Jusuf-al-Hafiz. And I am in your debt. A drink, wasn't it? But I never thought I should repay you like this.'

He smiled sympathetically as Philip took the sherbet, and gulped down the cool, bubbling drink. Never in his life had Philip imagined that such bliss could come from a drink. He could feel the energy flow back into his body, and his back straightened like a plant deprived of water for a long period, and then suddenly drenched with rain.

'Sir Hugo?' Jusuf asked.

'Dead,' Philip said.

'I am sorry. I would have wished to repay his hospitality.'

All the prisoners were being offered sherbet now. Their grimy, dust-streaked faces lost the expression of haggard strain and fear. The Kingdom might be lost, and they were helpless captives of the Infidels, but they were still alive, and they would not be killed now, for they knew the customs of the Turks.

'Jusuf!' an imperious voice called. 'Bring the knight of the Black Hawk here!'

Philip limped after Jusuf. Men stood aside with pity on their faces as he was led towards Saladin. Philip clenched his hands. A quick and a clean death, he hoped. He was too exhausted to endure torture.

Saladin inspected Philip in silence, running his dark eyes over the torn and stained surcoat, the battered hauberk, and the tired young face that returned his inquiring glance.

An elderly Emir stepped forward and pointed an angry arm at Philip. 'My lord, this is the knight who nearly killed you. It was he who killed the Emir Fahr-el-Din, may Allah's curse be upon him! He is a madman. I saw him surrounded by six of our men, and he killed them all!'

'Yes, this is the knight,' Saladin said quietly.

Philip shifted the weight from his wounded leg and waited with patient resignation for the signal. He could see the Negro executioners, their scimitars resting against the smooth black skin of their shoulders.

'You fought well, sir Frank,' Saladin said. 'A pity you fight for the faith of the unbelievers. I offer you a choice. Become a follower of Mahomet and you will receive much honour at my hands. Or . . .' and he paused.

Philip stared back at the Emir. He knew what the choice meant. He tried to find some indication of Saladin's intentions, but the dark eyes were quite expressionless. Philip shook his head.

Saladin smiled, and put out his hand.

'I have no love for renegades,' he said. 'Jusuf, is this the knight with whom you hunted on the coast last year?'

'Yes, my lord.'

'Then take him away, and treat him well. He is a man.'

Jusuf touched Philip's arm, and led him away.

PART TWO

PART TWO

Chapter Ten

DAMASCUS

PHILIP put down the heavy brass tray on the low
table, and set out the bowl of fruit and the cups for
coffee. The room was empty, but he could see the
Emir Usamah Ibn-Menquidh in the garden, walking slowly
towards the house, pausing to admire his flowers, and
keeping to the shade of the trees.

Philip folded his arms, and waited. Four years of captivity had taught him the value of patience, and much else
besides.

The old Emir had reached the shallow flight of steps
outside, and Philip went to help him, taking his arm, and

lowering him gently to a divan piled with cushions.

'Thank you, Philip,' the old man said. 'I suppose I must become used to being helped about the house like a child.'

'You are ninety, sir,' Philip said.

'Yes, yes, that is so. Allah has been good to me.'

Usamah nibbled at a few dates, and sipped his cup of black, treacly coffee. He was a frail-looking old man, with sunken, wrinkled cheeks. But even now, at the end of a long life, his profile was like that of a falcon, with the same fierce set of the eyes and mouth.

In his younger days he had been a famous soldier, a hunter and traveller. On several occasions he had visited Outremer, and had met the leading barons of the Kingdom. He often spoke of the Christians to Philip, with an odd mixture of respect for their courage, and loathing for their religion.

Usamah put down the cup with shaking fingers, and looked up at the determined brown face beside him.

'I expect you find it a little tedious, acting as nursemaid to an old man, eh, Philip?' he said.

Philip shook his head. But at his side his strong, capable fingers clenched themselves suddenly. Usamah's sharp eyes saw the quick gesture, and he half smiled, as if in sympathy.

As the old man went on with his simple meal, Philip's mind was racing. He stared out into the garden, with its bright splashes of colour against the dazzling white of the high walls, and the dark shadows thrown by the trees. He must not complain, he was thinking. He had been fortunate, he knew, compared to the lot of many Christians captured at Hattin. The King and the chief barons had been ransomed fairly soon, but many knights were still held by the Turks. As for the infantry, they had been sold as slaves, and it was better not to think of what had happened to them.

Jusuf had seen to Philip's future. He had sent him to Damascus, and for four years Philip had been a mixture of friend, secretary, servant, and nursemaid to Jusuf's father. And since Jusuf's death in a battle in Egypt, Usamah had treated Philip more as a son than a prisoner.

He was disturbed by the clink of dishes. Usamah had finished his meal.

'I will dictate, Philip,' he said.

Philip sat on a low stool, with paper and quill pen before him. Usamah was writing the story of his long life, more for his own amusement than for any other reason. He would have been startled and quite incredulous if he had been told that people would still be reading his memoirs seven hundred years later.

'You were describing the battle of Al-Balat, sir,' Philip prompted the old Emir.

'Ah, yes, that was the time when I chased a Frankish knight. The fool had no mail shirt on! He spurred his horse, but I knew I should catch him, may Allah's curse be upon all Franks!'

Philip smiled as he heard the familiar phrase. Usamah

never failed to use it when he mentioned a Christian; it was a habit more than a true indication of his feelings.

'Do you know why I was certain of catching him?' Usamah asked eagerly, his wrinkled face filled with animation as he recalled that distant battle.

'No, sir.'

'I noticed that the tail of his horse was waving. I knew I would catch him!'

'And did you, sir?' Philip asked.

'I ran him through with my lance.' Usamah chuckled grimly, and held out his trembling hand. The gnarled fingers were shaking, and he grunted with disgust. 'They were steady enough then,' he said. 'Do you know the secret of holding a lance, Philip?'

'Yes, sir,' Philip said quietly. His hands closed on the pen and the paper. A sudden vision swam before his eyes of the courtyard at Blanche Garde, and he could feel again the surge and power of his horse between his mail-clad legs.

Usamah had not noticed Philip's face or sudden twitch of the hands. He was far away, too, thrusting his spear again through the hated unbeliever.

'You must hold the butt well under your arm,' he said. 'Let the horse run. Never move your hand. Grip tightly, and keep your hand still.'

He paused while Philip wrote down the incident, and his comments on the fight.

'I expect you would like to hold a lance again, Philip?'

he said. 'But of course you would! Do you wish to spend all your life in the East?'

'No!'

'Oh!' Usamah was startled by the emphatic negative. 'Where will you go, then?'

'To England, sir.'

'England? Oh, yes, I have heard of it. A small island far to the north, is it not? I remember a Frank telling me about it years ago. Cold, wet, and foggy, he said. You would miss the sun, Philip.'

'I am tired of the sun, sir.'

Usamah grunted. 'But why England?' he asked curiously. 'Perhaps you have lands there?'

'None, sir. But my family came from there many years ago, and I may find some relations.'

Usamah stroked his bony chin, and watched Philip with affection.

'I often have it in mind that you once saved the life of my son,' he said. 'May Allah's mercy rest upon his soul,' he added fervently. 'I think you know, Philip, that if you became a true follower of the Prophet, I would make you my son. I shall not live much longer, and I am a rich man.'

Philip was touched by the old man's words. 'You have been very kind to me, sir,' he said. 'But this could never be my home.'

'Ah, well, I will not press you,' Usamah sighed. 'Unless you change your faith with a deep conviction, you can never be a devout servant of Allah. But if you plan to go to this far country, you will need money. I must see to it.'

He started to dictate again, and Philip wrote steadily in his fluent Arabic script. When the old man was tired, and dozed on his couch, Philip went out into the garden to sit in the shade of a tree, and listen to the tinkle of the fountain.

He had a great deal to think about. During the first few months of his captivity, he had hardly bothered to think. The death of Sir Fulk, of Joscelin, and then of his father, had reduced him to a state of utter despair. The later news had been like hammer blows on a brain that was already numb.

For the Kingdom was lost, swept away by the over-whelming rush of the Turks, exultant and invincible after their crushing victory at the Horns of Hattin. Jerusalem had fallen after the shortest of sieges, for there was no one to man its great walls. All the chief towns and castles had gone, too, Blanche Garde among them. It lay stripped and gutted now, so Philip had heard.

The Christians still held a few coastal towns; the Hos-pitallers clung grimly to their huge fortress of Krak des Chevaliers, up in the heart of the Lebanon mountains, just north of Damascus. But otherwise there seemed no future for Outremer.

And certainly, it seemed, there was no future for Philip. There had been no one to come foward with his ransom. He was unlucky, or perhaps still held for some reason. He had not minded. What was he to do if he were freed? And life with old Usamah had not been unbearable. In fact it was pleasant, and Philip had become resigned.

But all that was changed now. Great events were taking place. The Pope, horrified by the capture of the Holy City, had preached a new Crusade. Western Christendom was shocked by the news, and the richest rulers of Europe had sworn to go on a new Crusade.

They were in Outremer now. Philip of France had come to besiege Acre, and with him was Richard Plantagenet of England, reputed to be the finest soldier in Christendom, backed by a magnificent army and all the resources of the West. The siege must be over by this time. They would be free to march south, wheel inland, and storm the Holy City. Philip writhed and clenched his hands. He could take no part in these tremendous adventures. He must sit here in Damascus and nursemaid an old man. It was intolerable; it was more than he could bear.

He leapt to his feet, and paced up and down the garden, oblivious of the hot sun beating down on his bare head.

The silvery tinkle of a small bell aroused him from his fury. With a sigh he went back to the house. Usamah smiled at him, and went on with what he was doing. He did not like Philip to do too much for him; it was a reminder that he was really a very aged man who was nearly helpless.

Philip sat down on the divan, and watched the Emir

unlock a small chest, finely made by an Eastern crafts-
man, with metal scroll work on the lid and sides.
Breathing heavily, the old man shuffled back to his
divan, and sank back. He set down the leather bag he
had taken from the chest, and smiled again at Philip.
His thin fingers laboriously unravelled the knot at the
neck of the bag, and with a triumphant grunt, he held
the pouch upside down.

A shower of black pearls cascaded across the highly
polished surface of the table. They gleamed and sparkled in
the sunlight, black beads of inky fire.

'They are yours,' Usamah said abruptly.

Philip started, and stared at the pearls. He knew something of precious stones, and their value. These pearls
would make him a rich man, richer by far than he might
ever be as the lord of Blanche Garde.

'I can never thank you, sir,' he said at last.

'You have no need to, Philip. I have never paid you for
the life of Jusuf, may Allah rest his soul.' Usamah looked at
Philip's intent face, and smiled. There was little that escaped
his shrewd eyes, despite his age.

'I saw you pacing up and down in the garden,' he said.
'You reminded me of a caged lioness I saw once. Perhaps
these will help to unlock the cage.' And he touched one of
the pearls with his shaking fingers.

Philip nodded. He said nothing. Four years as a prisoner had curbed his tongue, and taught him discretion. He
gathered up the pearls, and then helped Usamah to his

bed-chamber, where the Emir would sleep during the heat of the day.

Philip went out riding the next morning with half a dozen of the Emir's servants. They were bound for a spot outside the walls where a falcon trap was set up, for although Usamah had long since flown his last hawk, he still loved to catch and train the birds. By the Beirut Gate they waited while a caravan passed into the city. The streets of Damascus were not very different to those of Jerusalem, Philip was thinking, as he watched the beggars. They were as filthy and repulsive as those Llewellyn had once driven away.

One of them rushed across to Philip. He held out his hands.

'Sheyan-lillah!' he howled. 'Something for the love of God!'

The same cry, too, Philip thought, and fumbled for a coin. The beggar took it, spat on it, and glanced up.

'You are Sir Philip d'Aubigny of Blanche Garde?' he asked quietly.

Philip's horse shied as he jerked roughly at the reins. For this scarecrow of the Damascus slums had spoken in the *langue d'oeil,* the language of France and the Normans, and his accent was that of a nobleman.

'Show no signs of listening!' the beggar hissed. 'Meet me tonight or any night at that tavern by the gate. Ask for Ali the Beggar.'

He was gone, running nimbly away, shrieking out his high-pitched plea for alms. Philip took a deep breath,

resisted the impulse to turn and watch, and shook the reins of his horse.

They rode through the circle of cultivated land that surrounded Damascus, through the green orchards and fields, and out into the flat, open country beyond, that stretched away monotonously to the ring of mountains on the horizon.

The falcon trap was a small stone building, about six feet high, covered with dry grass and vegetation, so that the bricks were concealed, and the shed appeared as a harmless mound of turf.

Two men crawled inside, and then their faces appeared at a small opening, where they held out sticks to which pigeons were tied. The procedure for catching wild falcons was simple enough, but demanded patience. The pigeons would flutter helplessly, and their noise and movement would attract falcons, who could not resist such a tempting bait. As they swooped down and grappled with the unfortunate pigeon, the stick would be pulled inside the hut, and the falcon grasped by expert fingers.

Normally, Philip would have followed the trapping with interest, for hawking was one of his passions. But the day passed with infuriating slowness, and he made little attempt to join in the work. He would see this beggar with the nobleman's voice tonight, he decided. There was no difficulty in leaving Usamah's house when he wanted to, and he would not be stopped or molested in the streets if he wore Turkish clothes. His Arabic was faultless now, and no one would take him for a Frankish knight in the dark, for his tell-tale grey eyes would not be seen.

Five hours later he was standing outside the inn, near the Beirut Gate. The single eating-room was more than half full, which reassured him, for there would be less chance of anyone paying him much attention. It was just as well he was wearing shabby clothes and a tattered cloak, he thought, for the inn was a disreputable place.

He pushed his way through the ill-lit room, and sat on a bench with his back against the wall. A Negro came up, and Philip ordered some food. As he waited, he glanced around the room. But he could see no sign of Ali the Beggar. With some difficulty Philip forced the unappetizing food down his throat. A few years ago he would have burst out with anxious questions about the beggar. But the silent man who bent his head over the bowl of stew was a different person from the young knight who had marched out of Blanche Garde Castle.

Philip pushed away the empty bowl, and beckoned to the Negro.

'Do you know Ali the Beggar?' he asked casually.

The Negro eyed him doubtfully, then shrugged his broad shoulders, and jerked a hand in the direction of a curtained doorway.

'Upstairs,' he said, accepting the few coins that Philip pushed over the table in payment for his meal, and shuffling away.

Nobody seemed to be paying any attention to Philip. Why should they? he thought, as he slipped through the curtain, and climbed the rickety stairs to the landing above. But one hand was under the cloak, and he could feel the hilt of the dagger that Jusuf had once given him.

There were three doors on the landing. One was open. Philip stood motionless, his tall figure throwing a long black shadow against the peeling plaster of the wall.

From below came the buzz of conversation and the clatter of crockery. But it was very quiet up there on the landing. Then from the open room came a cough, and the rustle of someone moving.

Philip went to the door, and raising the knife, he tapped with the hilt on the door. 'Ali the Beggar?' he asked softly.

'Come in,' said a voice in Arabic.

Philip braced himself, and moved his grip on the dagger. There was no particular reason why he should suspect treachery, but he had learnt to trust no man. Then he slid through the door, and pushed it shut behind him.

A single rushlight flickered on a low table in the centre of the room. The furniture was rough and battered; a truckle bed, two stools, and a chest by the window. The beggar was sitting at the table, and looked up as Philip shut the door.

'You will not need that knife, Sir Philip,' he said in his faultless French.

'Who are you?' Philip asked suspiciously. He still could not credit the familiar speech from the lips of this repulsive beggar.

'I am John de Vitry,' the beggar said. 'A knight of the Hospitallers.'

'De Vitry!' Philip suddenly had a vision of the waiting-room in the Palace at Jerusalem, a group of young men with scented handkerchiefs, and a voice, Joscelin's, saying something about a brother in the Hospitallers to young Jacques de Vitry.

'I knew your brother, Sir John,' he said.

'Yes, Jacques. He was killed at Hattin.' De Vitry pushed forward the spare stool.

Philip sat down, and slid the dagger back into its sheath.

'What are you doing in Damascus, de Vitry?' he asked. 'Are you in hiding, after escaping?'

'Oh, no. I came here of my own accord. From Krak des Chevaliers.'

'Of your own accord!'

De Vitry laughed. 'We have a regular connection with Damascus, you see, Sir Philip. I have been here before, because I speak fluent Arabic.'

'But why come here?'

'We like to know what is going on. And we are arranging the escape of prisoners. You are the next on our list.'

Philip shrugged his shoulders helplessly, and laughed. 'I think you had better explain, Sir John,' he said.

'It's quite simple,' de Vitry said. 'We have unlimited money, and even the most devout Infidel will do a great deal for money. We have succeeded in releasing several barons. Horses are the difficulty, you see. It's fairly simple for you people to get outside the walls, isn't it?' Philip nodded. 'But not so easy to go much farther. And that's where we help. We have a place outside, and a supply of good horses. There is one waiting for you. In two days' hard riding, you will be at Krak.'

'I want two horses,' Philip said instantly.

'Two?'

'Yes, Gilbert d'Assailly is coming with me. He's in Damascus, too.'

De Vitry shook his head doubtfully. 'But I only had orders about you, Sir Philip. The Grand Master was most insistent.'

'Who?'

'Sir Roger de Moulins. He was not killed with the other Hospitallers at Hattin, you know. He mentioned you particularly, Sir Philip. You see, you have some powerful friends. Sir Balian d'Ibelin and Guy of Lusignan asked that you should be helped to escape.'

Philip's eyebrows lifted slightly. Otherwise he gave no sign of surprise or gratification at the information that such important barons were interested in his fate. He had become very like his father.

Five minutes later he had persuaded de Vitry to allow him the use of another horse. It would have needed a stronger personality than the young Hospitaller to stand against such a forceful person as Philip had become.

De Vitry gave Philip a detailed description of the place

where the horses could be found, and the password which would ensure that the man holding the horses would hand them over. More instructions followed about the route to Krak, and the necessity for taking sufficient food and water for the journey.

'What about you, de Vitry?' Philip asked curiously.

'I must stay here. There is a good deal more for me to do.'

Philip seized his hand and shook it warmly. 'You are a brave man, Sir John,' he said. 'One day I will repay you for this.'

'Escape first, and then you can thank me,' de Vitry said.

Philip hurried back to Usamah's house. He would find Gilbert in the morning. They must leave Damascus the next night. There would not be much difficulty about that, for the house Gilbert was living in was on the wall of the city. The drop to the foot of the ditch was not too great for active men, with the help of a rope.

Philip went through the details as he walked through the dark streets, and let himself in by a side door to the courtyard of Usamah's house. Food, fruit, water, a rope, weapons; he went through the list in his mind. Everything must be ready by the next evening.

He met Gilbert in the bazaar early next day. The position of Christian knights in Damascus was a peculiar one. They were prisoners, but were allowed a considerable amount of freedom. As long as they did not attempt to escape, they were left alone. For the Turks were a curious mixture, friendly enough and respectful to old enemies of high rank, but ferociously cruel to men who were caught attempting to leave the city.

So Philip was able to meet Gilbert, and talk to him quite openly. Gilbert had changed little in the four years. He was still the grave young man who had arrived at Blanche Garde, slow of speech, lanky, and ungainly in movement, and regarding the world with a pessimistic air.

Like Philip, he was dressed in shabby clothes. In that way they escaped drawing too much attention to themselves in the streets, for an obvious Christian often received a kick or a passing blow, if nothing worse, from any Turk who felt so disposed.

They squatted down in the shadow of a high wall, two humble figures, and talked in low tones.

'We are going to escape tonight,' Philip said. He felt Gilbert stiffen by his side. 'Don't look excited,' he muttered.

'I'm not, Philip. I'm worried. Don't be such a fool. We can't get away from this infernal place. And if we're caught . . . remember what they did to Jacques de la Tort last month.'

Philip tried not to remember. Jacques had been a friend of his.

'This is different, Gilbert,' he said, and told him about de Vitry. 'The only difficulty is climbing down from your window. I can find the rope. But we dare not risk leaving a rope dangling down the wall. The sentries will see it. Is there anyone who can pull it up after we've gone?'

Gilbert was reassured by the story of de Vitry, and he settled down to give the plan his serious consideration.

'There's a Syrian slave in my place,' he said. 'He's a Christian, and he's grateful to me for some kindnesses. He gets a pretty rough time, you know. They flogged him last week for breaking a bowl in the kitchen, so he's not too fond of the Infidels at the moment.'

Philip did not like the idea much. 'He would be taking a dangerous risk in helping us, Gilbert,' he said doubtfully. 'It won't be a flogging if he's caught.'

'I know. But I think he'll take the chance. If we don't try him, who else is there?'

They decided to meet again that afternoon, when Usamah would be taking his afternoon siesta, and Philip would not be needed for dictation. Gilbert could report then about the Syrian, and, if that was satisfactory, they would escape that night.

Philip went back to Usamah. For one moment he nearly told the old man about his plans. He was fairly certain that Usamah would not stop him. Several times he had hinted at the idea himself. But it might be safer to take no chances. And Usamah might be glad to know nothing. The Eastern idea worked in a peculiar way, Philip had learnt.

He met Gilbert again, this time in Usamah's garden.

'Malik will do it,' Gilbert said, when they were sure that no one could overhear their conversation. 'But he wants some payment.'

'I haven't any money,' Philip said. 'Only the pearls.' He had told Gilbert about Usamah's gift. 'And one of those would be no use to Malik. A slave with a black pearl would be suspect immediately. They're far too valuable.'

'What about that cross around your neck?' Gilbert said.

Philip fingered the thin gold chain from which hung a small gold cross. His father had given it to him. His mother had once worn it. He was not very happy about the prospect of handing over such a gift to an unknown Syrian slave.

'It would make all the difference,' Gilbert said softly, reading Philip's thoughts.

'Very well. He can have the cross.'

The other arrangements were soon made, and they parted once more. Philip went about his preparations methodically, for nothing could be left to chance. There would be risk enough when they started to climb down the walls, and went off in search of the horses, if they got so far in the plan as that.

He pulled on his hauberk, and slipped dark, shabby clothes on top. He still had his chausses, but they would show beneath the cloak. The mail coif of the hauberk would hang down out of sight over his shoulders. His precious sword, polished carefully each day, and well greased, went in a long bundle, together with the chausses, the coil of rope, a supply of waterskins, dates, and figs, and some cold meat.

Philip did not see Usamah again that evening. Perhaps it was for the best. The old man was far too clever not to have noticed something, skilful as Philip now was in concealing his feelings. But Philip was fond of the Emir. He would have liked to bid him farewell.

An hour after the sun was down, Philip slipped through the side door of the garden into the narrow, high-walled street outside. On his shoulder was a long, sausage-shaped bundle. No one would stop to question a humble slave carrying a burden for his master, and Philip had his story all ready.

There were few people about in the ill-lit streets. No one was interested enough to look twice at the wearily hunched-up figure who shambled along with the clumsy package on his back, moving obsequiously aside to the walls to give free passage for any pedestrians coming towards him. Philip paused outside the house of Shuhab-al-Din, where Gilbert lived. Then he crossed the road, pushed open the door with his foot, and stepped inside.

The kitchens were on his right, and he could hear the sound of voices. If he was seen, he would say that he was bringing a present from the Emir Usamah to Shuhab. He had done such a thing before, and the servants knew him by sight.

But no one saw him. He pattered swiftly up the shallow stairs. The clumsy bundle brushed against the wall, and he slowed down. He did not want to make a noise now.

The passage was dark, but a faint yellow strip of light showed under Gilbert's door. Philip tapped lightly with his knuckles. The door creaked open, and Gilbert pulled him inside.

'All well, Philip?'

'So far. What about that Syrian of yours?'

'He'll do it. I told him to come here in half an hour. The sentries will be round this section of the wall in a few minutes. Then you'll hear the muezzin, and they come round again. There's over half an hour in between, and that should be enough.'

'You're sure of that?' Philip asked, though he knew it was unlikely that the methodical Gilbert would make a mistake on such a vital point.

'Quite certain,' Gilbert said. 'I've listened to them often enough in the last four years,' he added bitterly.

'Well, tonight will be the last night,' Philip said.

He was pulling on his chausses. Now he was covered from neck downwards in mail, and he adjusted the coif over his head. But for a helm, he was fully armed. Round his waist he buckled the wide sword belt; it was pleasant to feel once more the heavy drag of the long blade at his side.

'That mail will jingle a bit,' Gilbert said. He had lost all his armour after Hattin, and a knife was the only weapon he could muster.

'If we're seen on the wall it won't matter how much noise we make, or how we're dressed,' Philip said grimly.

For there would be no mercy from the Turks. And

there would be none on his side, Philip decided. His mouth closed in a thin line. There would be four years of humiliation to repay. Gilbert saw the expression, and sighed. This was a different Philip from the smiling young squire whom he had first met in Jerusalem at Sir Fulk's house. He had seen the gradual change during the last few years.

There was a faint scratching noise from the direction of the door. Gilbert jumped round nervously.

'Malik, I expect,' he said.

He heard a click from behind him as he opened the door. Philip was against the wall, knife in hand. He was not taking the slightest chance that night.

It was Malik. A slouching figure slipped furtively into the small room, jerking his head in sudden, swift gestures of sheer fright.

'Had all the stuffing whipped out of him,' Gilbert muttered.

Philip nodded. He was not impressed with the Syrian. This was not the man he would have chosen to hold one end of a rope while he slid down the walls of Damascus. But they had no other choice.

'Show him the cross,' Gilbert said.

Malik's claw-like hand closed over the thin gold chain, and he gloated over the cross with a grunt of satisfaction.

'You know what to do, Malik?' Gilbert demanded.

'Yes, my lord.'

'Now, remember, if that rope is seen on the wall after

we're gone, we shall all be caught. You, too, Malik. And you know what they will do to you if they catch you?'

It was only too clear that the wretched Syrian did know. His face went grey with fear, and his eyes rolled up until the whites could be seen against the darkness of his swarthy skin.

Philip sighed. He wondered if it had been wise of Gilbert to remind the man of his probable fate. His nerves were jumpy enough already. 'You're too heavy to lower by hand,' Gilbert said, picking up the rope. 'We'll have to make this end fast here.'

Fortunately the framework of the window was solid, and without much difficulty they knotted the end round the centre pillar. Philip put his weight on the loose end of the rope, and tugged. The window frame took the strain without even the faintest creak.

'Right,' he said. There had been no question as to who should go first. Philip was instinctively the leader of this expedition, and Gilbert never suggested anything else.

Philip let himself through the open window feet first. He took a firm grip with his mailed hands, and slid down cautiously into the warm darkness of the night.

He could see nothing. And he had enough sense not to look down at the sheer drop to the ground below. But he would probably have seen nothing if he had looked.

He had no idea of how far he had gone. Steadily he let himself down, taking most of his weight with his feet, twining them tightly around the thick rope.

Then his feet were free. He had reached the end of the rope. He must look down now, and he was afraid of what he might see. The drop to the bottom might be too far to take without a risk of breaking a leg.

He held on with his hands, and glanced down. For a moment he could see nothing. But his eyes were more accustomed to the darkness by this time, and he could distinguish the darker blur of the ground below. Not very far, he decided. There was no point in hesitating. He must let go sometime.

He let go. He held his breath, and tried to flex his knees so as to cushion himself against the shock of the fall. But the drop was shorter than he had estimated. His feet hit the hard ground with a jar that sent a painful jolt through his entire body, and he rolled over gasping.

He lay there for a moment, and then leapt to his feet. He was down, and unhurt.

The wall shot up above him, towering up into the night, so high that he could only just pick out the parapet against the lighter blackness of the sky. Coming down the rope was a gigantic spider, or perhaps a moth, Philip decided, seeing the dark grey cloak that Gilbert was wearing.

Gilbert came down quickly. Then he, too, came to an abrupt halt as his feet reached the end of the rope.

'All right!' Philip muttered. 'Only a few feet to come. Let go, Gilbert.'

He heard a grunt, and then Gilbert swooped down. With another grunt he crashed to the ground, and rolled over.

'All right?' Philip asked anxiously. He had been afraid of this. For Gilbert, with his lanky figure, and ungainly legs, might fall awkwardly.

Gilbert stood up, and swayed to one side. A groan of pain came from his lips.

'What is it?' gasped Philip, a sudden cold spasm of fear clutching at the pit of his stomach. If Gilbert had broken his ankle, they were lost.

'Sprained ankle, I think,' Gilbert said.

Philip knelt down, and gently ran his fingers over Gilbert's foot and ankle. 'Try your weight on it,' he said.

'Just do it, I think,' Gilbert said. 'But we'd better wait here for a few minutes now.'

Philip fought down the inclination to run, to get clear of the wall. In a few minutes the patrol would be back.

'The rope!' Gilbert said. 'Why doesn't Malik pull it up?'

They stared up fearfully. The sentries might not see them at the foot of the wall. But they could not cross the gap quickly to the thick cover of the orchards, for Gilbert could only hobble, and he would never reach those blessed trees before the patrol came round. If the rope was still on the wall then, they were certainly lost.

The rope lay still, like some enormous serpent against the wall. Philip stood up, and tried to reach the end with the idea of twitching it frantically as a signal to Malik. Then it moved, paused, and slid upwards.

With a sigh, Philip sank back to the ground. He could

feel the chilly sweat on his forehead, and that agonizing cramp of fear in his stomach subsided slowly.

Gilbert moved suddenly. 'The muezzin,' he said.

Through the still night came the voice of the muezzin from his lofty minaret, calling the Faithful to prayer.

'*Hai ala-as-salah! Allahu-akbar! La ilaha illa'lah!*'

Philip smiled grimly. Old Usamah would be kneeling down in obedience to that cry, his bowed face towards Mecca, his thin, reedy voice muttering the prescribed prayer. '*Allahu-akbar*, prayer is better than sleep. There is no God but Allah. He giveth life, and he dieth not. My sins are great; greater is thy mercy. I praise his perfection. *Allahu-akbar!*'

'May it be many years before I hear that cursed cry again,' Gilbert whispered fervently.

The clear, ringing voice fell silent. They both pressed themselves against the wall, crouching down on the dry earth. The patrol would be above their heads at any moment.

How long they waited, Philip had no idea. Probably not for more than a few minutes, but it felt and passed like an hour. Then he heard the clank of armour, and voices far above. They passed, and died away. He breathed out deeply, surprised to find that he had held his breath during that tense minute.

'Right,' Gilbert said. 'Another half hour before they're round again.'

Philip helped him to his feet. They hobbled as quickly

as poor Gilbert could move for the direction of the orchards. The night was still very dark, and Philip knew that they could not possibly be seen, for neither was wearing anything white. But the moon would be up soon, and they must be in the trees before that.

A black mass loomed ahead, and with a final rush, Gilbert trying to stifle his groans, they dashed into the trees. Philip turned to look back.

A yellow moon was rising behind the walls of Damascus. In that bright light the spires and minarets shone whitely. It seemed a fairy city of lovely buildings and romantic walls.

But Philip did not waste time admiring the beauty before him. He took his last glance at Damascus, turned and grasped Gilbert by the arm, and led him through the orchards.

Chapter Eleven

THE ASSASSINS

D E VITRY had given Philip detailed instructions for finding the barn where the horses were waiting. There was no difficulty, apart from the slow pace of poor Gilbert. But they found the river bank, as de Vitry had said, and turned to the right there. The moon was bright enough for them to move without stumbling over stones and roots of trees, which was some help to Gilbert.

'There!' Philip whispered, and pointed.

In the shadow of a clump of trees was a tumbledown

barn. Gilbert took a step forward, but Philip pulled him back.

'No, wait,' he hissed. 'There may be something wrong. It's not worth taking a risk. I'll go and have a look.'

Gilbert sank down thankfully, and felt his ankle gingerly. Philip pulled out his sword, his long fingers flexing themselves lovingly around the grip. Every night, in the privacy of his room, he had carried out his sword exercises. His wrists and arms were as supple as they had ever been, he thought. But he was to discover that four years had given him a far greater strength than he had ever possessed before.

He moved slowly towards the barn. His hauberk and chausses jingled softly, but to his anxious ears the sound was far louder than that. The gurgle of the stream close by drowned the noise, though, and he reached the door of the barn without pausing or slowing down.

The woodwork of the building was warped, and Philip put his face close to the nearest gap. Ten feet away he could see the flicker of a small oil lamp. The shape of two horses could just be distinguished beyond, and Philip heard them whinnying impatiently, as if they were disturbed. That sound made him stiffen. For he knew and trusted horses. There was something wrong, something unusual, in that barn. And in the next second he learned what it was.

Two Turks suddenly moved in front of the yellow light. One was dragging a limp object on the ground. Philip drew in his breath. For the light threw a faint gleam on the white face of a dead man.

'Dead,' one of the Turks said. 'No use, Rubal; you hit too hard. Why didn't you do as I told you? I could have made this fellow talk, and tell us why he's keeping two Frankish horses here.'

'May Allah render him helpless,' the other man growled. He aimed a vicious kick at the body.

Philip stepped back. He yearned for his shield at that moment. He could rush the men, hold off the attack of the one on the left, and cut down the other. But now he would have to rely on speed and surprise. It was a matter of two minutes to bring Gilbert to the barn, and explain his plan. Gilbert was to hobble round to the other side where Philip could see another door. He was not to attempt to rush in, but merely to batter on the wooden wall, and make as much row as possible. Philip would do the rest.

The Turks were still arguing over the dead man. Only one had a weapon drawn, a curved scimitar. He would take him first, Philip decided, working out his plan with complete calmness. Only the pounding of blood in his heart gave any indication of his feelings.

The stillness of the night was suddenly broken by a battering of hands on wood. The Turks whipped round. In that instant Philip kicked the rickety door open, and leapt inside. As he bounded forward, he let out a high-pitched shriek.

Round jumped the two Turks. They had a brief and horrifying glimpse of a figure hurtling towards them out of the gloom. The man with the scimitar opened his mouth in dumb surprise, and automatically brought his weapon up. But he was given no time. Philip's sword came down in a hissing arc, full on the top of his turban, and he went down as if a section of the wall of Damascus had fallen on him.

Philip pivoted to his left like a cat, his blade flickering out in a swift jab. He felt a slight jar, and he had spitted the second man like a fowl on the kitchen fire at Blanche Garde.

'All right, Gilbert,' Philip said. 'They won't give any more trouble.'

'They won't,' Gilbert said. He smiled wryly as he saw Philip's grim face in the faint light.

Philip made straight for the horses. They quietened down as he ran his hands over them. They were beautiful beasts, and obviously in magnificent condition. Philip sighed with relief. The last hurdle was over. In a few hours they would be clear of Damascus, and in the depths of the hills to the north.

When the sun rose with its Eastern abruptness, the two riders were at the foot of the Ante-Lebanon mountains. On their left towered the desolate peaks and rocky gorges, running in an irregular line towards the north. Philip had never seen them before, but he knew roughly where he was, thanks to de Vitry's thoroughness.

They were to ride steadily northwards until they reached the Lake of Homs, which was large enough for them to find without much difficulty. To the west of the lake there was a wide gap in the mountains, separating the northern tip of the Lebanon range from the southernmost peak of the Gebel Alawi. If they rode through this gap— and de Vitry had assured Philip that he could not miss it—they would come to Krak, for the castle had been built for the express purpose of covering this natural gateway into Outremer.

Philip rested the horses soon after the sun came up. He watered them carefully, with an anxious eye on their supplies. Food was not his chief concern; Hattin had shown him that thirst was his greatest danger. Then he and Gilbert made a rough breakfast of figs and dates, and rode on once more.

Gilbert was tiring already. His ankle was badly swollen, and he had not been given so much opportunity as Philip to ride during their captivity. But he stuck to his saddle uncomplainingly. The horses were superb, and there was little risk of being caught by any pursuit from Damascus.

They were in wild country now, a hard and relentless landscape of jagged peaks and deep ravines, bare of any vegetation or any sign of softness. The earth was a brownish red, as if some giant hand had stirred the whole land with a stick, and then left the tumbled mass to dry and crack in the sweltering sun.

'Do you really like this country, Philip?' Gilbert asked curiously.

Philip looked up at the rock-strewn mountains.

'I hate it,' he said curtly.

'Do you?' Gilbert turned in quick surprise. 'But it's your home, Philip.'

'Not after we recapture Jerusalem. And I doubt if we shall hold Outremer even if we get as far as that. Not as long as the barons go on with their squabbles and their infernal plotting.'

Gilbert watched his friend, stroking his beaky nose reflectively. Philip had been bottling up all this, he decided. Perhaps the years of waiting in Damascus had brought out this sudden explosion.

'What do you want to do, then?' he asked.

'I shall go to England,' Philip said decisively. 'Will you come with me, Gilbert?'

'Wherever you like, Philip,' Gilbert said without any hesitation; and they rode on in silence.

They spent the night in a deep gully, sheltered from the cold night wind, for the air was chilly in the mountains once the sun went down. They huddled together for warmth, wrapped in their long cloaks, stirring uneasily on the hard ground, while behind them the horses stamped and whinnied. But towards dawn they all slept soundly, horses and men alike.

Philip awoke with a start. He heard a sharp exclamation of alarm from Gilbert, and he half rose, one knee on the ground, and his right hand clenched on the hilt of his sword.

A ring of silent men surrounded them, brown-faced Turks in bright turbans, armed with sword and bow.

Philip stood up slowly, and his hand fell from the sword hilt. There was nothing he could do, he decided. In the pit of his stomach he felt the sharp stab of sheer despair. It seemed to well up towards his throat, and he closed his lips firmly to stop the groan of fury that nearly escaped him. In a few hours' time he and Gilbert would have been riding safely through the gap in the Gebel Alawi, with the great walls and battlements of Krak rising before them, manned by friends waiting to welcome him after the four years that had been cut out of his life.

No one spoke for a moment. The leader of the Turks stepped forward; a middle-aged man with a yellow turban that had a single jewel clipped to the front. He was examining the two Christians with a somewhat puzzled expression on his face. His eyes, burning with a curious intensity, ran over their equipment. Clearly he had seen Christian knights before, and he was unable to account for Philip's armour, and the lack of a helm or a shield.

'Who are you?' he asked abruptly in Arabic.

'We have come from Damascus,' Philip said. There seemed little point in denying the fact now.

The Turk's thin eyebrows went up. 'Prisoners?' he asked, as if that explained his first surprise at their appearance. 'Your name, sir Frank?' he went on as Philip nodded.

'I am Philip d'Aubigny, and this is Sir Gilbert d'Assailly.'

The Turk looked at Gilbert, and then back to Philip. 'You will come with us,' he said curtly, and raised his hand as a signal to his men.

For a second Philip wondered if he could rip his sword out and make a fight of it there. But he sensed that a man was immediately behind him. He could see the shadow cast by the rising sun. Perhaps his chance might come later. He was determined on one thing; he would not be taken back alive to Damascus.

And then came the first surprise. The Turks did not take the pass leading to the south. They wheeled north. Going to Hama, Philip decided. He did not know this part of Outremer, but he had studied the excellent map that de Vitry had shown him.

Hama was to the north of Lake Homs, he knew, but the Turks swerved to the west when they passed the shore of the blue lake. In an hour they were deep in the mountains, and all that day they rode steadily towards the west.

Philip was even more puzzled. He tried to visualize de Vitry's map, and the memories of other maps he had seen at Blanche Garde. By this time, he reckoned, they must be in the Nosairi Mountains, close to the borders of the County of Tripoli and the Principality of Antioch, two Christian states that had been wiped out by the Turks after Hattin.

The Nosairi mountains, he was thinking idly. What did he know about them? The Nos ... A sudden suspicion shot through his mind. He glanced sharply at the silent men riding on either side. He knew what to look for now, and he found confirmation on these men's faces of what he had dreaded to see; their burning eyes, their dull, expressionless faces, and their air of well-drilled and disciplined confidence.

The leader of the men was riding beside Philip. He saw Philip looking at him, and he returned the glance from his dark, restless eyes.

'Who are you?' Philip asked. 'The Hashishiyun?'

'Yes, sir Frank.' He might have said more, but at that moment the leading riders paused, and he cantered forward to point out the route they were to take.

Philip had let out a low grunt. Gilbert, who was immediately behind came up to his side. He had heard the question and answer, but the name had meant nothing to him.

'What did you ask him?' he said in the *langue d'oeil*.

'I asked him if they were the Hashishiyun, and he said they were,' Philip said dully.

'But who are they?' Gilbert was bewildered and a trifle disturbed by the sudden change in Philip.

'Haven't you heard of them?' Philip said in surprise. 'No, I suppose you wouldn't have. They are the Assassins.'

'The what?'

'They're a religious sect of the Turks,' Philip said. 'They've always been opposed to the southern Turks, and are spread out over the north now, I think. Even Saladin is afraid of them, Usamah told me once.'

'But why? Why are they so frightening?' Gilbert persisted.

'Because they murder anyone who opposes them. It

doesn't matter where you are, even in your own tent with a dozen guards outside, they still murder you.'

Gilbert stared at his friend in amazement. 'Nonsense, Philip!' he said. 'Are they magicians?'

'Perhaps they are,' Philip said wearily. 'No one really knows. But they don't mind being caught. They seem to welcome death. Count Raymond of Tripoli's father was murdered outside his own castle and in his own city by them.'

'Why did they kill him?'

'Nobody knows. Probably they wanted him to do something, and he refused. He thought he was safe. But nobody's safe from the Assassins. Not even Saladin.'

'Have they tried to murder him?'

'Oh, yes, old Usamah told me about it. Saladin came up into these mountains with a large army to storm the Eagle's Nest, as they call it—the home of the Old Man of the Mountains.'

'Who's he?' Gilbert asked, feeling that he was listening to some nightmare of the East.

'The Sheikh Rashid ed-Din Sinan of Basra,' Philip said. 'We used to call him the Old Man of the Mountains in Outremer. He's the leader of the Assassins in this part of the East.'

'Well, they missed Saladin, then,' Gilbert said. 'He's still alive, unfortunately.'

'I know. But he only escaped because he called off the siege. The Old Man was away from his castle when the siege started, and he hurried back. Saladin's men tried to capture him, but they were stopped. By magic, Usamah said.'

'Rubbish!' Gilbert said; more to bolster up his own growing fears, than from conviction.

Philip shrugged his shoulders. 'If you had lived in the East as long as I have, Gilbert,' he said, 'you wouldn't be so sure. Anyway, Saladin didn't like the look of things. He slept badly, and had terrible dreams. One night he woke up. There wasn't anyone in his tent, but on his bed were some hot cakes, flat ones, specially cooked, the sort that only the Assassins make.'

'What!' Gilbert was catching the infection of the dread in Philip's quiet tones.

'There was a poisoned dagger, too, and a threatening letter. Saladin thought the Old Man of the Mountains must have been there himself, and he gave way. He asked the Old Man for forgiveness, and called off the whole campaign.'

'Phew!' Gilbert glanced round at the silent men riding on either side of them. They had watched the two Franks without interest, not understanding anything of what they were saying.

'But what will they do with us?' he asked uneasily.

'I wish I knew,' Philip said. 'All I do know is that we'd be ten times better off in the hands of the Turks at Damascus than prisoners of the Old Man of the Mountains.'

He relapsed into a gloomy silence, and they rode for

the next hour without a word passing between them. The Assassins showed them no particular hostility. At the various halts they were brought food. Gilbert was handed a small, brown cake, flat and round. He looked at it, glanced inquiringly at Philip, who nodded, and with a shudder gingerly bit into the cake. But the taste was pleasant enough, and he finished it off.

As the sun was setting, they rode into a narrow gorge. The rocky slopes on either side rose up precipitously to a great height, and the air was chilly and damp. There was a well-defined track running down the centre of this ravine, which suddenly turned to the right. The gorge opened out to a width of perhaps half a mile, and Philip saw one of the Assassins raise his hand and point upwards.

Philip looked up. The track swerved in towards the right-hand side of the ravine, and then crept like a snake up the side, curving and winding to the summit. Perched right on the edge of the cliff, for so it looked from the bottom of the gorge, Philip could see grey walls and towers.

'Masyaf!' he muttered to Gilbert. 'The Eagle's Nest.'

The leading horsemen began the climb. The next ten minutes were terrifying ones for Philip and Gilbert. The track was narrow, and strewn with fallen stones. On the left was the frightening drop to the gorge below. One false step by the horses, and they would be flung into space. Philip shut his eyes frequently during that dreadful ascent, and once, when his horse stumbled, cold sweat broke out on his forehead, and he could have vomited with sickening fear.

His hands were shaking when they reached the summit. But the prospect of the unknown dangers that awaited them made him pull his tired and shaken nerves together. As they rode across a deep ditch cut out of the solid rock, and entered the main courtyard of the castle, he had recovered.

There was nothing unusual about the fortress in design. There were the usual curtain walls and round towers, a large gatehouse, and a cluster of residential buildings against the wall that overlooked the gorge.

Philip and Gilbert were told to dismount, and obediently followed their guide to a door at the foot of the main block. One man gestured to the broad sword belt around Philip's waist, and held out his hand. The casualness of the action, the calm assumption that there would be no refusal, that disobedience was impossible, or even anticipated, made Philip hesitate for the briefest of seconds. He sighed, and unbuckled the belt.

They were ushered into a room. The heavy door clanged behind them, and they heard the rattle of chains and bolts. But they were in no ordinary prison cell. The apartment was a spacious one, comfortably furnished with beds, divans, and chairs. The sun shone cheerfully through the wide windows, cut from the solid rock, and much larger than the normal slit-windows of a castle, for there was no siege engine in existence then that could have flung a missile to such a height.

Philip went straight to the window, and looked out. He

recoiled with a shudder. The wall fell sheer for hundreds of feet to the gorge below. The stream alongside which they had ridden was a thin and winding streak of white. A bird fluttered past the window, wheeled, and then swooped downwards with a flicker of its wings.

Philip grinned mirthlessly. He would have to grow a pair of wings to escape from this room.

Gilbert collapsed with a groan of relief on one of the beds. He pulled off his sandal, and stroked his swollen and discoloured ankle with a rueful face.

'There's water in those jars,' Philip said. 'I'll bathe it for you. We can both do with a wash, too. Do us good.'

They washed and tidied themselves after the long ride and the night they had spent in the open, and felt the better for it. Philip had recovered his nerve now, and his cool brain was calculating the position and their chances with all the logic and keen intelligence that he had acquired in four years of waiting and reflection.

He knew that they were both in danger, terrible danger, but there was a chance that a calm head might save them yet. And both Sir Hugo and Usamah had drilled into Philip's head the maxim that the danger least to be feared by a wise man was the danger he could foresee and understand.

Philip knew a great deal about the Assassins, thanks to Usamah. The Emir had acquired a vast store of varied knowledge in his ninety years, many of them spent travelling throughout the East. His acute and inquiring mind had studied the methods and mysteries of the Assassins, and he had imparted much of his knowledge to Philip's retentive brain during those long, sunny afternoons in Damascus, when the fountain tinkled musically in the garden, and the sun threw long shadows across the flower-beds.

'Listen, Gilbert,' Philip said. 'Everything depends on the impression we make on the Old Man of the Mountains. You see, he's not altogether opposed to the Christians. In fact, he's made treaties with us several times. If he thinks we could be useful to him, he may well let us go, and even send us to Krak with a message for the Hospitallers.'

'How could we be useful to him?' Gilbert asked. His short time in Outremer had not given him a very full grasp of the constantly shifting manoeuvres of the many different groups and nationalities of the East.

'The point is that the Assassins would not be altogether sorry to see Saladin smashed. The Old Man has a wonderful spy service, and he's bound to know what's happening at Acre. He knows that Philip and Richard have landed with big armies, and intend to march on Jerusalem. It might suit him to help them. He'll want some contact with them. It's a faint hope, I know, but there's a chance. If not . . .'

'Well, it may be a quicker death than the Turks would have given us,' Gilbert said, one hand rubbing his long nose.

Philip opened his mouth to speak, changed his mind, and went slowly over to the window.

'I'm not so frightened of dying,' he said. 'At least, I hope not. I don't *want* to die. But there may be something worse than dying, Gilbert.'

Gilbert looked up with a shocked expression. 'What do you mean, Philip?' he said in a low voice.

'You can lose your soul,' Philip said.

Gilbert hobbled across to the window. 'For heaven's sake tell me what you mean, Philip,' he said urgently.

'I will. The more you know, the better you can face it.' Philip sat down once more on the stool. 'The Old Man has some extraordinary hold over his followers. They will do anything he tells them. Anything! They will even die, and be glad of the chance.'

'It can't be possible,' Gilbert said incredulously. 'How does he gain this hold over them, Philip?'

'Usamah thought he knew the answer. The Old Man drugs them with some drink. They call it Hashish. That's how they got their name of *Hashishiyun*, the Assassins.'

'But what effect does it have?' Gilbert was beginning to realize now what Philip had meant by something worse than death. He too, had all the superstitious awe and dread of the unknown that belonged to his age.

'I don't know for certain,' Philip confessed. 'But I think you have strange dreams. Your willpower is weakened, and in the end you are ready to do anything you're told. That is what terrifies me. I can't bear to think of myself growing like those men who brought us here. You saw their faces, and their eyes. They were as dead men who are still alive. There wasn't anything behind their eyes at all.'

217

There was silence in the room for a time. Gilbert limped back to his bed and sat down slowly, forgetting for a moment the pain in his ankle.

'But will this Old Man of the Mountains do that to us?' he asked.

'I don't know. Our only hope is that he may decide we could be of more use to him as we are. We've got to persuade him, somehow, that we shall be more efficient, and able to carry out his orders without this drug.'

'You mean, promise to do what he wants, and then just snap our fingers at him when we're clear of this place?' Gilbert looked up eagerly.

'Yes,' Philip said with as much conviction as he could.

But he knew better than that. He knew that no one could escape the long reach of the Assassins; he remembered the men in Outremer who had lived in terror, waiting for the knife in the back, knowing that no amount of protection, not even the most alert of sentries, could ward off the servants of the Old Man.

But that would be in the future. First escape from the Eagle's Nest, and there was a chance. There was always a chance, Sir Hugo had said. Climb your mountains when you come to them.

They were brought food that evening, and then left to their gloomy thoughts. But they were both exhausted after their two days travelling, and the comfortable beds were tempting after the stony ground on which they had tried to sleep the previous night.

Two men in white robes came for them in the morning after they had been given a meal. They were led through the stone passages of the castle, and then pushed into a large audience hall, long and narrow, with a high, painted ceiling.

Philip paused, and then slowly walked forward, Gilbert a few paces behind him. Philip's hauberk jingled softly as he went. He would find the mail but little protection, he thought, for the assault would be on his mind, not his body. He had no defence there, except his intelligence and what calmness of spirit he could muster against the devilish onslaught of the Old Man of the Mountains.

The hall was most magnificently decorated, even by the luxurious standards of Outremer. The finest craftsmanship of the East had been poured out with a lavish hand, on a beautiful mosaic floor, slender marble pillars with delicate graining, and a profusion of silken hangings.

The guides had prostrated themselves flat on the floor, and left the two knights to make their own way to the low dais at the far end. A marble chair was set there, with two immense Negroes on either side, standing so still that at first Philip took them for marble statues. But as he drew closer, he could see the gleam of perspiration on their naked black chests, and the flicker of their eyes as they followed his every movement. Resting on each muscular shoulder was a curved scimitar.

Philip came to a halt, and folded his arms. But inwardly he was the reverse of composed, and he fought down his growing uneasiness as he examined the hunched up figure before him on the throne.

As the jingle of Philip's mail died away, silence fell on the hall. The Old Man was, indeed, an old man in fact as well as in name, small and withered, wearing a long white mantle, and a turban of the same colour. His skin was yellow, stretched tightly over the sharp bones of his face, making his features sharp and pointed. His beard was white, cut short to a pointed tuft that jutted out from his bony chin. He might have seemed a benevolent old man at first sight, but for his eyes, which dominated his entire appearance.

They were a light green, sunk deeply in the cavernous sockets, hard and expressionless as coloured stones, and yet burning with a fire of flaming fanaticism and single-minded purpose.

Philip shuddered inwardly as he caught the cold stare of those horrible eyes. The man radiated evil, ruthless greed, and ambition. Philip could feel the malignant personality of the leader of the Assassins play over him like the rays of the sun out in the desert.

The Old Man shifted his eyes to Gilbert's tall, ungainly figure, took him in from head to foot with one sweeping and comprehensive inspection, and then switched his icy stare back to Philip's determined face, assessing the strong chin and firm mouth, the calm eyes and air of steady self reliance with all the practised skill of one who had weighed the character of many men.

'You are Sir Philip d'Aubigny of Blanche Garde in the Kingdom of Jerusalem?' he said in a soft and gentle voice.

Philip nodded. The remark was more of a statement than a question, and he was not surprised at the Sheikh's accurate knowledge. The Assassins had their spies everywhere. The Old Man must have a detailed knowledge of all the leading personalities in the East.

'Sir Gilbert of Assailly?' the Sheikh said to Gilbert. 'A relation perhaps of the late Grand Master of the Hospital?'

'My uncle.'

For the next half-hour Philip and Gilbert were cross-examined about their experiences during the last few years. Philip answered truthfully. There was no point in doing otherwise, and it was clear that the Old Man paid little heed to the accuracy of the answers; he knew all about them. He was more interested in their minds, and his stony eyes never moved from Philip.

The interview was brought to an end by a curt order to the prostrate guards. They led the Christians back to their room, and another meal was brought to them.

'Phew!' Gilbert said, and collapsed on to his bed, for he found it tiring to stand on his bad ankle. 'Have you ever looked into the eyes of a snake, Philip? That's the impression he gave me.'

'I wonder what impression we made on him,' Philip said grimly.

They were left alone until the late afternoon, when the

same silent guards took them out into the open air, on to a broad parapet of the castle so wide as to form a terrace.

The view across the rolling mountains was superb, but Philip was in no mood to admire the scenery now. He disliked this impression of height, used though he was to walking on the lofty walls of castles. But here he felt as if he were on the summit of a mountain—as was, of course, the fact—and he was very conscious of the terrifying abyss below the low parapet.

Standing a few feet away was the Old Man, flanked by his Negro guards, so still that they might have been stone figures lifted from the audience chamber, and put down in precisely the same posture as that of the morning. The two other guards fell back a few paces, and went down on their knees, their faces to the ground.

'You are wondering, I expect, what I intend to do with you?' the Old Man said. He smiled bleakly. There was no trace of friendliness about his smile, though. He might have been a cat gloating over a mouse.

'Yes,' Philip said curtly.

'I shall send you and your friend to Krak. The castle is just over a day's ride from here, and my men will show you the way.'

Philip's heart jumped. But he kept his eyes on the Old Man. There was more to come.

'That is good of you,' he said.

'In return for my kindness, I shall require your services when I call upon them,' the Sheikh said in his silky voice.

'And what will you want me to do?' Philip demanded.

'I find it necessary to dispose of men who refuse to obey my orders,' the Old Man murmured. 'My followers usually do that for me. But for you, it would be simple, with your rank, and your friendship with important persons. There would be a saving of time.'

'And whom do you want me to murder?' Philip asked, deciding that there was no risk now in evading the issue.

'Oh, come, Sir Philip,' and the Old Man laughed. 'It may be the King of Jerusalem, Richard of England, or the Grand Master of the Hospital. Until I present my demands to them, I don't know who will refuse.'

'Do you really think I shall murder the Master of the Hospitallers for you?' Philip said incredulously.

'Why not?' was the calm answer. 'It would be your life or his. But perhaps you think I am exaggerating. My followers will carry out any orders I give them, however great the danger. And they would certainly find you and deal with you if you refuse to obey me. I will show you.'

He half turned, and snapped his fingers at one of the kneeling guards.

'Abu,' he said, still speaking in his soft voice, a dull monotone. 'The time has come for you to die.'

The man looked up without any change of expression on his blank face. 'Yes, lord,' he said.

'Leap from that parapet, Abu.'

'Yes, lord.'

The man rose to his feet. He hesitated only to bow to

the Old Man. Then he ran towards the low parapet, jumped on to the narrow ledge, paused while he raised his arms into the air, and leapt out into space.

For a second, or so it seemed, he paused in the air like a huge hawk, then his body plunged down, turning over slowly, the white robe fluttering, his arms and legs sprawling limply, like a rag doll that Philip had once flung from the battlements of Blanche Garde in his childhood.

Gilbert shrank back with a cry of horror, hands to his face. The two gigantic Negroes had not moved a muscle; they were watching Philip and Gilbert. The unfortunate wretch who had flung himself to a swift death might not have existed for them.

Philip felt a swift wave of nausea surge up to his throat. But he turned slowly from the parapet towards the Old Man, and schooled his face to a polite expression of inquiry.

The Sheikh had not turned to watch his servant disappear. He was watching Philip.

'You see, Sir Philip,' he remarked pleasantly.

'Very impressive,' Philip said.

He was searching for the response he wanted in those green eyes, and he thought he saw it; a swift gleam of appreciation.

'I think you will prove a valuable servant to me, Sir Philip,' he said.

'I doubt it,' Philip said bluntly. He was glad he had folded his arms, so that he could conceal the clenching of his hands. He yearned with all the force of his violent temper that he had learnt to control that he could seize that frail and evil figure in his arms, and fling him after his poor dupe to the deep gorge and the merciless rocks below. But one slight move, and those Negroes would pounce upon him before he had the slightest chance of reaching the Old Man.

'Well, we shall see,' the Old Man said. 'But be sure of this, Sir Philip. If you do not carry out my orders, then you will not live to obey anyone else.'

He swung round, and walked away.

Chapter Twelve

KRAK DES CHEVALIERS

THE escort of Assassins whom the Old Man of the Mountains had sent with them had returned to Masyaf, and Philip and Gilbert were alone. Krak, they were told, was about ten miles ahead. If they kept to the track that wound through the tangle of gullies and ravines, they would eventually reach the wider pass where the great Hospitaller fortress lay.

They rode in silence. Gilbert was still shocked and horrified by what he had seen, and uneasily conscious that they were not yet out of the reach of the Assassins. Philip was quite sure they were not. He had no intention of carrying out any orders he received, but he knew with a feeling of icy certainty that his life was in the hands of the Old Man.

'Horsemen!' Gilbert exclaimed.

Philip stood up in his stirrups. He caught a brief glimpse of sun flashing on steel, and then the party was hidden again in one of the innumerable folds of the rocky ground.

He roused himself from his fit of gloomy depression. Here was something concrete to handle. These men might be Hospitallers; but equally likely, they might be Turks. If they were, he would go down fighting. There would be no tame surrender this time. A clean end would be better than the knife of an Assassin in his tent one night.

He eased his sword in its scabbard, and Gilbert did the same, for the Assassins had armed him. But they were hopelessly outnumbered. It would be wiser to hide, and fight only if cornered.

'That will do,' Philip said, and cantered to a spot where the gully opened out. The rocks here rose to a considerable height, enough cover to conceal the horses.

They dismounted, and tethered the horses. Philip drew his sword, and, for the first time since he had left Damascus, left more like his own self. They could hear the approaching horsemen now, the clatter of steel hooves on the rocky path, and the jingle of mail. In a minute they would be past.

Then from behind Philip, his horse whinnied loudly.

The noise seemed deafening to Philip's anxious ears, and he muttered softly under his breath. From the direction of the track he heard the high-pitched blare of a trumpet, and shouted orders. They had been heard, after all.

Two horsemen shot into view, one on either side of the gully. Philip saw them, and leapt to his feet, waving his hands, and shouting hoarsely. For he had recognized the black, fluttering cloaks with the white crosses on the shoulder. These were Hospitallers.

The nearest horseman saw him and swerved towards him, his lance dropping to the charge, his head behind the big helm tucked down behind the shelter of his shield.

Philip dropped his sword, and shouted again. The Hospitaller saw the distinctive hauberk and mail coif, never worn by any Infidel, and swept past, raising his spear to the salute as he did so.

In a few seconds Philip and Gilbert were surrounded by a group of Hospitallers examining them with interest, for without his surcoat, Philip's identity was uncertain, and Christian knights did not wander in this way through the mountains of the north, now that the kingdom had collapsed.

One of the Hospitallers pulled off his helm, and rode forward. He was a man of middle-age, a stranger to Philip, who had met many knights of the Order.

'Who are you?' he asked curiously.

'I am Philip d'Aubigny, and this is Gilbert of Assailly.'

'D'Aubigny, Assailly!' The Hospitaller flung himself

from his saddle. 'We have been expecting you, Sir Philip. You met de Vitry in Damascus? We thought to see you several days ago.'

'Oh, we were lost in the mountains,' Philip said smoothly, and was relieved to hear his explanation received without any comment. For he had warned Gilbert to say nothing about the Assassins; so feared was the sect that few men were ever really trusted again if it was known that they had been in close contact with the Assassins.

'I am Hugh de Caimont,' the Hospitaller said. 'You will not remember me, Sir Philip. But I saw you fight de Nogent by the Pool of Siloam.'

They started back for Krak, the Hospitallers plying Philip and Gilbert with questions about their experiences. Philip realized that he would have to tell his story many times in the near future.

The track they were following led them into a wider valley. At the far end lay Krak, a vivid and beautiful sight to find in that wild and savage landscape. The white walls and round towers gleamed in the fierce glare of the sun, perched on the reddish earth of the mound, with the purple hills of Lebanon as a background, and the deep blue of the eastern sky above.

Philip had often heard Krak described, its great size and strength, the enormous store-rooms, and the accommodation for a garrison of over a thousand men. But now, as he reined in his horse, he was filled with awe and astonishment, seeing the stupendous castle with his own eyes.

A natural spur of high ground sprang from the centre of the valley. The sides had been cut away to form a precipitous cliff, and perched on this almost unassailable mound the Hospitallers had sited their castle, the greatest in the world, the supreme achievement of the military art of the Crusaders, built on a scale of such immensity and grandeur that it was never to be equalled or surpassed in the centuries to come.

The details became clearer as the party drew closer. Philip could see the lines of the outer ward, a plain wall broken at intervals by round towers. Rising behind this was the real core of the castle, the colossal ramparts of the inner ward, in a complicated network of enormous walls and towers.

Their Hospitaller guides rode round to the eastern flank where the mound was not so steep. They crossed a moat, rode over a drawbridge that was lowered for them, and then waited while the main gate was opened. Philip followed de Caimont, and found himself in a covered passage-way of stone, a sort of sloping ramp that led up into the heart of the fortress. The ramp turned and twisted like a snake until it reached the summit and passed through the last gate into the inner ward at the top.

Philip could not have complained about his reception. He and Gilbert were shown to luxurious quarters, provided with servants, a bath, and a change of clothes. Afterwards they were taken across the ward to the loggia, or covered cloister, that ran the length of the huge banqueting hall. The roof of this loggia was vaulted in stone, and each graceful archway was beautifully carved. Many of the knights of the garrison were waiting here, and they crowded round the two arrivals with polite curiosity.

Philip had never met any of them before. The Hospitallers he had known had been massacred after Hattin; these men were recruits from the West, and they treated Philip and Gilbert with an open admiration and deference that both found embarrassing, though extremely pleasant after their years of captivity.

Philip was startled to find himself famous. His exploits at Hattin, and his brief conversation with Saladin after the battle, had become exaggerated in the telling, as such stories often are. Young men, of the same age as himself, and others much older, were listening to him with the respect due to a baron of the High Court, and a knight who bore the reputation of being the most formidable swordsman in Outremer.

De Caimont interrupted the conversation. 'The Grand Master wishes to speak to you, Sir Philip. I will take you to him. He is in the Warden's Tower.'

'Who is the Grand Master now?' Philip asked, as they crossed the inner ward.

'Oh, still Roger de Moulins. You have met him before, Sir Philip?'

'Once, in Jerusalem. My father knew him.'

The Warden's Tower was on the south face of the Inner Ward, overlooking the highest section of the walls and the inner moat below. Philip followed de Caimont up a flight of winding stairs, and was ushered into a large, circular apartment with a high, vaulted roof. The floor was covered with bright carpets, and the furniture was of delicate Eastern design.

In contrast to this magnificence, the two great officers of the Hospitallers were grim and sombre figures in their black robes with the white cross at the shoulder.

One of them, Armand de Montbrun, the Warden of Krak, rose to greet Philip. He was a corpulent and heavy man of middle-age, slow in movement and deliberate of speech, but a fine soldier by reputation, as Philip knew. The dominant figure in the room was Sir Roger de Moulins, Grand Master of the Order of St John of the Hospital. But by the side of the bulky Warden, he was small and almost dwarfed. It was his personality, and his air of authority, his brisk, alert manner, that made him stand out. In appearance he made Philip think of an intelligent fox, with his sharp twitching nose and features, and the stiff grey moustache that bristled fiercely across his sunken cheeks.

He waved Philip to a chair, and, without wasting any time on compliments, plunged into a detailed cross-examination. He wanted to know all about conditions in Damascus, the latest news of Saladin, the possible movements of Turkish armies, their strength, their weakness, and any other information that Philip could give him.

Philip gave him a great deal, for he had not wasted his time in Damascus, and he supplied the information in a clear and lucid manner that could not but impress the two experienced men facing him. Towards the end of the interview, the Grand Master was treating Philip with the respect due to a much older man, and on one occasion he paused to throw a significant nod of his grey head towards the silent Warden.

'Thank you, Sir Philip,' the Grand Master said, when he had exhausted his list of questions. 'And now, what are your plans?'

'That depends upon what is happening at Acre, sir,' Philip said.

'Nothing is happening at Acre,' Sir Roger snapped acidly. 'They are all sitting around a table arguing.'

'But the town has fallen?' Philip said in consternation.

'Oh, yes, we have captured it. Philip of France and his army are now about to go home.'

'Go home!' Philip half rose from his seat in horror. 'Before the march on Jerusalem has even begun?'

'Exactly,' the Grand Master snorted, his moustache bristling with anger. 'Philip has quarrelled with Richard of England, or he's jealous. Both, I suspect. Richard is our only hope now. He's a magnificent soldier, with a fine army behind him.'

'And the King?' Philip asked.

'Guy of Lusignan? You can hardly call him King now. Conrad of Montferrat has claimed the throne. The barons of the High Court favour him. Guy has lost a lot of support since his defeat at Hattin.'

Philip suppressed a bitter smile. The little man on the other side of the table was one of those who had talked the unfortunate Guy into the disastrous march to Tiberias.

'Which side will you take, Sir Philip?' Sir Roger asked.

Philip looked up in surprise. He thought he detected a note of more than ordinary interest in the question.

'Does it make any difference which side I take?' he asked curiously.

'It makes a great deal of difference, Sir Philip. There have been many changes in Outremer since you were taken prisoner, you know, and in the composition of the High Court. You forget that you are now a baron of the Court since your father's death. You are the lord of Blanche Garde and Montgizard.'

'Montgizard!' exclaimed Philip.

'Of course. You are the heir to the Grandmesnils. That makes you the holder of one of the largest fiefs in the Kingdom.'

'With both fiefs in the hands of the Infidels,' Philip said harshly. He thought of his father, and Joscelin, and the cheerful red face of Sir Fulk.

'But not for long, Sir Philip. All Outremer will soon be in our hands. And you have many friends. You must number me amongst them. There is Balian d'Ibelin, for instance, Guy of Lusignan himself, and the younger barons will follow your lead.'

Philip went away in a thoughtful mood. Whether he liked it or not, it seemed that he was to be pushed into a prominent place in the endless squabbles of Outremer. And he was beginning to loathe the sound of them. The fall of the Kingdom after Hattin should have taught the barons a lesson, he thought, for there was no doubt that their incessant quarrels were the main cause of the disaster. But they were worse than ever, if the Grand Master was correct.

He and Gilbert spent a week at Krak. They were to ride to Acre with a strong detachment from the castle. It was to fetch this large contribution to the Crusade that the Grand Master had come from the coast.

On the afternoon before they left, Philip was strolling on the battlements of the Inner Ward. The day was hot, but at that great height a cool wind whistled gently over the great walls. Far below, the plain and the distant valleys were spread out like a map. Philip was leaning over the wall, and thinking of the similar drop from the parapet at the castle of the Old Man of the Mountains, when he saw the dapper little figure of the Grand Master approaching.

'Sir Philip,' Sir Roger said abruptly, coming rapidly to the point in his usual manner. 'I wish to have a final talk with you before you leave Krak. Why not join our Order?'

He held up a protesting hand as Philip turned in surprise.

'No, listen to what I have to say first. You are the type of knight we stand most urgently in need of in the Hospitallers. You have a long experience of Outremer. You speak and write Arabic. You know the Turk as few men in

Outremer do. You are of noble rank, and you are one of the most famous soldiers in the Kingdom.'

Philip leant against the parapet, and looked down at the sheer drop of the walls to the moat below. Only a week ago he had stood on a similar height and listened to another offer, from the Old Man of the Mountains. He wondered if the Grand Master would have appreciated the bitter irony of the two positions if he had known of them.

'You would rise rapidly in our Order,' the Grand Master was saying in his persuasive, courtier's voice. 'I would see to that, Sir Philip. I see in you a future Grand Master of the Hospitallers.'

This last remark made Philip swing round in startled surprise.

'You are exaggerating, sir,' he said.

'Indeed I am not,' Sir Roger retorted. 'I have been watching you. A Grand Master needs more than the mere ability to ride a horse and use a sword, you know. Our order is a great one, with fiefs, castles, and lands all over Christendom. You have the abilities for such a post. I do not often make mistakes of this kind. I am used to judging men. Think about it, Sir Philip. Let me have your decision at Acre.'

Philip whistled softly when he found himself alone again on the walls. Grand Master of the Hospitallers! He did not need the information that Sir Roger had given him about the importance of such a post. The wealth of the Order was immense, its influence throughout Christendom widespread. It was almost a kingdom in its own right. And the Grand Master was the ruler of all this.

Gilbert was packing their few possessions when Philip reached their room.

'That old fox been at you, Philip?' Gilbert inquired.

'How did you know?'

'Hugh de Caimont told me. They're all hoping you will join the Order. You're not going to, are you?'

'I don't think so. I shan't decide until we reach Acre. There's someone there I want to see first.'

'Oh, who's that?' Gilbert asked curiously.

'Richard of England,' Philip said.

Chapter Thirteen

RICHARD OF ENGLAND

PHILIP had not seen Acre for over four years. His first thought as he rode in from the north with the Hospitallers was that the port did not appear to have changed a great deal.

Acre had always been a busy port, but never more so than at that particular time, Philip soon discovered. Now all the hopes and resources of the Christians were concentrated there. Hundreds of men swarmed over the white walls and the ditch, repairing the damage inflicted by the long siege. Soldiers of many nationalities thronged the narrow streets, while outside the walls there stretched the lines of the tents and encampments, the long rows of horse lines, and the forest of pennons and banners bearing the devices of knights and barons from all over western Christendom.

The harbour itself was crammed with shipping. Out in the bay, the long transports were moored bow to bow, and at the quays squat cargo boats were tied, with chains of men unloading the contents of their deep holds on to wharves already piled high with an immense accumulation of stores of every description.

It was an inspiring sight, and Philip felt it to be so, despite the gloomy reports given to him by the Grand Master, that the vast explosion of effort which had brought all this concentration of power and strength to Acre was being frittered away by the squabbles of the leaders. Philip was soon to learn that precious time had been wasted on the journey from Europe by petty quarrels and sheer laziness; that now, when at last Acre was captured, and the time had come to advance into the heart of Outremer, Philip of France had already left for home through jealousy of Richard, and that the bulk of his army had either sailed with him, or was on the point of doing so; that Richard, still determined to march on Jerusalem, was shackled to Acre by the childish intrigues of the barons of Outremer, who could not agree on the man who should occupy a throne that no longer existed, and might never do so until they dropped their stupid jealousies and became a united body of Christians against the Infidels.

Philip and Gilbert did not make any attempt to enter into all this for the first few days. Philip took three of Usamah's pearls, and after examining the shops of the merchants, selected a Venetian jeweller. The Venetian glanced at the black pearls, and then dropped his eyes quickly to conceal the sudden gleam of satisfaction on his swarthy face. He had done good business in the last month. Needy French knights, recklessly selling equipment and loot from Acre to pay for their passage home, had not quibbled at the knock-down prices he had offered. Here was another knight with an empty purse, he decided, as he took in the details of Philip's shabby clothes. He rolled the pearls over on his table with his plump fingers, pursed his thick, red lips with an air of disgust at being offered such inferior jewellery, and named a figure of about one eighth of the actual value.

He was unprepared for the storm that descended upon his long, greasy hair. Philip knew all the arts of haggling in Jerusalem and Damascus. And he knew, too, the value of the pearls.

At the end of an hour Philip walked away. He had sold the pearls for a sum that was only a fraction below their real worth, and he and Gilbert had enough money to last them for a long time. But they spent a considerable amount in the next two days, on new clothes, tents, bedding, helms, spare hauberks and shields, and above all, on horses. For there was no lack of any equipment for a knight in Acre then. The departing French were only too pleased to find a buyer. So Philip bought six magnificent horses, the true chargers of the West, and when he had finished, he and Gilbert were as well, if not better, equipped than when they rode out from Blanche Garde four years before.

It was a superbly dressed Philip who went to attend the next meeting of the High Court in the citadel of Acre. He was one of the last to arrive, for the streets were very full, and he was uncertain of the way.

An officious Syrian secretary bustled up and demanded his name and business as he strode towards the council chamber. He listened respectfully as Philip gave his name in his fluent Arabic, and the door was flung open.

Philip had had no intention of doing so, but he could not have timed his entry more dramatically or effectively if he planned it carefully beforehand. For the barons of the High Court were on the point of taking their places at the long table. The loud hum of conversation had died away, and in the silence they suddenly heard the announcement of: 'Sir Philip d'Aubigny, Lord of Blanche Garde and Montgizard'.

Philip paused in some inward embarrassment when he saw the faces turned towards him, and again, without any design on his part, gave the barons an opportunity for examining with curious interest his tall figure and impressive demeanour. He had learnt much from the Turks in the airs and graces of deportment.

Then a portly figure hurried towards him, hands outstretched in welcome. It was his godfather, Sir Balian d'Ibelin, a trifle fuller in the face and waist than he had been when Philip had last seen him, but still the same with his expansive smile and flashing, white teeth.

'My dear Philip! How delightful to see you again.' A podgy hand patted Philip with sincere pleasure, while a pair of very shrewd eyes ran over the young knight.

Sir Balian, that experienced and practised diplomat, approved of what he saw, for he nodded with satisfaction, and then stood back to allow the other barons to crowd around Philip. There were many there who had liked and respected Sir Hugo, and were pleased to welcome Philip for his own sake. Others were curious to see the young knight who had made such a great reputation for himself at Hattin. And there were some who regarded Philip as another important piece to be used on the chess board of the High Court, with its continuous struggle for power.

Philip responded to the greetings with the quiet dignity he could now assume so readily. He bowed politely to Conrad of Montferrat, a sleek cat of a man, olive of complexion, and long of face, with white, fluttering hands, and a silky voice that reminded Philip for a moment of the Old Man of the Mountains. Conrad made much of Philip. He needed every supporter he could win for his struggle with Guy of Lusignan for the throne of Jerusalem. Philip knew Conrad's motives. He had often heard Sir Hugo discuss the man, and now that he had met the count for himself, Philip could understand his father's scathing remarks.

It was a relief to shake hands with Guy of Lusignan, still the same charming and handsome figure, with his deep voice and the irresistible smile that had won Philip's affections at the Pool of Siloam.

But the man whom Philip had really wished to see was not at that meeting. For although the High Court made a practice of inviting distinguished visitors to attend their discussions, Richard of England was not present. He was, so Philip heard, recovering from a fever.

Philip took no active part in the discussion that morning. He listened, and was filled with a growing weariness and disgust. The barons were still arguing about the throne. Sir Hugo had once said that they had been arguing and plotting about the throne since it was first set up a hundred years before. Philip came to the conclusion that a hundred years hence the same thing would be happening.

He had a short conversation with Sir Balian after the Court closed.

'And whom will you support, Philip?' Sir Balian asked. 'Conrad or Guy?'

'Does it matter?' Philip said wearily. 'I want to ride for Jerusalem.'

'So do we all,' Sir Balian said blandly. He was possibly one of the most skilled intriguers in Outremer. 'But we have our feudal obligations, you know, my dear Philip.'

'Have we? I am under no feudal duty now to the King of Jerusalem, whoever he may be. No fiefs, no duty, is the law of Outremer.'

Sir Balian shrugged his ample spread of shoulder. 'None of us have any land now,' he said. 'At least, not many. But what have you in mind, Philip? You seem in no lack of money,' he added, glancing significantly at Philip's clothes and jewellery.

'I would like to meet King Richard.'

'O-ho!' Sir Balian fingered his beard, and eyed Philip with added interest. 'So that's how the land lies. Well, you might do worse. He's a fighter like yourself.'

'Do you know him, sir?'

'Yes. He's better now, I believe. Meet me at his quarters an hour before sunset. I'll present you.'

Richard of England was living in a small house near the south gates of Acre. The simplicity of the place impressed Philip. He would have expected the King of England to have taken over the most luxurious quarters in the city.

And he was impressed, too, by the sentries outside. They were well equipped, neatly turned out, and obviously under strict discipline. Good stuff, Philip decided, as he was shown into a hall, and asked to wait. Sir Balian, he was told by a secretary, had not yet arrived.

Philip strolled across the hall towards the windows that overlooked the crowded harbour. He was not alone. A group of knights were chattering close by, all Englishmen, Philip thought, judging by their dress, which was drab enough in comparison with his, or with any other nobleman of Outremer. Where their faces were burnt a brick-red by the sun, Philip's was a dark mahogany, and with his

Eastern clothes, he might have been taken for a Turk. So, apparently, thought the English knights, too.

'One of these Pullani,' Philip heard as he walked across the hall.

'Look at him,' remarked another man with disgust, making no attempt to lower his voice. 'Dressed like a peacock, and probably stinking of scent. The mere sight of an Infidel would give him a fit of hysterics.'

Philip looked out of the window, and smiled ruefully. There was no love lost between the natives of Outremer and new arrivals from the West. There never had been. And relations were more strained than ever. He could not blame the Westerners, he thought, remembering the discussions he had heard that morning in the High Court.

He heard the Englishmen moving across towards him. He hoped they would not be too offensive. His temper was well under control now, and he could probably pass off without an open quarrel anything but the most outrageous insults. If he wished to meet Richard, he might be well advised not to be presented as the man who had soundly thrashed a handful of his knights.

'And what do you want?' a voice demanded from behind him.

Philip turned slowly. A thickset English knight, hands on hips, was eyeing him with open contempt. A pleasant-looking fellow, Philip thought, with his cheerful face and air of simple cheerfulness. His light blue eyes were quite startlingly at variance with the brown of his cheeks and forehead.

'I am waiting for an audience with the King,' Philip said quietly.

'Well, he won't think much of you, I can tell you that,' the Englishman said bluntly. 'I'll say one thing for the King. He may be tactless, but he has no use for dressed-up dummies, and he doesn't mind saying so. You take my advice, and . . .'

He did not finish the sentence. A door was pushed open violently at the end of the hall, and a loud, imperious voice, thick with anger, was heard. The Englishmen swung round, forgetting Philip.

Two Genoese merchants were backing out through the door, scared and flurried, and raising their hands in pleading apology.

'You charge enough!' roared the voice. 'If that cargo is not unloaded by midday tomorrow, I'll come down and wring your fat necks with my own hands!'

'Yes, your grace,' the merchants cried, 'the cargo will be on the quays tonight.'

They backed away, and disappeared hurriedly as a tall man strode through the door. Philip stiffened. For here at last was the man he had come to see. He had never seen Richard before, but he could not mistake that reddish hair and beard, the three lions sprawling on the surcoat, and the tall, arrogant figure. Richard paced across the hall, reminding Philip of a panther he had once seen caged in Damascus.

There was the same impatient grace and suppressed energy, the urge to move and smash and rend.

'Can't anything be done quickly in the East?' Richard demanded, turning his head to a man who had emerged from the room behind him, whom Philip recognized as Sir Roger de Moulins. 'We've practically settled this ridiculous squabble about the throne of Jerusalem, but we're still sitting here at Acre, and unless someone makes a move, we shall be rotting in this pestilential hole in six months' time. I tell you, Grand Master, I am riding out of Acre next week if I have to go by myself!'

'You won't ride alone, your grace,' the Grand Master said quickly. 'The Knights of St John of the Hospital will be behind you. We have never turned our backs on the infidel yet.'

Richard shrugged his broad shoulders, and some of the fury left his face. 'I wish there were more like you in Outremer,' he said moodily. 'Those Syrian barons of the Kingdom! I'd like to batter their thick heads together until some sense was knocked into them!' He raised his long muscular arms, and shook his fists in the air.

Philip smiled. Here was someone after his own heart. The Grand Master's quick eyes had seen him, and the grey head bobbed a swift greeting.

'Well, your grace,' he said, 'here is one Syrian baron of the kingdom who believes in fighting. This is Sir Philip d'Aubigny of Blanche Garde. He has just escaped from the Infidels, as I expect you have heard.'

'D'Aubigny!' The King swung round. 'Yes, I have heard about him.'

He stared down from his superior height at Philip, examining him from head to foot. Philip returned the inspection. He was there to be looked at, and to stare in his turn.

Richard noticed the cool grey eyes that were watching him. He was not accustomed to such a frank inspection, and his blue eyes gleamed.

'Well, Sir Philip,' he said, 'what can I do for you?'

Philip did not hesitate. His mind was made up in a flash. 'I should like to take service under you, your grace,' he said.

'Under me!' Richard was surprised, and the Grand Master's sharp features twitched with interest.

'But you are a baron of the High Court of the Kingdom of Jerusalem, Sir Philip,' Richard said. 'You owe your allegiance and your feudal service to the King.'

'I have no lands, and therefore no feudal obligation by the law of Outremer,' Philip said. Then his mounting bitterness boiled over. 'And is there a Kingdom of Jerusalem, or a king?' he added.

Richard looked at him for a moment, and then threw back his red head in a roar of laughter that rose to a bellow. He did not believe in doing anything by halves, Philip was to discover.

'You've put the question that's been in my head for the past month,' he said. He cut the laughter short, and submitted Philip to another sharp and short inspection. He nodded.

'Yes, I shall be glad to see you ride behind me to the Holy City, Sir Philip,' he said. 'Because that's where I am going, and you're the sort of man I would like to have, if what they tell me is true. You speak Arabic, and write it?'

Philip nodded.

'And you know the Turks, and everything worth knowing about Outremer? Good! You're just what I want. I will attach you to my personal household, Sir Philip. Berkeley!'

The thickset knight who had insulted Philip hurried forward.

'Yes, your grace.'

'See to Sir Philip d'Aubigny here. I will speak with him in the morning. An hour after dawn, Sir Philip.'

He nodded, and turned on his heel. The heavy door of his room slammed behind him, and suddenly the hall seemed emptier, as if something vital and alive had left it.

The little group of knights were looking at Philip in a somewhat scared silence. Berkeley coughed, and shuffled his feet uneasily.

'I am William of Berkeley, Sir Philip,' he said apologetically. 'We did not realize who you were, and . . . er . . .'

The others crowded round. 'What does Saladin really look like, Sir Philip?' 'How did you escape from Damascus?' 'Did you really tell Saladin to his face that you would not change your faith, Sir Philip?'

Philip smiled. Gilbert would have recognized it as the grin of the young squire of Blanche Garde, and a relieved expression crossed Berkeley's worried face.

'About the other matter of the dressed-up dummy, Sir Philip,' he muttered. 'If you . . .'

'Oh, please, seigneurs,' Philip protested. 'If we are to ride to the Holy City together, we must be friends.'

'Well, I'm very glad to hear it,' Berkeley said with an engaging candour that was his most pleasant characteristic. 'They say you are the most dangerous jouster and swordsman in Outremer. And the standard here is somewhat higher than ours.'

Philip left an hour later. He felt he had made new friends. And above all, he had found a man he could follow. He hurried outside, returned the salute of the English archers, and waited for his horse to be brought. If Richard has enough of these archers, he thought, inspecting them with a professional eye, and comparing them with the unreliable infantry who had lost their nerve and the battle at Hattin, then we shall teach the Turks a lesson.

He put one foot in the stirrup. A loud cry came from the far side of the courtyard, and he heard the jingle of armour and the sound of rushing feet.

'My lord, my lord!'

Philip froze. For that shouting voice with its hoarse note was strangely familiar. It could not possibly . . . He swung round to see a man-at-arms fling himself at his feet. His hand was seized and covered with kisses.

'Llewellyn!' he gasped. He bent down, and pulled Llewellyn to his feet, staring into the brown face with the old crooked smile. Tears were rolling down his old servant's cheeks, and Philip felt the prickle of tears in his own eyes.

'I thought you were dead, Llewellyn,' he said, his own voice hoarse with emotion. 'I thought you were killed at Hattin.'

'Oh, not me, my lord. It would take more than an army of Infidels to finish me. And you, my lord? You have grown. Sir Hugo would be proud of you now, my lord.'

They smiled at each other, finding it difficult to speak.

'Who is your lord now, Llewellyn?' Philip asked at last.

Llewellyn's face split in a lop-sided grin of delight. 'Until a minute ago I was serving Sir William de Bohun. He's an English knight. But I'll serve you again now, my lord, if you'll make my peace with Sir William. He's been a good master.'

'I'll see him in the morning, Llewellyn,' Philip said. 'I met him just now.'

He gave Llewellyn directions for finding the house that he and Gilbert had rented, and rode away, pushing his way impatiently through the crowded streets, along the busy quays by the side of the blue water and the lines of ships, and nearly singing in his mood of excited gaiety.

Gilbert took one look at his face, and smiled, rubbing his long nose with deep satisfaction. This was more like the Philip he had known, he thought, and he listened to Philip's hurried report of what had happened.

'I'm going to change, and then we'll have dinner,' he went on, leading the way into his bedroom. 'We'll try that wine we bought ...'

He broke off, and stiffened. Gilbert turned, and saw Philip staring at the low bed.

'What is it, Philip?'

Philip did not answer. He bent down and picked up a small, round cake. The design of a dagger was scratched across the brown crust. In silence he handed it to Gilbert, whose face had gone white.

'The Assassins!' he whispered.

Philip nodded. There were two other articles on the bed, a long knife, and a roll of parchment. Philip broke the red seal, and read the single line written on the paper.

'*Conrad of Montferrat must be killed. See to it.*'

For a long minute Gilbert and Philip stared at the sprawling Arabic script. Then Philip tore the thick parchment across, and hurled the fragments on to the floor.

'But why Conrad?' Gilbert asked.

'I can guess. He's opposed to Richard's plans. And the Old Man of the Mountains must be anxious to see us defeat Saladin. With Conrad out of the way, Guy of Lusignan will have the throne of Jerusalem, and Richard can march for the Holy City.'

'I suppose so,' Gilbert said. 'What are you going to do, Philip? Warn Conrad?'

Philip laughed harshly. 'Do you think for one moment that he would believe me? And if he did, would he trust me? You can be certain of one thing, Gilbert. If I don't murder Conrad, the Assassins will do it. And if I am suspected in any way . . .' He broke off.

'You mustn't breathe a word to a soul about this,' Philip said urgently. 'Llewellyn and that new Saxon servant of yours—what's his name, Gurth—must be warned that robbers are after us. They can be trusted to keep a close watch on our quarters. And don't move a step in future without a knife within easy reach.'

Chapter Fourteen

PETER DE CHAWORTH

THE sea was an intense blue on the right flank of the Crusaders. The ships of the Venetians and Genoese, who were carrying the vital supplies for the army, dipped and bobbed in the slight swell.

On the left was the plain of Sharon with the hills of Samaria in the background, a green and well watered countryside, but covered now by the great clouds of dust thrown up by the columns of the Christians as they plodded steadily down the old Roman road to the south of Outremer.

Philip was happy. He was busy though, as a member of

Richard's household, an essential link between the King and the other sections of the mixed army, a man who was on good terms with the Syrian barons and the two Military Orders, which, with the English, made up the bulk of the force.

This march was no haphazard affair, as the advance to Hattin had been. Richard insisted on watching every detail. The men marched ten miles each day, moving in the cool of the evening; they rested on alternate days, when ample supplies were landed from the accompanying ships. There had been little fighting so far. The Turks moved parallel with the Christians, keeping to the shelter of the hills and forests. They had made isolated attacks, but the only other sign of their existence were the tell-tale dust clouds that drifted over the trees throughout the day.

The long march from Acre was nearly ended. Another day would bring the Crusaders to Jaffa. With that port in their hands, they could turn inland, and strike boldly for Jerusalem.

Philip shared a tent with Gilbert. They were lounging in the evening sun after the day's march, enjoying the cool breeze from the sea.

'I'd better go,' Philip said, and stood up. He was due to attend the daily conference held in the King's tent, when the plans for the following day were made.

'Warn Llewellyn and Gurth as usual,' Philip said. 'Who's on guard first tonight?'

'Llewellyn.'

Philip nodded. Since the incident of the Assassin's cake in Acre, they had always seen to it that one man was awake and on guard outside their tent. Gilbert's new man, Gurth, was a stolid lump of a fellow, fair-haired and blue-eyed, and almost inarticulate. But he was immensely strong, and when his slow temper was roused, he was a dangerous and formidable fighter.

Outside the King's tent there was the usual knot of men chatting. They greeted Philip, and he was about to go inside the tent, when a young squire touched his arm.

'Sir Philip d'Aubigny?' he asked, stammering slightly.

'Yes.' Philip had never seen the boy before. He was short and slightly built, not much more than nineteen, Philip thought, with a snub-nose and a freckled face.

'I am Peter de Chaworth, sir,' the squire said.

'Oh, yes,' Philip remarked, wondering what the boy wanted.

'I am from the Marches, sir,' de Chaworth said, as if he expected Philip to know all about the Marches. 'The Welsh Marches, sir. My father's castle of Kidwelly is quite close to Llanstephan.'

'Llanstephan!' Philip was suddenly interested.

'Yes, sir. You are a d'Aubigny of Llanstephan?'

'My grandfather came from there many years ago,' Philip said. 'But I was born in Outremer.'

'Oh, I know that, sir,' de Chaworth said quickly. 'But I have just had letters from Wales. My father tells me that Robert d'Aubigny is dead.'

'He must be a cousin of mine,' Philip said.

'That is what I thought, sir,' young Peter stammered excitedly. 'He is the last of the family. There is no heir to the fief, my father says.'

'What!' Philip gripped Peter's arm, and then apologized quickly as the squire winced. 'I'm sorry, Peter. But your news startled me. I must go to the conference now. Come to my tent afterwards.'

The King's tent was full. The two Grand Masters were there, Guy of Lusignan, recognized now as the King of Jerusalem, the leaders of the other sections of the army, and several of the senior English and Norman barons.

They waited for Richard to open the discussion. For the Crusaders had made their one gesture of common sense, and had elected the King as the commander-in-chief.

'Now, I want information,' Richard said briskly. 'Jaffa is ten miles ahead. What is the country like between here and the port?'

'I can tell you, your grace,' the Grand Master of the Templars said promptly. 'The road hugs the coast, and then crosses a river. There is a good ford, and we can cross easily. For the first part of the march our left flank will be covered by a marsh. But after that comes the danger.'

As he went on to describe the lie of the ground, Richard scratched out a rough plan. Once clear of the marsh, the Crusaders would march with the great forest of Arsuf on their left, and a narrow strip of plain between them and the sea on the right.

The Turks were obviously still following, and would almost certainly attack soon, if they were to stop the steady Christian advance. The forest of Arsuf was an ideal spot from which to attack.

Richard considered his map, his long, muscular fingers tugging at his red beard. The others waited in silence. They had learnt to trust his military judgement.

'We will march at dawn,' the King said. 'The column must be so arranged that we can change without delay from an order of march into an order of battle. The baggage train will be nearest the sea, and the mounted men next. The archers and footmen will move on the extreme left flank.'

The men in the tent nodded. There could be no argument about such sensible dispositions.

'The two vital points are the van and the rear,' Richard said, looking significantly at the Grand Masters. By the tradition of Outremer, the Military Orders covered those two sections in battle. The order of march was soon arranged; the Templars with the van were told to march steadily for the little town of Arsuf, and not to halt unless the situation in their rear was hopeless. Behind them would ride the remnants of the French force, then the Syrian barons, the English and Normans who made up the solid core of the army, and finally the Hospitallers.

'Any suggestions?' Richard asked.

Guy of Lusignan leant forward. 'We must not charge until the Turks are fully committed to the attack,' he said.

All nodded. This was the invariable advice of all who had experience of fighting against the Infidel.

'We shall not charge at all, I hope,' Richard said. 'First reach Jaffa, and then we can consider a pitched battle.'

'But surely we must charge, my lord, if the opportunity arises,' Roger de Moulins said anxiously.

Philip smiled. Trust the Hospitallers to yearn for a wild rush at the Infidels.

'Not until I give the order, Grand Master,' Richard said firmly. 'When you hear six trumpets blown together, then you may charge. But not before. That is vital, Sir Roger.'

The conference ended soon afterwards. As each man left the tent, Richard watched their faces intently, his elbows on the table, his bearded chin cupped in his enormous hands. Philip could guess what the King was looking for. He had learnt a great deal about the art of leadership from Richard. The King was looking for confidence. But there was no doubt about that. Probably no Christian army had faced the Turk with such high morale, or so well equipped and led.

Now only the English and Norman barons were left. Richard glanced at them, and laughed. 'The trumpets won't sound at all, if I can help it,' he said.

'I think you may have to, my lord,' Philip said in his capacity as the expert adviser on the characters of the leaders of Outremer. 'I know the forest of Arsuf. I've often hunted there. It's an ideal spot for Saladin to attack. And if he does, then the Hospitallers will charge.'

Richard looked round the table. 'Well, we must hold them back,' he said. 'I will ride up and down the column. You will attend me, and I shall use you as messengers.'

He pushed away the map, and a servant brought wine. 'You're looking very happy tonight, Philip,' he said. He had taken one of his swift likings to Philip. 'What is it? The chance of revenge for Hattin?'

Philip smiled. 'Partly, my lord,' he said. He told the King what Peter de Chaworth had said.

'But why are you so interested, Philip? You don't want to go to England, do you? Your home is in Outremer.'

'Not after we have taken Jerusalem, my lord,' Philip said firmly.

'Oh, so you plan to return with us? I must see what I can do.'

Richard did not believe in wasting time. He sent for a clerk, and promptly dictated a letter to England. Philip's claim to Llanstephan was to be investigated.

'And if you don't have that,' he added with a burst of his usual generosity, 'I shall see to another fief for you, Philip.'

Philip flushed. He had not expected this. 'How can I thank you, my lord?' he stammered.

'By killing a lot of Turks tomorrow. Or better still, by holding back Roger de Moulins. He likes you, and may listen to you.'

Gilbert was chatting to Peter de Chaworth when Philip reached his tent. They lay in the short grass in the evening sun and talked until it was dark.

Philip did not sleep well. And there were others in the camp who were sleepless, to judge by the roaring songs from the tents beyond. Perhaps these men felt that this might be their last night.

Gilbert was sleeping, breathing evenly. Philip envied him. He was thinking of that still, hot night before Hattin when he had talked with his father. Sir Hugo, he thought, would have approved of Richard. Well, things would be different this time. Philip turned on the hard mattress. Some insect rustled close by. A rat perhaps, Philip thought with distaste, and turned back again on his side.

A dark form leapt at him. A heavy weight pressed him down on the bed, and something thudded into the mattress. Philip writhed under the man lying across his chest. A hot breath panted in his face. In the gloom he saw an arm go back, holding a curved knife.

Philip heaved himself upwards, and struck out blindly with his clenched fist. He felt his knuckles smash against bone, and the murderer half sprawled sideways under that unexpected thrust of Philip's body.

Philip reached out frantically. The knife came down, and flashed past his cheek to bury itself once more in the mattress. Philip's clutching hands slithered over bare, greased skin.

'Llewellyn!' he bellowed. 'To me, to me!'

The flap of the tent was torn aside, and Llewellyn blundered in. Gilbert was awake now, calling out in alarm.

Philip was on his knees, grappling with his unseen murderer. The other two could do little to help or hinder the two figures threshing about on the floor.

'Got you!' Philip grunted, as his hand closed over the man's wrist.

A knee caught him in the stomach, and he fell back, gasping. A dark shape leapt for the open flap of the tent. Philip flung himself forward.

'Stop him, Llewellyn!' he yelled. 'Don't let him get away!'

Llewellyn jumped forward. With a crash he collided with Philip, and they burst through the flap, sprawling on the ground outside. The Assassin was dodging swiftly to the left. In a second he would vanish in the darkness.

An immense shape loomed in front of him. The Assassin swerved, and Philip heard Gurth grunt. With a crunch, Gurth brought the iron bar in his hand down, and the Assassin collapsed and lay still.

'Bring him in here,' Philip said. 'Llewellyn, a torch.'

Wiping the cold perspiration from his forehead, Philip bent over the limp figure, while Llewellyn held a spluttering torch above his head.

'Dead, my lord,' Llewellyn said. 'Thanks to Gurth.'

Philip nodded, and shivered as he picked up the murderous knife which had dropped from the Assassin's hand. It had been a close call. If he had been asleep . . .

'A camp thief, my lord,' Llewellyn said. 'There are plenty of them about.'

Philip caught Gilbert's anxious glance, and shook his head. This was no ordinary camp looter.

'Listen, Llewellyn,' he said. 'No one must know about this. You and Gurth must bury this fellow under your tent.'

'Bury him under . . .' Llewellyn gasped, and looked at his master in astonishment. He turned to the dead man, and then his eyes widened. He had spent a lifetime in Outremer; nobody could do that, and not learn about the Assassins.

'Yes, my lord,' Llewellyn said. 'And I'll see that Gurth keeps his mouth shut. Too much noise outside for anyone to have heard.'

Philip slept after that. Gurth squatted inside the tent, and took it in turns with Llewellyn to keep watch. In the morning, Llewellyn reported that the Assassin's body had been disposed of, and that no one had remarked on the disturbance inside Philip's tent.

'They'll try again, my lord,' he said quietly.

'I know. You and Gurth must never leave my tent unguarded after this.'

Llewellyn nodded. He knew better than to ask questions, and went away to bring up the horses. An hour later the Christian army marched out of the camp, and took the long, straight road for Jaffa.

Chapter Fifteen

THE BATTLE OF ARSUF

THE Turks did not show their hand for over two hours. By that time the Templars in the van were within sight of the little town of Arsuf with its shattered keep. The Christians marched steadily alongside the blue sea, their heads turned to the left, watching in grim silence the ominous clouds of dust over the trees. They could hear the din of a great army advancing towards the plain. It would not be long before the storm broke, Philip thought. He could feel the old sensation of cramp in his stomach, and he was shifting restlessly in his saddle, his steel-mittened hands clenching and unclenching on the butt of his spear.

But he felt confident. The cross-bowmen would turn the scale, he thought, even though he had never seen them in action yet. But he knew that the range of their weapons was greater than that of the short Turkish bow. For once, perhaps, the favourite tactics of the Infidel, their charge of mounted bowmen, would be countered.

The clamour from the green slopes of the forest grew louder and more menacing. Philip heard the familiar clang of the cymbals and the deeper roll of many drums. Here they were, he muttered to himself, and grinned at Gilbert, who was leaning forward in his saddle, his long legs dangling down on either side, his serious face watching the forest, and one hand rubbing his nose in his usual gesture.

A mass of mounted Turks suddenly burst out into the open, and a growl of loud-spoken comment ran down the long columns of the Crusaders. Knights bent down and began to fit their ponderous helms over their shoulders; the files closed up, and the pace of the march began to quicken automatically.

Richard rode through a gap in the infantry, and out into the open where his army could see him clearly. He watched the Infidel advance coolly, and gestured to his household knights to come forward.

'Who are they, Philip?' he asked, pointing to the first waves of the enemy.

'Those Negroes are Soudanese archers, my lord. And I think they are Bedouins behind.'

'And Saladin's best troops?'

'Oh, they're still in reserve. Those will be the Mamelukes of Egypt and the troops of the Emirs of Syria and Mesopotamia. Once they come on to the plain, Saladin will be fully committed.'

The King nodded, and turned back to watch. The bulk of the first advance was directed towards the Christian rearguard. Saladin's tactics were clear enough. If he could crumple up the Hospitallers, then the whole pace of the march would falter, and eventually come to a standstill. Possibly gaps would open up, and then the Turks could make a general charge, split the Crusaders into groups, and throw them back to the sea in a final attack that would smash them into helpless and panic-stricken fugitives.

From the rear the din grew in volume. The Hospitallers were already at grips with their old enemies. Then the cymbals clashed, the drums thudded, and to the accompaniment of shrill yells, a dense wave of mounted archers swept down on the centre of the Christian army.

This was the first test. Philip watched tensely. The English and Norman infantry had never yet faced a Turkish charge in the open field. If they faltered now the battle was lost. Richard's careful plan would be ruined, and his army annihilated.

The English cross-bowmen watched their enemy

advance with a stolid curiosity that heartened Philip. He was accustomed to the temperamental and unreliable Syrian footmen of Outremer. He could see the precisely dressed lines of the English, and hear the shouted orders that sent hundreds of backs down to wind the thick cords, the trained fingers that fitted the heavy bolts into place, and then the simultaneous raising of the bows to the shoulder.

But would they have the nerve to wait, or would they blaze away while the Turks were still out of range? That was the true test of disciplined infantry.

Philip groaned. 'Too soon!' he muttered.

But he had underestimated the range of the cross-bow. The stumpy bolts whirred through the air, flatter in their flight than the arrow. The leading files of Turkish horses went down with a crash. Those behind piled into the chaos of kicking and screaming men and beasts. The English sergeants shouted out their crisp orders, and another volley flew into the centre of the shrieking mob.

Philip laughed and cheered. The Turks were being pounded at a range that left them helpless. They turned and fled, leaving behind a grim litter to show the effectiveness of the cross-bow.

The Christians had won the first round. All down the column, hands and lances were waved exultantly and men cheered loudly.

Philip could see nothing of the struggle in the rear now. Thick dust clouds blotted out the picture, but to judge by the din, there must be a desperate fight going on there, he thought, and he wondered how the Hospitallers were feeling.

Richard's thoughts were the same. He beckoned to Philip.

'Ride back, Philip,' he said. 'Roger de Moulins knows you, and may listen. Tell him the day is ours if he will continue the advance.'

Philip turned his horse, trotted through a gap in the infantry, and rode down the column, past the big wagon on which fluttered the standard of England, and past the long lines of mounted men, every head turned to the left, and watching the enemy as they deployed in increasing numbers on to the plain.

Then Philip was enveloped in the swirling dust of the battle. Occasional arrows flickered overhead, or bounced drunkenly on the hard ground. He stopped, and pulled on his helm, and the clamour seemed to grow fainter and more distant.

He could see the huge black standard of the Hospitallers, and he pushed his way through the files towards the familiar white cross on the dark background. Sir Roger de Moulins was there, a slight, dapper figure in hauberk and cloak, peering through the dust at the struggle in front.

As Philip rode alongside, he turned and saw the black hawk on the white surcoat and shield. He grasped Philip by the arm.

'We must charge!' he shouted through his helm, his

voice high pitched and muffled. 'The King must sound the trumpets. We have the Infidel at our mercy!'

He turned away to shriek fresh orders to his men, and Philip took in the situation. It was a confused picture at first, swiftly moving figures appearing and then vanishing in the dust, rearing horses, and straining knights, with a deafening row that made it difficult to think.

But Philip was more accustomed now to the sight of a battle. He could pick out the cross-bowmen on foot, marching forward while they reloaded, then wheeling swiftly to fire on the thick mass of Turkish cavalry who had pressed their way towards close-range.

The cross-bows were inflicting heavy casualties. But rapid and accurate as was their fire, they could not completely prevent the Infidels from coming on. Many horses had been shot down; Hospitaller knights were trudging along on foot, their long lances at the trail, while others had snatched up cross-bows from dead archers, and were firing back at the enemy.

Fresh from the comparative calm of the centre, Philip could visualize the battle as a whole. But to the Grand Master of the Hospitallers, the scene was confined to the grim struggle in front of his eyes. Could he make the hot-tempered little man realize the whole picture, Philip wondered. He must try, but it was difficult to do so in shouts and bellows through the thickness of two helms and above the thunder of the battle.

'The van and centre are clear, sir!' he shouted. 'The King

prays you to march on. Saladin will have committed all his army to the plain within an hour.'

'An hour!' the Grand Master shrieked. 'We shall not have a horse left to charge with by that time! Still, I will obey the King. We will do what we can.'

Philip rode back. The pace of the advance had slowed. That was to be expected with the pressure on the rearguard. The Turks were still deploying on to the plain, but the centre of the Christian line had still not made any contact with the enemy.

Philip stopped by the English knights, and spoke to young de Chaworth.

'Put on your helm, Peter!' he said sharply.

'But I shall be suffocated.'

'Better that than a Turkish arrow through your throat,' Philip said, a swift vision of Sir Fulk reeling in his saddle passing through his mind.

Richard was still riding up and down outside the infantry, and the sight of his tall figure, calm, and immensely inspiring, gave all his men a feeling of supreme confidence. They needed it, too, for the bulk of the Turkish army was deployed on the plain now, a menacing and fearsome sight as they surged slowly forwards under the continual pressure from behind.

The attacks on the Christian centre were increasing, and clouds of mounted archers were galloping up, firing, and wheeling away. But their casualties were high, for the cross-bowmen had their range now.

Philip noticed that the Infidels were finding it increasingly difficult to retire, for the plain was narrow, and the continual deployment of more troops from the hills and forest made it impossible for the archers to carry out their usual manoeuvres. He remembered the charges that Balian d'Ibelin had made on the march to Hattin. They had kept the column on the move.

Richard listened to his suggestion, and nodded. 'I had the same idea, Philip,' he said. 'Bring up the knights of the household. Warn them that they must not charge too far. Watch me.'

Gilbert and Llewellyn closed in on either side of Philip in the narrow wedge formation they had found so valuable. The other household knights fell in behind Richard, and he waited coolly for his opportunity.

Philip seated himself tightly in his saddle, and rammed his knees into his horse's sides. This was the first time he had ridden the beast in a battle, but he was not worrying about that. The horse was a superb one, well trained by its former French owner, and, thanks to Llewellyn's care and Philip's riding, in magnificent condition.

Richard raised his lance in the air, and spurred forward, a bulky mass of hauberk and helm and shield. Philip had often heard stories of the King's furious fighting skill and determination. He saw something of it in that brief flash of vision as Richard thundered down on the nearest Turkish archers and cavalry.

Then Philip was choosing his own target, the wind

whistling through the eye-slits of his helm as he peered over the rim of his shield, and saw the tiny pennon fluttering far ahead, as it seemed, on the tip of his lance. He felt the powerful muscles of his horse beneath him, galloping with a beautiful smoothness of rhythm.

The Infidels seemed to leap towards him. He felt the shuddering jar as his lance went home, and saw a turbaned figure fly from the saddle. His horse hit the Arab pony in the flank, and ploughed on through the dense pack of Turks, mad with the thrill of the charge.

Philip had kept a tight grip on his emotions. He knew how the wild excitement of a battle and a charge could transform him into a raging fury. This must not happen yet. It would come later. He pulled hard on the reins and swept round in a circle, knocked another Turk from the saddle, and obediently Gilbert and Llewellyn followed him round, cutting a narrow passage through the Turks.

Then they were back in front of the cross-bowmen once more, and the patient lines of Christian knights were waving their lances, and riding steadily forward towards Arsuf.

That was the pattern of the battle for the next hour. Richard made his limited charges with his household, and farther down the column the same tactics were repeated. They kept the Infidels from pressing too hard on the Crusader infantry, but the pace of the march was slowing down. Frantic appeals to be allowed to charge out came up from

Roger de Moulins. Each time Richard sent back an emphatic 'No'.

But the crisis of the battle was approaching, the brief moment when the fighting would rise to the highest pitch, and the issue would be decided one way or the other. Richard, experienced soldier that he was, felt it instinctively. He was watching the struggle at the rear now, or what little could be seen through the dust.

Saladin had brought his entire army into the open at last. He was still concentrating his main attack on the Hospitallers, confident after his years of victories over the Christians.

The Grand Master of the Hospitallers sent his usual frantic appeal for the trumpets to sound the charge. Once again Richard sent back his refusal. He could guess what the position was like back there, but he kept grimly to his plan. The game was in his hands now, and he would not throw it away unless he was forced to do so.

And then the climax came. The Hospitallers could wait no longer. Their Grand Master pushed his way to the front ranks, his banner behind him. With a deep roar of 'St George! St George!' the great Military Order swept forward, the Grand Master in the lead.

Philip heard the roar. For a few seconds he saw the banner rush forward, and caught a glimpse of the Hospitallers as they crashed into the tightly packed ranks of the Infidels, the big Western horses rearing above the smaller Arab ponies.

Then the dust cloud closed over the wild picture, and only the deep roar of the fight and the bellows of 'St George!' could be heard. The Hospitallers had charged.

The roar of that charge, the drumming of hooves, and the surge forward was seen and heard by the whole army. The infection spread, just as a great breaker on the shore turns slowly over all along the length of its crest, until the seething torrent of water is thundering up the beach in a welter of spray and overwhelming force.

Richard saw the charge, and the gradual breaking of his column. He could not stop it now, and he knew that his perfect plan was ruined. But he knew, too, that few generals can hope to fight the perfect battle, and that those who can achieve the greater part of their design will win the fight.

So he did not hesitate. He waved his lance in the air. On the wagon, beneath the banner with the leopards of England, the trumpeters saw the signal for which they had been waiting. They raised their trumpets in the air.

High above the turmoil of the battle sounded the sweet, clear calls. The last notes were drowned in a tremendous roar of cheering; the deep, confident shouts of men who knew that the battle was theirs. 'Save us, Holy Sepulchre, help us, Holy Sepulchre!' they cried, and forced their way past the patient infantry.

The long, thin lances came down to the charge with a ripple of tiny pennons. Blank faces of steel crouched down behind the shelter of shields, and with a rumble of drumming hooves the chivalry of Christendom rode out against the Turk.

Philip had only the vaguest recollection of the last stages of Arsuf. For, as he had done at Hattin, he abandoned himself to the exultant fury of the charge. The battle was won now, he knew. There was no need for caution. He could charge home, and burst his way through; the farther and deeper the better. He had many scores to settle.

The first shock of the Christian charge swept the leading Infidels from the field. The pressure was still weak opposite the Crusader van and centre, and then the Christians swung to the left, and rolled the Turks into a tightly packed mass opposite the Hospitallers.

There Saladin rallied his best troops, the mailed Mamelukes from Egypt, and for a few desperate moments he staved off the destruction that threatened his army, as he had done at Hattin. But he was not faced by men exhausted by heat and driven frantic by thirst this time. He had been out-manoeuvred and out-generalled, and an overwhelming attack of fresh and confident knights, on huge Western horses, and more heavily armoured than his men, was being hurled at him from all sides.

Philip saw the orderly lines of the Mamelukes, the men who had won Hattin, killed his father, and Sir Fulk, and Joscelin, sent him to captivity for four bitter years, and destroyed his heritage of Blanche Garde. His lance was broken. He threw away the splintered and useless stump,

and pulled out his sword. To his left, Richard of England had flung himself upon the Turks, and Philip rushed in to his right.

He was surrounded once more by the dark, snarling faces, white turbans and steel helmets, the gaping, red nostrils of frightened horses. In a frenzy of hatred and fury he cut, stabbed, and hacked until he had cleared a space, as Richard was doing on his left.

Into those two narrow gaps the leading English and Norman knights hurled their weight and speed, and behind the two raging figures that led them, they split the Mamelukes into small, struggling groups, cut their way through, then turned and annihilated Saladin's picked men.

Philip suddenly realized that it was all over. Through his eye-slits he saw a distant mob of panic-stricken horsemen racing for the shelter of the forest. He drooped wearily in his saddle, his body glowing with heat, his face dripping with perspiration. His breath came in harsh sobs of exhaustion as he felt the weight of his shoulder straps dragged down by the shield. Even the sword seemed a dead weight in his hand, and his fingers on the hilt were trembling with fatigue.

Slowly he sheathed the long blade and tugged at his helm. He could see the blue sea, and the ships beating in towards the beach. The plain was littered with the debris of the battle, the piles of horses and men, the spent arrows, the swords dropped in flight, the shields and dust-covered evidence of what had happened in those last furious minutes.

Gilbert was smiling at him, and there was Llewellyn with his lop-sided grin, and a smear of blood trickling down his face. Philip laughed. From the depths of the forest he could hear the wild pursuit as the Turks rode away in terror to report the greatest defeat that Islam had suffered since the far-off days of Dorylaeum.

PART THREE

Chapter Sixteen

THE JOUST AT CARDIFF CASTLE

PETER DE CHAWORTH grunted as a sudden shower of rain raced across the heath. He huddled under the shelter of his cloak. 'Do you still like the English climate, Philip?' he asked.

Gilbert d'Assailly chuckled. 'Oh, you must wait, Peter,' he said quickly before Philip could answer. 'He hasn't seen an English winter yet.'

Philip shook his head and grinned. He was watching the grey curtain of rain drift across the heather.

'I'm longing for the winter,' he said, and grinned again as a chorus of protests went up from the others. 'And I love the English summer. Look, it's clearing already.'

He sniffed delightedly at the warm, moist scent of the

earth as the sun broke through the clouds. A million tiny rain drops sparkled on the leaves and bushes.

'Is England always as green as this?' he asked.

'Not in the winter, Philip,' William de Berkeley said. 'You'll be glad enough then to huddle in front of a smoky fire.'

Philip laughed and shook his head once more. The others watched him with amusement and some surprise. For this was a new Philip to them, a very different person to the serious and often grim knight of Outremer, who had not spoken much, and whose one object in life seemed to be the killing of Infidels.

But Gilbert rubbed his nose with vigorous satisfaction. This was the young squire of Blanche Garde, he thought, the pleasant and happy person with whom he had ridden and hawked on the hills above Ascalon. A great improvement, he decided, on the man who had watched unmoved the wretched slave of the Old Man fling himself over the battlements at Masyaf.

They were outside London now, heading for the west, where Philip was to see the fief that King Richard had granted him. After that they were to stay with William at Berkeley, and then ride across the Severn into the Welsh Marches.

For Philip had left Outremer. He did not think he would ever return again to that burning sun, to the tawny landscape with the savage hills and rocky ravines. There would be little there for him if he did. Arsuf had been a crushing victory, but even that had not opened the road to Jerusalem.

Richard's army had dwindled, the Crusaders had squabbled again, and at the end of a year's indecisive fighting, a truce had been arranged between Turk and Christian.

Richard had made himself famous during that year. Some of the stories were probably exaggerated, for legends will always grow up around the name of a famous man. But he had done astonishing things on the battlefield, such as the last fight at Acre, when he had held off the entire Turkish army with only a handful of knights to help him.

Philip had been one of those knights. He was recognized now as one of the greatest of the Christian knights, a man whose name was mentioned with respect wherever people talked about the Crusade and the Holy Land. His knowledge of Arabic and the Turk had made him useful to Richard during the truce talks. Philip had met Saladin again, and that great man, as generous and chivalrous as Richard, had loaded him with gifts. The horse Philip was riding now across an English heath was a present from the Emir. The truce was the best that Richard could do for the Christians. The Turks still held Jerusalem, but Christian pilgrims were to be allowed to visit the city. The barons of Outremer remained in possession of the chief ports, and the Military Orders clung to their great castles farther inland.

Richard had hurried home, impatient to reach England, and in his haste had chosen the overland route through Germany. And there his enemies had caught him, and thrown him into prison. They were demanding an enormous ransom now for his release.

Philip had visited Blanche Garde during the truce. The castle had been dismantled by the Turks, and the old fortress was a ruin. But underneath the piled stones Philip had unearthed Sir Hugo's chest, and the contents of this, added to the pearls of old Usamah, had made him a very wealthy man. He had sailed to France, ridden leisurely northwards to Normandy, where Gilbert had seen Assailly once more, and then they had crossed the Channel to England.

They reached Norham, Philip's new fief, after three days. It was a rich and pleasant fief, with a comfortable manor-house that, Philip decided, could be made luxurious with the wagon-loads of furniture that he had brought with him from the East. But the portly and lazy steward had allowed everything to lapse into chaos, and for a week Philip inspected everything, and flayed his new servants with his tongue. He would be back in six months' time, he told them, and he left them in no doubt of what would happen if there was not a great improvement by that time.

Gilbert watched and listened with quiet amusement. This was all very like Sir Hugo, he thought.

At Berkeley they spent two weeks, for William would not allow them to go on until he had shown them around his fief, entertained them to many feasts with his neighbours, and hunted over the best parts of the countryside. He was anxious, too, to rebuild his castle on the lines of the powerful fortresses of Outremer, and to make the building more comfortable.

'And well he might,' Philip said on their first night at

Berkeley. He was standing in the room which he was to share with Gilbert. 'Why, the servants at Blanche Garde had better quarters than this!'

Gilbert said nothing. But he smiled as he saw Philip inspect the bare and comfortless room. It was circular in shape, following the design of the corner tower in which it was built. The stone floor was bare except for a few rushes, and they, as Philip's twitching nose told him, had been there for some time. The walls were of rough stone, dripping with damp. A gloomy light filtered in through the three slit-windows, and the low ceiling only added to the general air of depression. Smoke billowed out from the wide fireplace, and Philip coughed as the acrid fumes caught his throat. Perhaps the English climate had its drawbacks after all. He looked round for somewhere to hang his cloak. Some wooden pegs were driven into the crevices between the stones by the door. The furniture was limited to two stools, a couple of rickety truckle-beds, and a chest.

Llewellyn came in that moment with hot water. He glanced around, and sniffed.

'Not quite what we are used to, my lord,' he said. He caught an angry gleam in Philip's eyes, and backed out hastily.

They left William with regret, though, for Philip had grown to like him. But as he would be travelling fairly frequently between his two fiefs of Llanstephan and Norham, he would be able to visit Berkeley each year.

The season gradually changed around them as they

made their leisurely way across England. Autumn came slowly to the lovely, empty countryside, changing the colours and hues of the wide forests and broad heaths. Philip found some new beauty to admire at every mile, as they followed the old Roman road that ran with such mathematical straightness towards the west.

On several occasions they spent the night at monasteries. The monks greeted them with lavish hospitality as Crusaders home from the Holy Land, and when they discovered Philip's identity, and the fact that he was a scholar who could read Arabic, they brought out all the treasures of their libraries for him to see.

They crossed the Severn at Gloucester, and stayed at the abbey there. Philip was taken into the great Norman nave of the abbey church, and knelt reverently by the side of Duke Robert of Normandy's tomb, one of the leaders of the First Crusade, the man who had knighted his grandfather, and who had fought his way into the Holy City by the side of Godfrey of Lorraine.

As they rode through the Marches, Peter de Chaworth told Philip something of their history, and of the conditions farther west. Llanstephan would be no peaceful fief, Philip learnt. The Welsh bitterly resented the intrusion of the Normans, and there were frequent risings. Peter's home, Kidwelly, had been captured quite recently, and Llanstephan lay even farther to the west. Philip did not think he would mind that. There would be plenty for him to do. The castle would have to be rebuilt, of course, for it had not taken him long to realize that England was a hundred years behind Outremer in the art of castle building.

Two days after leaving Gloucester, they clattered over the wooden bridge of Newport. The grey walls of the castle rose from the muddy river banks on the farther side, and in the courtyard they were greeted respectfully by the steward. They could, of course, stay there for the night, he said, but his master was away at the joust at Cardiff.

Peter de Chaworth was immensely excited at the news. 'We must go, Philip!' he exclaimed. 'It's the biggest joust in the Marches. And my father is sure to be there. He'll fall off his horse when he sees me ride into the courtyard with you!'

Philip turned to the steward. The joust, he learnt, was to start on the next afternoon, and Cardiff was about ten miles from Newport.

'We'll ride there first thing in the morning,' he said.

Peter's freckled face flushed with delight. He was a knight now, but in heart he was still the excitable young squire who had spoken to Philip outside Richard's tent. Philip used to watch him, and feel very old.

'You and Gilbert can enter for the open event,' Peter said. 'You'll knock them all over the place, Philip! And I can go in for the young knight's joust. I wasn't old enough the last time I was there. Oh, I'll show them now!'

Philip grinned, and gave Llewellyn orders for the next morning.

They rode fully armed for Cardiff, and Philip inspected his men before they left Newport. In addition to Llewellyn and Gurth, and some servants whom he had taken on in London, he had brought a dozen mounted men-at-arms with him from Outremer, all of them experienced soldiers of mixed Saxon and Norman blood, and first-class cross-bow-men into the bargain. They had been glad enough to follow so famous a baron, and one who paid so well. And Philip had fitted them out without much regard to expense.

Llewellyn had seen that the turn-out was immaculate, but he would have been disappointed if Philip had not inspected his work. So Philip went slowly down the line, with Llewellyn stalking behind him.

Philip knew what to expect; well groomed horses and carefully polished leatherwork; helmets and hauberks burnished like silver, and freshly laundered white surcoats bearing the device of the black hawk. But he was more interested in the men themselves; they looked as he had hoped they would, veteran soldiers, sturdy and reliable, obviously fit and cheerful, carrying themselves with an easy confidence.

'I expect there'll be a big crowd at Cardiff,' Philip said to Gilbert as they rode out of Newport. 'So we must make a good impression.'

'Oh, I think you'll do that,' Gilbert remarked dryly.

He exchanged glances with Peter behind Philip's broad back, and they both smiled. Philip could be delightfully naïve sometimes, Gilbert thought. He remembered his acute embarrassment at his reception in Acre after their escape from Damascus, and his constant surprise at finding that his name and reputation were so well known in England.

And both Gilbert and Peter knew the West, as Philip did not. They had a very shrewd suspicion of the sensation that Philip's arrival would cause at Cardiff. He might think that his troop of men, mounted and armed with a lavishness that many knights would envy, his servants, his wagons loaded with the luxuries of the East, were the normal accompaniment for a baron of Outremer. Perhaps they were, Gilbert thought, thinking back to his life at Blanche Garde, but there were few barons in the whole of England who travelled in such state, or were rich enough to put such a troop of men into the field.

An hour's leisurely riding brought them within sight of the round keep of Cardiff Castle.

'It hasn't changed much,' Peter observed in surprise. 'In fact, it looks smaller! I suppose that's the result of seeing the castles of Outremer. Why, you could put the whole place down inside the inner ward of your castle of Blanche Garde, Philip.'

Llewellyn brought up Saladin for Philip. He had rested the horse until now in preparation for the jousting. Gilbert winked at Peter as they watched Philip mount. There was certainly not a horse in England to compare with Saladin's parting gift.

Llewellyn issued his last orders in his hoarse, parade-ground voice. 'Now, sit up straight in your saddles! Remember you're Crusaders, and not recruits. Stick your chests out! That's more like it.'

The joust was about to begin in the ward of Cardiff

Castle. A line of ropes and stakes marked the narrow strip of the lists, set up at the foot of the steep mound on which stood the keep. A cluster of coloured tents had been erected at one end for the competing knights. The pennons of Marcher lords and barons from across the Severn and the Bristol Channel fluttered in the bright autumn air. Their owners were making last-minute adjustments to armour and equipment, while servants walked their great horses up and down.

From the other side of the lists came the deep hum of a large, expectant crowd, drawn from all the surrounding towns and villages—men, women, and children in their hundreds, packed ten deep or more along the line of the ropes. A small stand had been erected on the opposite side for the more distinguished visitors, and this was already filled with the nobility of the Marches, the men in gaily coloured cottes and cloaks, and their ladies resplendent in silks and brocades, their hair covered by wimples and stiff white caps.

On the edge of the lists was the herald, a portly and pompous man, dressed in a gorgeous tabard and holding the staff of his office. He was waiting for the Earl of Gloucester to give the signal for the opening bout.

Richard de Clare, Earl of Gloucester, the most influential of the Marcher lords of South Wales, and one of the richest feudal barons in England, was talking to two elderly knights. Like himself, they were not taking part in the joust, and wore the ankle-length cotte and richly furred cloak of the Norman nobleman. The Earl, despite his importance, was a comparatively young man, red-haired like the majority of the Clares, tall, and slimly built, with a pallid face from which the bones and features stood out sharply; high cheekbones on either side of the thin, inquisitive nose, and below, a pointed and obstinate chin. He turned his restless eyes towards the herald, and had half raised his hand when a raucous trumpet call sounded from the other side of the gatehouse.

The Earl's sandy eyebrows shot up in surprise. Visiting knights or barons seldom announced their arrival in such a peremptory tone outside his castle. The hum of the crowd died away, and in the sudden silence the hollow rumble of many hooves was heard on the wooden drawbridge.

The formidable and imposing figure of a knight in full armour and spotless surcoat rode into the ward. A brightly painted, curved shield covered his left side from shoulder to knee; below that could be seen the long scabbard of his sword, and a highly burnished helm was strapped to his saddle. Above his head the pennon of a baron fluttered from the tip of his lance.

The beauty and superb breeding of his great horse roused the silent crowd to a buzz of comment which increased in volume as the rest of the long column appeared through the arch of the gatehouse. First came two more knights, and then a compact body of heavily armed cross-bowmen, bronzed and burly veterans, all splendidly mounted, and riding in perfect formation.

Behind them creaked six large wagons in charge of mounted servants.

'In the name of the saints, who's this?' the Earl demanded in astonishment. 'I've never seen that device before! A Black Hawk? Have you, Sir Henry?'

The elderly knight by his side shook his head. 'Never, my lord.' He tugged at his grey beard in perplexity. 'It's very strange. There can be few barons in the kingdom who travel in such state.'

The leading knight led his troop around the end of the lists behind the tents, and towards the enclosure at the foot of the mound. He held up his mailed arm. A hoarse shout came from the leading man-at-arms, and the column came to a halt, the men sitting erect and motionless in their saddles.

'That horse must be worth a baron's ransom,' the Earl muttered, running an expert eye over the magnificent charger. 'Not bred in this country, though.'

'They don't look like Normans, my lord,' the other knight remarked. 'Those hauberks are foreign made. And the face of that leading knight has been burnt by a hotter sun that we ever see in the Marches.'

'You're right!' the Earl exclaimed. 'Look, that third knight has the Chaworth martlets on his shield. Didn't Geoffrey de Chaworth's son go on the Crusade?'

'Yes, of course. They're Crusaders!' Sir Henry cried. 'But who's their leader?'

The word *Crusaders* went round the big crowd in a flash of excited comment. The Crusades, with their danger and romance, had gripped the imagination of Christendom, and anyone returning from the distant Holy Land was greeted with awe and admiration. And few Crusaders had as yet come back to the Marches. In the stand the knights and ladies stood up, craning forward curiously to see these famous men. A circle of squires and menservants flooded round the cross-bowmen and the three knights.

'Where's Bohun?' the Earl asked. 'He'll probably know who this baron is.'

A sunburnt knight limped hurriedly down from the stand, and was hailed by the earl.

'I can't believe it!' he exclaimed. 'That's d'Aubigny of Blanche Garde!'

'What!' the Earl and the other men swung round to stare at Philip, who was just dismounting. 'Do you mean the Syrian baron who fought at Hattin, and then with the King at Arsuf and Acre? But he's one of the greatest barons in Outremer, isn't he? What's he doing in the Marches of Wales?'

'Well, that's Philip d'Aubigny all right,' Bohun said. 'I'm not likely to forget him. I was behind him at Arsuf when he and the king broke through the Mamelukes. And that's his man-at-arms, Llewellyn. I had him for a time when d'Aubigny was prisoner of the Infidels. Best fellow I've ever had.' He limped off to greet Philip.

'I have heard that the King has given him a fief in the midlands,' old Sir Henry said, 'and there are d'Aubignys at Llanstephan, you know.'

Philip smiled with delight as he recognized Bohun, and they shook hands warmly.

'My dear d'Aubigny!' Bohun said. 'What brings you to the Marches?'

'I have a fief at Llanstephan, Sir William. And your wound? Better, I hope?'

Bohun glanced down at his leg. 'Makes me limp a good deal,' he said. 'Now, come and meet the Earl.'

The group of men watched Philip approach, eyeing with curiosity the dark, resolute young face and the graceful ease with which he walked under the weight of his hauberk and chausses, as though he were more used to them than the lighter feel of cotte and cloak.

The Earl held out his hand. 'You are very welcome, Sir Philip,' he said. 'We have heard a great deal of you in the Marches.'

Philip bowed with the quiet dignity he had learnt in the East, and answered as best he could the eager questions thrown at him. But the Earl twitched his arm, and led him out of earshot of the others.

'A word with you, Sir Philip,' he said in low tones, his sharp features working anxiously. 'The King? What news of the King?'

'He is still in Germany, sir.'

The Earl gnawed the knuckles of his left hand, his brown eyes roving over Philip's face. Influential and wealthy though he might be, and the more so because of that, his position as a supporter of Richard could easily turn to his disadvantage if Prince John gained the upper hand.

'You are a friend of the King?' he asked abruptly.

'I have sworn allegiance to him,' Philip said without any hesitation. He smiled at the anxious face. 'You need not worry, sir. The King will soon be home, if I know anything of him.' He spoke more accurately than he knew, for many miles away at that moment a white-faced Prince John was staring with horror at a curt message that had just arrived from France: *The devil is loose. Look to yourself.*

The Earl's face cleared, and he shook Philip warmly by the hand. 'I think we shall be friends, Sir Philip,' he said. 'Now, I expect you are anxious to take part in the joust. We are looking forward to seeing you ride.'

Philip, together with Gilbert and Peter, was given a tent at the end of the lists, and the plans for the joust were explained to them. As the various knights varied so greatly in skill and experience, they were divided into three classes. Competitors would be drawn against each other in each class, and the prize awarded on a knock-out system. Philip and Gilbert were automatically placed in the first group, and Peter, much to his disgust, in the third.

Philip had to wait an hour for his first bout. But he began his methodical preparations long before. A man-at-arms held out a selection of blunt lances, and Philip made a careful choice, running his eye down the shaft for uneven knots, feeling the butt in the palm of his hand, and then holding the lance in the air to test the balance.

Everyone knew his name by this time. Many knights

gathered round to watch Philip make ready for the bout, eager to pick up any tips from so experienced a fighter.

Llewellyn was testing the harness on Saladin, tugging at each piece of leather. A faulty strap could snap at the critical moment, and hurl the rider from the saddle. Philip watched him for a moment. He could safely leave that to Llewellyn, and he turned to pick up his helm. A small page was holding it, a sturdy boy with red hair. The three red chevrons of the Clares were emblazoned on his surcoat, and he was looking up at Philip with a rapt expression of hero worship on his small face.

'Hullo!' Philip said. 'What's your name?'

'Richard de Clare, sir.'

'Oh, I see. The Earl is your father?'

The small red head nodded. 'Is this where an Infidel hit you, sir?' the boy asked. His finger traced a faint mark on the burnished top of the helm.

'Yes, I got that at Acre.'

Saladin put down his beautiful head and sniffed delicately at the boy.

'Is this the horse the Emir Saladin gave you, sir?'

'Yes. Do you like him?'

'Oh, yes, sir!' Richard stroked Saladin's smooth neck. 'I wish I could ride him. Fancy riding the same horse that Saladin once rode!'

Philip ruffled the red hair, and smiled. 'Well, you can, tomorrow,' he said.

'Can I, sir? Really? Oooh!'

Philip caught the heavy helm just before it slipped to the ground. Llewellyn slid it over his head, and adjusted the straps. Then he held out the shield, and slung the strap over Philip's shoulder before he helped him into the saddle.

Philip eased himself into a comfortable position, and then automatically his hand went to his sword hilt to see that the blade would slide out easily.

'You won't want that,' Gilbert said.

'I know. But it's a habit.'

'Well, be careful,' Gilbert muttered.

Philip looked at his friend in surprise. 'Of course I'll be careful. Why, is this fellow I'm fighting so good?'

'Oh, I don't mean that! You could probably knock him out of the saddle with a broomstick under your arm. These fellows aren't used to the sort of fighting you're trained for, Philip. Aim for his shield. If you hit him on the helm you might break his neck.'

Llewellyn handed up the blunt lance, and Saladin trotted proudly into the narrow lists. Philip reined him in then, and sat motionless. But for the skirts of his surcoat fluttering in the slight breeze, he might have been a stone effigy in some great cathedral church.

A storm of applause greeted his appearance. For the crowd could appreciate and forecast for themselves the exhibition they were about to see. The knights who had fought so far were highly skilled amateurs, to whom the management of horse and lance was part of their training as noblemen. But with Philip, it had been a grim business of life or death, and the crowd at Cardiff that day knew instinctively that they were about to watch a fighter who had been tested and proved in the most searching conditions in the world.

Up in the small stand Bohun was rubbing his hands together in anticipation. 'Now we're going to see something!' he said.

'Is he really as good as they say?' de Clare asked.

'Oh, yes,' Bohun said emphatically. 'I saw him at Arsuf. It was he and the King, you know, who broke the Mamelukes in the last charge. And I watched him in the joust at Acre— the one Richard held just before we all sailed for home.'

'Did you ride in that?' a knight asked.

'Good heavens, no! I'm not in that class,' Bohun said. 'The flower of the knights of Christendom were there; the best men of Outremer, the Templars and the Hospitallers, the finest lances from France, and the pick of our men. I've never seen such riding.'

'What happened?' the Earl asked.

'Well, the Outremer fellows thought d'Aubigny would win; they reckon him their best man, you see. On the first day he won all his bouts quite easily. We thought there was only one man who could touch him, William de Molembec from Poitou. Unpleasant fellow, a loud-voiced drunkard, but a fine horseman for all that.'

Bohun paused, and his audience prompted him impatiently. 'Now, don't spoil the story,' he said. 'That night the King gave a big dinner, and Molembec was drunk, as usual.

He was infernally rude to some of the Syrian barons, and singled out d'Aubigny, as luck would have it. He made some remark about Philip's father, who was killed at Hattin. I don't think Molembec quite knew what he was saying, and his friends hustled him out. Anyway, he and d'Aubigny met in the final bout the next afternoon.'

'That must have been worth seeing,' a knight observed enviously.

Bohun chuckled. 'It was! They were to have the best of three runs. The first was a draw. Both hit each other's shield. In the second d'Aubigny hit his man's helm, a lovely piece of riding, and de Molembec just managed to stay in the saddle.'

'And the third?'

'Molembec went for the helm, and missed. D'Aubigny hit him full on the shield.'

'D'Aubigny's fight, then,' the Earl said.

'No doubt about that. But that wasn't the end. D'Aubigny threw his lance away, drew his sword, and they went for each other like two wild cats.'

'I should like to have seen that!' several men said.

Bohun beamed at his audience. He was enjoying the story. Men returned from the Crusades had a host of good stories to tell, and a ready audience.

'De Molembec wasn't in d'Aubigny's class with the sword. He was knocked out of his saddle by a tremendous crack on the side of his helm. And then the fun began! The herald ran forward to end the bout, but d'Aubigny jumped off his horse, and went in to finish de Molembec off. The King waved the herald back, and the crowd whooped d'Aubigny on. They were all backing him, you see. I'll say one thing for Molembec. He had guts. He stood up, and fought back, but d'Aubigny is a wonder with the sword. His speed is uncanny, and he uses the point a lot. Anyway, he hit his man as he liked, and then caught him on the side of the neck; his favourite stroke, so I was told. Molembec started to sway, and then d'Aubigny hit him again, exactly on the same spot. Didn't go through the mail, but Molembec went down as if half the walls of Acre had fallen on his head.'

'Badly hurt?'

'Oh, he died a couple of days later,' Bohun said casually. 'Ah, they're ready. There's the herald.'

All eyes switched to the narrow strip of turf below. The herald was standing in the centre of the lists, raising his staff for silence.

'A bout between Sir John Maurice of Taunton,' he bellowed, 'and Sir Philip d'Aubigny of Blanche Garde in Outremer, Baron of the High Court of the Kingdom of Jerusalem, Defender of the Holy Sepulchre!'

Philip smiled behind his helm. The herald was making the most of the titles of the unusual entrant; he would expect a large tip for that.

Sir John Maurice was manoeuvring his horse at the far end, and Philip watched him closely. The art of jousting was one of the most difficult arts of all. There were two essentials; the lance must be held rigidly, and not allowed to sway from the line by a fraction; and at the moment of impact, horse, rider, and lance must be moving at top speed, with the combined weight and momentum all concentrated on that supreme and vital second. Only long and tireless practice could ensure perfection, and even then a poorly trained horse might offset the highest skill of the rider. Philip knew that he could rely on Saladin; he knew the horse would gallop unhesitatingly in a straight line, and he knew, too, the exact distance and time it would take to work him up to a full gallop.

He considered the tactics to adopt, and remembered the warning that Gilbert had given him. There were two possible targets at which a jouster could aim; the shield, or the helm. The first was the larger, and therefore the easier mark, for a rider showed only the top of his helm. But a full hit on the helm was a certain win; if the rider did not sway back to the blow, or fly from the saddle, the appalling jerk might snap his neck. The expert knights went for the helm, and in the grim jousts of Outremer, Philip invariably chose that target if he was fighting in earnest. Well, he had better not do so now, he decided. Probably there would be no need. Maurice's horse seemed very restive.

The herald looked from one rider to the other, saw that they were ready, and lifted his staff. The trumpets sounded, and the crowd craned forward as the two horses cantered forward, picking up speed rapidly, and the two slender lances came down to the charge.

Philip hunched himself in his favourite position; the

cool wind flowed in through the eye-slits, and he stared rigidly at Maurice's shield, ignoring, like all good jousters, the tip of his lance jutting out ahead. He saw the shield leap towards him as Saladin reached his top speed. The tip of the lance was in a straight line for the centre of the other man's device. Philip clamped his knees like two vices into Saladin's sides, threw his weight forward and gritted his teeth.

Where Maurice's lance went he never knew. But he felt the familiar jolt under his arm pit as his lance went home, and the butt jarred violently. As he hurtled past he caught a brief glimpse of a figure sprawling backwards in the saddle.

He brought Saladin round in a tight circle. A riderless horse was trotting across the grass, and his rider was on his knees on the ground. From the crowd came a storm of applause; coloured handkerchiefs fluttered in the stand, and Philip raised his lance in acknowledgement.

Sir John's squire lifted off his master's helm, and Philip bent down. 'I hope you are not hurt, Sir John?' he asked.

Maurice's face was flushed with annoyance, as well it might be after such a spill in front of that large crowd. But at Philip's words he laughed and shook his head.

'No, no, Sir Philip. I am honoured to think that I have ridden against you,' he said courteously.

Both Peter and Gilbert won their bouts, and Philip rode again later in the day. Gilbert had no difficulty with his opponents. He fought as one might have expected him to, with caution, methodically and competently, and Philip knew that it would take a very experienced jouster to beat him.

The great hall of the keep was crowded that night for dinner. Extra tables were set on the dais for the visitors, and the body of the hall was filled with the garrison and the servants who had come with their masters. Philip found himself in the seat of honour on the right of the Earl, with the Lady de Clare on his other side. She was a dark-haired, imperious-looking woman, most magnificently dressed, and by her manner fully conscious of her position as the leading lady of the Marches.

Philip looked round the hall and half smiled to himself as he caught Gilbert's amused glance. No doubt this was a scene of magnificence and luxury, judged by Western standards, but Philip still found it all very barbaric and crude. The walls were bare; logs spluttered in the yawning fireplace, and the smoke billowed out across the hall. The uncertain light came from torches stuck into holders on the walls, and from wax candles on the high table. Most of the hall was in shadow, and the high, raftered roof was almost in complete darkness. The hall was draughty, too. Philip had been persuaded by Gilbert to buy a furred cloak in London, and now he was glad that he had done so as he felt the draughts eddy round his feet and shoulders.

He found that he was being treated as the guest of honour. To a great extent this was due to his reputation as a Crusader, but partly also to his friendship with King Richard. Before the meal had ended, Philip had consented to take young Richard de Clare as his page. The boy, as a member of such a great family, would normally have gone to the Court for his education, but that was hardly possible now, when the de Clares were bitter opponents of Prince John.

Philip was more interested in finding some news of Llanstephan. It was Peter's father who supplied the information. Sir Geoffrey de Chaworth was a gloomy looking man. His forehead was creased with permanent lines of worry; two deep lines ran from the corner of his nostrils, and his mouth drooped at the corners with an air of perpetual dismay. Even his voice was mournful.

'Bad news for you, Sir Philip, I'm afraid,' he said. 'De Braose is at Llanstephan now.'

Philip had never heard the name before. 'Who is that?' he asked.

'He's a cousin of the last d'Aubigny. He claims the fief now.'

'I know the man,' the Earl said in tones that showed quite clearly his dislike. 'But you are the rightful heir, Sir Philip?'

'So the lawyers told me in London.'

'Well, you'll have to throw the fellow out by force. We shall all be glad to help you,' the Earl said. 'Braose is a friend of Prince John.'

Sir Geoffrey shook his head sadly. 'Won't be easy,' he said. 'Llanstephan is a strong castle, Sir Philip. You'll need siege machinery and a large force.' He seemed almost pleased, Philip thought, to be the bearer of such depressing news.

Chapter Seventeen

KIDWELLY CASTLE

THE jousting went on all the next day. In the stand they were discussing the chances of the various competitors. 'Who've you got here likely to give d'Aubigny a fight?' Bohun asked.

'Belleme's the only one, I should think,' the Earl said.

'Ivo de Belleme!' Bohun shrugged his shoulders with disgust. 'I wonder you allow him to ride inside your castle, my lord.'

'It might be awkward to turn him away,' the Earl said. 'I know he's one of the Prince's strongest supporters, and . . .'

'And an unpleasant scoundrel into the bargain,' Bohun said emphatically. 'Well, I hope he does meet d'Aubigny. I'd better have a word with Philip.'

'For heaven's sake, no!' the Earl said. 'I don't want

trouble here. Hullo, Belleme is riding against d'Aubigny's knight, d'Assailly, now.'

Philip had noticed Belleme. He knew nothing of the man, but he had taken an instant dislike to him on sight. Belleme was of medium height, but obviously of immense strength. He had a chest like a barrel, and his wide shoulders drooped like those of an ape Philip had once seen in Damascus. But it was the man's manner that repelled Philip. His servants were in dread of him; they sidled up to him with the air of dogs expecting to be kicked, as indeed they frequently were. His small page was brutally cuffed on the head for a trifling mistake. Belleme's face matched his manner; coarse, brutal, and arrogant.

'You'd better watch out for this fellow, Gilbert,' Philip said. 'He's good.'

Gilbert glanced placidly across at his opponent. 'I'll be all right, Philip. Don't worry.' He mounted and rode down to the other end of the lists.

Philip felt uneasy. He watched Belleme choose his lance. There was an air of competence about the man, and he caught snatches of the conversation.

'Well, let's see what you can do against these Crusaders, Ivo,' a knight was saying.

'I'll break his neck for him,' Belleme said. 'Give me that helm, boy.' His page held up the heavy helm. 'The other way round, you young fool!'

He brought his mailed hand across the boy's face with a backhanded slap that sent the page reeling back with blood streaming from his nose. Belleme rammed the helm on his head, waited impatiently while a servant adjusted the straps, and then hoisted himself into the saddle. As he jerked the reins, the horse reared. With a muttered curse Belleme dug his long prick spurs deep into the animal's side, and sent him galloping forward into the lists.

Philip watched it all, and smiled. A man who treated his horse like that was asking for trouble in a joust.

The herald stepped forward importantly. 'A bout between Sir Ivo de Belleme of Shrewsbury,' he shouted, 'And Sir Gilbert d'Assailly of Blanche Garde in the Kingdom of Jerusalem.'

He signed to the trumpeters, and as the long instruments went up in the air, and the loud notes rang out, the two mounted men shook their reins and cantered forward. Philip watched Belleme. The man could ride, he thought. But Gilbert was experienced enough to look after himself. He would probably go for the shield, while Belleme was obviously trying the helm thrust, to judge by the angle of his lance. They met in the centre of the narrow strip of turf. Gilbert's lance hit Belleme's shield with a crack, and splintered, the broken shaft flying up into the air. His opponent's lance tip caught him a glancing blow on the side of the helm, and wisely he let himself sway back and to the left. But it was Belleme's bout, and a mild splutter of applause came from the crowd who knew of his friendship with Prince John, and had heard tales of his life that shocked even the people of that time.

Peter de Chaworth was waiting his turn to ride. He had won each round so far, and the next would make him the winner of the entire event.

'You'll be all right, Peter,' Philip said. 'Watch for his horse. I noticed him in the last round. He has a tendency to swerve away. So keep close in to him. And whatever you do, don't look at his lance. Or yours! Just keep your eyes on his shield.'

Peter nodded nervously, and Philip heard him swallow convulsively. But it was excitement, not fear. He had seen Peter in action. With a final slap on his back, he heaved him up into the saddle.

Peter did as he was told. He had developed into a good jouster, and his horse could be relied upon to run straight, for he was a present from Philip. Both knights went for the shield, but Peter closed in as Philip had advised. The other man's horse swerved away, made his rider miss his aim, and Peter triumphantly got home full on the shield.

The sun was beginning to sink when the last bout of the day was announced by the herald. The high curtain walls threw long shadows across the inner ward as the crowd pushed eagerly forward to catch a good view of the event that would decide the winner of the main prize. Even the sentries on the battlements deserted their posts, and turned their backs on the parapet to watch, while the steep slopes of the mound were covered with people who had scrambled up there to find a clear view of the lists.

As the experts in the stand had predicted, Philip and Belleme were the final pair. Bohun was quietly confident, and smiled grimly as he heard the men around him discuss Belleme's chances.

Philip made his preparations with unhurried calm. Peter fussed about him anxiously.

'You must watch out, Philip,' he said. 'I heard Belleme a minute ago. He's out to break your neck with a helm thrust if he can. You see, he knows you are a friend of the King, and if he can't do it here, he said he would deal with you afterwards.'

Philip chose his lance, and turned towards Peter. 'Is that what he said?' he remarked quietly.

'But he's dangerous, Philip! I've often heard stories about him.'

Philip shrugged his mailed shoulders, and signalled to Llewellyn to bring Saladin closer. Gilbert, who had been in the stand, walked up at that moment. He knew his Philip. And one glance at that set face with the thin line of the lips told him that something was wrong. But he had no chance to ask what it was, for Llewellyn was holding out the big helm, and in a few seconds Saladin was trotting out to the lists.

'What's the matter with Philip?' Gilbert asked quickly.

Peter told him. Gilbert wheeled on him, his eyes blazing with anger. 'You young fool!' he cried. 'I warned Philip to be careful, and now you go and make him lose his temper.'

Peter's freckled face flushed. 'But that won't put him off, will it?' he exclaimed in alarm. 'You don't . . .'

'Put him off!' Gilbert snorted. 'It means that Ivo de Belleme had better see a priest before he rides into the lists!'

'But he's a killer, Gilbert! They say he has killed five men in tournaments.'

Gilbert sighed wearily. 'I could cheerfully hit you over the head, Peter!' he said angrily. 'After three years in Outremer, haven't you yet learnt the difference between real fighting and this playing at jousting? Belleme may be as good as you say. But he'd be safer now if he had been locked naked in a cage with a hungry lion!'

The crowd had fallen silent. It was possible to hear the faint jingle of mail from the two jousters as they brought their horses round to face each other. The herald made his announcement, and the trumpets rang out.

The long, slender lances came down to the charge. The two horses sprang forward, and the riders crouched down. The steel-shod hooves of the horses flung up clods of soft turf, and the white surcoats fluttered in the wind. A gasp of escaping breath came from the tense crowd as the two figures seemed to leap towards each other in those last few yards. The menacing lances were high; each man was trying for the helm thrust.

'Philip's wide! He's too wide!' moaned Peter.

'Of course he is, you fool! Shut up!' Gilbert's hand closed like a vice over Peter's arm. 'Now, Philip! *Now!*'

In the last fraction of a second before the lances hit, Philip gave a gentle twitch to his reins. The well trained Saladin veered to his right, a few inches, perhaps a foot, and in towards the other horse. But it was enough. Belleme's lance flickered past, missing by the thickness of a sheet of parchment. With a crack that was heard all over the ward, Philip's lance went home, full on the helm, driven on by the furious speed and momentum of his charge, his arm, hand and wrist all braced like steel bands to withstand the shuddering shock of the impact.

Belleme was bent back in the saddle like a bow. The straps of his helm broke, his feet were torn from the wide stirrups at which they were clawing convulsively, and he was thrown clear as his frightened horse reared and galloped on. With a thud and then a loud jingle of mail, Belleme hit the ground, arms and legs sprawling drunkenly as if they did not belong to him. His shield flew away, stood for a second on its rim, then fell and lay as motionless as its owner.

The silence was broken. From the crowd came a concerted gasp, then a rumbling bellow of applause, deep and rolling like thunder. Arms waved wildly in the air, men and women shrieked, instinctively relieved after the tense strain of watching and holding their breath.

Philip trotted back to his tent. He dismounted, and Llewellyn, his mahogany-coloured face creased in a crooked grin of delight, tore off the helm.

'You've broken his neck,' Gilbert said accusingly.

'I don't think so.' Philip wiped the sweat from his

forehead, and looked down the lists to where men were bending over the motionless figure on the grass. 'The straps of his helm snapped. That saved him.'

He was surrounded by smiling faces, all watching him with awed respect. The Earl of Gloucester eyed him with an odd expression.

'I have never seen such riding,' he said at last. 'That last minute change of direction with your lance. How do you do it, d'Aubigny?'

'It's a question of timing,' Philip said. 'That, and a horse you can trust.'

'Well, don't try it again in a joust,' Gilbert said crossly. 'You would insist on using that trick against de Molembec at Acre, and Saladin didn't swerve in close enough. You nearly missed altogether.'

'But I didn't, did I?' Philip said cheerfully, his burst of temper having evaporated now that he had dealt with Belleme.

They waited until a surgeon inspected Belleme, and announced that the man would recover.

'Anyway, he'll have a stiff neck for a few months,' the Earl said happily, and bore Philip off to the keep.

They kept Philip busy that night with stories of Outremer. In those days people had to rely for news of what was happening in the world from travellers. A silent high table listened intently to Philip as he described the great Saladin, and held up his hand for them to see the ring that the famous Infidel leader had given him.

'And that was once worn by Saladin,' the Lady Clare murmured as she touched the ring with her fingers. 'Now, tell us about Damascus, Sir Philip. You escaped like St Paul, down the walls, didn't you?'

It was raining when Philip rode out the next morning with Sir Geoffrey de Chaworth. And it was still raining the following afternoon when they came within sight of Kidwelly Castle. Philip was wearing the new fashion of the hood attached to a shoulder cape, and a very sensible idea it was, too, he thought, as he huddled in his saddle, and watched the grey curtains of rain sweep in from the sea, over the sand-dunes on their left and across to the dim blue of the mountains.

'Kidwelly!' Peter flung up his arm and pointed.

Philip peered without much interest through the rain. He could distinguish a tall keep in the distance. But his mind was running hopefully on hot water and a change of clothing. Perhaps, after all, Gilbert was right about the English climate. Saladin seemed to think so as well, for he was stepping disdainfully through the thick mud of the road, throwing up his beautiful head, and snorting peevishly at the misty rain.

'We shall have to alter it, Father,' Peter was saying. 'I've learnt a lot about castle building in Outremer. And Philip can advise us.'

'I daresay, boy,' Sir Geoffrey said pessimistically. 'But where's the money coming from?'

'Oh, my ransom money will help.'

Sir Geoffrey grunted. 'That won't go far. But you can make a start if you like,' he said gloomily.

They were greeted warmly at the castle. It was not every day that the son and heir to the fief returned safely from the Crusades. The Lady Anne de Chaworth was a tall, spare lady with a determined chin and a rasping voice. Her eyes missed nothing as she watched her servants, and even her mournful husband obeyed her instructions with a meekness that made Philip smile. Perhaps this explained Sir Geoffrey's gloom, he thought, as he and Gilbert were shown to a small room at the top of the keep.

Kidwelly Castle was fairly small at that time. It would be many years before the changes begun by Peter de Chaworth would transform the simple Norman keep and outer ward into one of the most formidable fortresses in the Marches.

Meanwhile, Peter apologetically ushered Philip into the damp and badly lighted cell, for that was all it was, above the hall.

'I'm sorry, Philip,' he said. 'I know what your castle of Blanche Garde was like, and your house in Jerusalem. But I'm going to change all that.'

'Don't worry,' Philip said hastily, trying not to notice the wicked gleam in Gilbert's eye. 'But I would like some hot water. Llewellyn can see to it.'

Llewellyn sniffed loudly when he saw the room, but he knew better than to make any comment. He unpacked the contents of several large chests, and the room began to look more comfortable. A cheerful fire roared in the big grate, and three torches burned in the wall sockets. The bare, dirty floor was covered with rugs from Outremer, and Philip's travelling bed and mattress were laid out carefully.

'There's no need to be uncomfortable, my father used to say, unless you can help it,' Philip remarked.

'Exactly,' Gilbert murmured, and covered his mouth with his hand.

But Philip was watching his new page, who was fussing about happily arranging clothes, and unpacking.

'Come here, Richard. I want to have a look at you.' Philip turned the small figure around like a top. 'As I thought. You're filthy! Tomorrow you will have a good bath.'

Richard looked in horror. 'What, all over, my lord!' he gasped.

'All over, and every day. I'll inspect you in the morning. If you're not spotless then, I'll thrash you.'

'Yes, my lord,' Richard said meekly, and sidled out of the room, too soon to see the grin on Philip's face.

They bathed and changed into dry clothes. With some difficulty they stumbled down the narrow stairs to the hall, for no light came in through the tiny slits in the thick walls.

The Lady de Chaworth, as might have been expected, was a good housekeeper, and dinner that night was a lengthy meal. Sir Geoffrey, as Philip discovered, had one weakness, and that was food. He ate with great gusto and much noise, and became almost cheerful about the quality of the fish.

'We'll ride to Llanstephan in the morning,' he said, speaking with difficulty, as his mouth was full. 'Ach! a bone!' He explored the inside of his mouth with a long finger, brought out a piece of fish and hurled it on to the floor, spitting noisily at the same time. 'Not that we shall do any good, Sir Philip. De Braose won't let us put a foot inside, if I know anything of him. Ah, the roast!'

The plates were whipped off the table, and hastily wiped by the servants standing behind. Philip had left some fish on his plate. In doing so, he had been lacking in English table manners, he decided, for Sir Geoffrey had emptied his on to the floor, much to the delight of the dogs who were snarling in the rushes. Sir Geoffrey watched anxiously as his plate was piled high with meat. Philip could smell the spices; they disguised any flavour that the meat might have possessed. Probably just as well, he thought, as he chewed steadily at the tough gristle; the beef must have been salted originally.

'Aaah! That's better,' Sir Geoffrey remarked, and sneezed violently, for he had caught a cold after the wet ride from Cardiff.

For one second there passed through Philip's mind a picture of old Usamah in his beautifully decorated dining-room, his table covered with gold and silver dishes or graceful Damascus glass, eating daintily and fastidiously, with the bright Eastern sun streaming in through the tall windows. Then a sudden gust of wind eddied down the chimney, and a billow of acrid wood smoke enveloped Philip. He coughed, and wiped his eyes.

They rode to Llanstephan soon after dawn the next day. The castle, as Sir Geoffrey explained, was quite close to Kidwelly as the crow flew, but a river ran in between, and as Llanstephan was built near the mouth, where there was a wide estuary, it was necessary to ride up-stream for a mile to reach the ford.

They took with them all Philip's troop of cross-bow-men, and several men-at-arms from Sir Geoffrey's garrison. Too many, Philip thought, for such a large force would only arouse de Braose's suspicions. But Sir Geoffrey's distrust of the man was such that he refused to go unless his men went with him.

Their route followed the sea for a couple of miles, and then ran along the edge of a quite considerable cliff. The view out to sea was lovely, and Philip's spirits rose. The sun was shining, too; a pleasant change after the last two days. The road suddenly dropped down to sea level again, and Peter nudged Philip. 'You can see the castle now,' he said.

Philip pushed Saladin forward, and looked ahead eagerly. The wide estuary was filled with the high tide, the water lapping the cliffs on the farther side. Above the low cliffs rose a natural mound, long and narrow, and perched on this ridge was the castle from which his grandfather had ridden so many years ago when he went on the First Crusade.

'Well, what do you think of it, Philip?' Peter asked.

'The position is magnificent,' Philip said. 'I can't see much of the lay-out from here, though.'

'Oh, the usual keep, and curtain walls,' Peter said.

They rode up-stream, and splashed across the shallow ford. A winding track led towards the castle, and Philip could see more of the details now. The curtain walls were high, but not covered by projecting towers as was the invariable custom in Outremer. But there was a substantial little gatehouse, a toy compared to the immense erection at Blanche Garde, but stronger than was usual in the Marches of Wales at that time.

The wooden drawbridge was up when they arrived, and they halted on the edge of the dry ditch that followed the line of the walls.

'Sound, Morgan,' Sir Geoffrey said to his trumpeter.

There were sentries on the wall, but they did not move. Sir Geoffrey muttered angrily, and his trumpeter blew again in response to a curt order.

'Ah, there's de Braose,' Sir Geoffrey said.

The distance was too great for Philip to distinguish the features of the man who had laid claim to his fief. He was dark-haired and tall, but that was all he could see.

The figure on the wall leant over, and shouted down. 'What do you want, Chaworth?' he cried.

Sir Geoffrey's temper rose. As he had explained several times to Philip that morning, the fish at dinner had not agreed with him.

He stood up furiously in his stirrups. 'What the devil do you mean by keeping us hanging about like this?' he bellowed. 'Is this the way you greet all your visitors, de Braose?'

'When they come armed and with cross-bows,' de Braose said. 'Who is that with you?'

'This is Sir Philip d'Aubigny, the rightful heir to this fief.'

'I thought as much. Go home to Outremer, d'Aubigny. There is nothing here for you. As for you, de Chaworth, unless you are out of sight in two minutes, I will bid my men fire.'

Peter put out his hand, and pulled his father back. Sir Geoffrey shook him off, and waved his arm furiously at the high walls. Philip glanced behind. He had heard a series of deep clicks. His men were winding their cross-bows.

'Don't fire unless I give the order,' he said quietly. 'I think we had better ride back, Sir Geoffrey,' he added. 'There is nothing we can do now.'

On the way back to Kidwelly he rode in silence, and shook his head when Peter asked him several times for his plans. But by the time they had reached the castle, and were sitting down to the midday meal, he knew exactly what there was to be done.

'Can you find wood for four scaling-ladders, sir?' he asked Sir Geoffrey.

'I expect so, Philip.' Sir Geoffrey was munching happily at cold meat, his temper restored again. 'But they won't be any use against the walls of Llanstephan, you know.' He shook his head sadly, and attacked the meat once more.

'Well, we can but try,' Philip said. 'De Braose will be expecting an attack, but if we try at night, and can gain even a footing on the walls, we should be safe enough. How large is his garrison?'

'About thirty,' Sir Geoffrey said, 'and not well armed at that. But his archers are good. They're Welsh. You'll never mount your ladders.'

'I think we will,' Philip said. He was not completely sure himself, but at all costs he must give the others confidence. 'My cross-bows have a longer range than ordinary short bows; we learnt that at Arsuf. And they're good shots. They can keep the top of the walls clear until we are up.'

'At night?' queried Sir Geoffrey.

'The moon was nearly full last night,' Philip said. 'If we approach the walls just before it rises, we won't be seen very clearly, if at all. A full moon will give enough light for my men to shoot by.'

'If the moon gets through the clouds,' Sir Geoffrey said. 'It will probably be raining, you know.'

Philip shifted impatiently in his chair. Sir Geoffrey could be very irritating, he thought. No battle would ever be won if a general didn't take a risk occasionally. Fortunately, Sir Geoffrey felt less despondent after a heavy meal, and gave orders for the scaling ladders to be constructed. Philip suggested that they should be made in two sections for greater ease of carrying, and then, satisfied that the

Kidwelly men knew their job, he wandered away to the walls.

The sun was shining for a change, but had little heat. Philip was looking for a sheltered spot where he could sit and think. He was not too happy about his plan. It was a good one, but full of risks. One single factor that would tip the balance in his favour, Philip thought, and he would feel more confident.

Voices broke in on his thoughts, and he glanced around the corner of the parapet. There were three people sitting in the angle made by the walls. One was little Rowena, Peter's youngest sister. She was sitting on a low stool, chin on her small hands, her long black plaits falling down her back, and her round, blue eyes fixed unwaveringly on Llewellyn. By her side was Richard de Clare, balancing Philip's helm on his lap. At his feet was a pot of grease, but like Rowena, he was looking at Llewellyn.

Llewellyn was very much at his ease, his back propped comfortably against the parapet; Philip's hauberk lay across his knees, and in his hand was a burnishing cloth. The sleeves of his cotte were rolled up to the elbow, exposing his thick forearms with the curling black hair, and the thin white line of an old scar.

'Was that a wound from an Infidel, Llewellyn?' Rowena asked, pointing with a chubby forefinger at the scar.

'Oh, yes, my lady. At Arsuf. One of them Emirs with a white turban covered with jewels. Caught me when I was fighting with another fellow.'

'Did you kill the Emir, Llewellyn?' Richard asked eagerly.

'Cut his head right off, master Richard. Back-handed cut, like this.' Llewellyn's big, brown hand swept out in an arc, narrowly missing Richard's red hair.

Philip bit back a chuckle, and sat down on the parapet, out of sight. To his certain knowledge Llewellyn had gone through Arsuf without a scratch. The scar had come from the knife of a drunken Syrian footman in a brawl at a tavern in Jerusalem. Sir Hugo had ordered his Arab physician to bind up the long cut, and had then thrown Llewellyn into a cell for a week to cool his heels and his aching head.

'Go on with your story of that battle, Llewellyn,' pleaded Rowena. 'What was the Emir's name?'

'Habis Jaldak, my lady. We was with Count Raymond of Tripoli on a cavalry raid. Our party was out scouting, as I told you. There we were, down by the river, and thousands of Infidels up on the hill above. Now, master Richard, get on with that helm! His lordship will flay you alive if he finds a speck of rust on it in the morning!'

Richard obediently smeared a blob of grease on the top of Philip's helm. 'Yes, go on, Llewellyn,' he said. 'What happened? You were in a pretty tight fix, weren't you?'

'That we were! But Sir Hugo was in command. His lordship's father. Nothing ever upset him. Cool as a glass of sherbet, he was.'

'What's sherbet?' piped Rowena.

'Don't ask silly questions, Rowena!' Richard said

impatiently. 'It's a drink the Infidels make. I say, Llewellyn, is it nice stuff to drink?'

'Now you're asking silly questions, Richard,' Rowena retorted indignantly.

'It's not silly! I'm going on Crusade to the Holy Land one day, and I've got to learn these things. I might get taken prisoner by the Infidels, as Sir Philip was, and if they offered me sherbet, I might think it was poison if I didn't know any better. Sir Philip was offered sherbet by Saladin himself after the battle of Hattin, wasn't he, Llewellyn?'

'What's that got to do with it?' Rowena asked.

'Now, now, you two,' Llewellyn said reprovingly. Philip choked as he heard the cooing note in the hoarse voice that could reduce tough bowmen to a state of gibbering fright.

'Well, there we were with the river at our back,' Llewellyn went on, giving Philip's hauberk a perfunctory flick with his rag. 'We was tired and hot. You've no idea how hot it can get in Outremer. Scorches you like a flame, it does. Why, you can put a hunk of raw meat on a slab of rock, and in a matter of minutes it's done to a turn!'

He shot a swift glance at the two intent little faces to see if they had swallowed this appalling lie. Apparently they had, for four eyes opened in wonder, and Rowena's feet in their scarlet shoes wriggled with delight.

'Really as hot as that, Llewellyn?' Richard asked in awe.

'Of course, master Richard. I wouldn't be telling you lies, now, would I? And you going to the Holy Land one day? You ask his lordship. No, perhaps you'd better not,' he added hastily. 'He'd only curse me for not getting on with my work.' And he polished furiously for a few seconds.

Philip covered his twitching lips with his hand, and tiptoed away. He could hear the deep, hoarse voice as he went out of earshot. 'Well, then the Infidels charged. Hundreds of 'em, thousands . . . and we . . .'

He met Gilbert in the inner ward, and they sat down on the steps leading up to the keep.

'I've been thinking about your plan, Philip,' Gilbert said. 'I've an idea.'

Philip nodded eagerly. He had a high opinion of Gilbert's sound common sense.

'Why not make a diversion, Philip? I don't think these Kidwelly men will be much use storming the walls. They haven't any armour except helmets. If Sir Geoffrey took them round opposite the gatehouse, they could create an alarming disturbance there in the dark.'

'That's a good idea,' Philip said enthusiastically. 'Give them plenty of torches and trumpets, and ask Sir Geoffrey to shout out orders as if he had hundreds of men with him.'

'That will split the garrison, you see,' Gilbert said. 'If Braose has only thirty men, he'll have to send some to the gatehouse.'

Philip felt easier in his mind. This might be the one factor for which he had been searching. But that night one more incident occurred that finally tipped the balance.

Chapter Eighteen

THE STORMING OF LLANSTEPHAN CASTLE

THE scene in the solar at Kidwelly Castle was a peaceful one. The Lady de Chaworth was sewing industriously, while her husband dozed in front of the fire. Dinner had been a satisfying meal, and on Sir Geoffrey's melancholy face there was, for once, an expression of deep contentment. In one corner of the room Philip was discussing in low tones the plans for the next night with Gilbert and Peter.

Suddenly the curtain rings over the door rattled noisily, and in hurried the castle steward, his portly frame quivering with agitation.

'A man-at-arms from Llanstephan Castle is here, my lord!' he exclaimed to Peter, who was nearest the door.

'What does he want?' Peter asked in surprise.

'He wishes to speak with Sir Philip d'Aubigny, my lord.'

Sir Geoffrey opened his eyes, and sat up with a jerk. 'A trap!' he said decisively. 'Don't let him near you, Philip. A knife in the back, that's what you'll get!'

Philip exchanged glances with Gilbert. To both minds there had sprung the recollection of the Assassins and their methods. He hesitated. But his instinct was telling him that this might be the chance for which he had been praying.

'I think it would be wiser to see what he wants, sir,' he said slowly. 'He can be searched before he's brought in.'

'I'll see to that,' Peter said, and hurried out.

'Well, don't say I didn't warn you,' Sir Geoffrey grumbled.

Philip smiled. But he noticed a slight movement of Gilbert's hand to the knife at his belt.

Peter returned a few minutes later, followed by two of the Kidwelly garrison holding the wrists of a third man whom they pushed into the room. He must have recognized Philip after seeing him outside Llanstephan that morning, for when, at a signal from Peter, the men-at-arms released him, he stepped forward and went down on one knee in front of Philip.

'What do you want with me?' Philip asked, examining the man closely.

'I am Gerwyn, my lord, a man-at-arms from Llanstephan.' He returned Philip's searching glance unflinchingly. An elderly, grey-haired man in his fifties, he was a typical old soldier with an air of sturdy reliability.

'I was servant to Sir Robert d'Aubigny for over twenty years,' he added, 'and a good master he was to me, my lord.'

Philip nodded. Sir Robert had been the last of the old line at Llanstephan. 'Well, what of it, Gerwyn?' he asked.

'My father was at Llanstephan all his life,' Gerwyn said. 'We have always served the d'Aubignys, my lord. I have no love for Sir Walter, and there are others in the garrison who think as I do.'

Philip felt his hopes rising. Then he paused. There was still the possibility of a trap here.

'You are a descendant of Sir William d'Aubigny who went on Crusade to the Holy Land, my lord?' Gerwyn asked.

'He was my grandfather.'

Gerwyn's weather-beaten face lit up. 'I often heard him spoken of when I was a boy,' he said. 'Then you are the rightful lord of Llanstephan.'

Philip hesitated no longer. His mind was made up. 'If you will help me, Gerwyn,' he said. 'How many reliable men can you vouch for in the garrison?'

'Four, my lord,' Gerwyn said instantly. 'There may be more, but it would be dangerous to talk to others now if you have some plan in mind.'

Whatever doubts Philip may have had about Gerwyn's

honesty were pushed aside by that last remark. He ignored a warning rumble from Sir Geoffrey.

'How many men are there in the garrison?' he asked quickly.

'Fifty, my lord.'

'He's lying!' Sir Geoffrey exclaimed. 'Thirty at the most!'

'Not now, my lord, I swear!' Gerwyn said. 'Sir Walter has sent for twenty Welsh archers from Howel ap Meredith.'

'The infernal scoundrel!' Sir Geoffrey roared. 'That's treason! Howel is the local Welsh chief, Philip. De Clare will see that de Braose hangs for this when he hears of it!'

But Philip was not particularly interested in what the Earl of Gloucester might do to Sir Walter de Braose. He was far more concerned at the prospect of meeting twenty experienced archers on the walls of Llanstephan. His plan had been a risky one before this; now it was rapidly becoming a gamble. He had nothing to lose by giving Gerwyn all the details of the attack, and there was always the chance of finding some help.

'I am storming Llanstephan by ladder tomorrow night,' he said.

Gerwyn's face brightened instantly. 'Come to the west wall, my lord,' he said eagerly. 'There is a fall in the ditch there where you can mount your ladders.'

'How can I find the exact spot in the dark?'

'I will see that a torch is burning on the wall above,' Gerwyn said. 'I shall post myself on the west wall with the four men I can trust. There may be others on guard,' he added, 'but we can deal with them.'

At the end of ten minutes Philip had given Gerwyn his full instructions, and then, remembering how King Richard had asked for precise details of the ground before the battle of Arsuf, he made Gerwyn explain to him the exact lay-out of Llanstephan Castle. Satisfied, he gave the man a present of money, and sent him away.

The four scaling-ladders were completed early the next morning. Philip had no way of estimating the height of the Llanstephan walls, but he had made a guess, based on his one inspection of them, and then added an extra ten feet, for the ladders would have to be erected at the bottom of the castle ditch.

Speed was the most essential part of the plan, so the ladders were put up against the walls of Kidwelly, and for two hours under Philip's critical eyes, his men practised climbing in full equipment.

'Who's going up first?' Gilbert asked.

'I'll take the right-hand ladder, you the next, and Peter the one on the extreme left. I'm not certain yet about the other.'

'Llewellyn?'

'No, I want him in the ditch,' Philip said. 'He won't lose his head, and we'll need someone down there to keep a regular stream going up the ladders.'

'What about Gurth?' Gilbert suggested.

Philip grinned. 'Yes, he'll do, if the ladders don't break

under his weight. Now, listen, Gilbert. As soon as we're up, we'll take a staircase each. Gerwyn says there are four from the walls leading down to the inner ward. They've got to be kept clear until everyone is up.'

'And then we rush the keep,' Peter said eagerly.

'You won't, Peter,' Philip said. 'Your job is to make for the gatehouse. Knock out the guards there and open up for Sir Geoffrey and his men.'

'What about the keep?' Gilbert said, raising the problem that lay at the back of everyone's mind.

For in the castles of that time the keep was regarded as the last line of defence. Usually it was built quite separately from the rest of the fortifications, and if they fell, the garrison would retreat to the keep.

'That's worrying me, too,' Philip said. 'I think the crossbowmen, or some of them, at any rate, must work their way along the walls, and get as close to the keep as they can. They should be able to shoot down most of the men running back.'

'The Llanstephan keep has a pretty steep mound,' Peter said. 'They won't run up that very fast. That will give the cross-bows a chance.'

'Anything else?' Philip asked. 'Any suggestions, Llewellyn?' For the old soldier had joined the discussion.

'Yes, my lord. No surcoats. Sir Hugo never allowed them on a night attack. Said they showed up.'

'Yes, I hadn't thought of that,' Philip said. 'Tell the men, then, Llewellyn. No surcoats to be worn.'

'Not that surcoats are much use in this climate,' Llewellyn grumbled. 'Not enough sun here to raise one blinking drop of honest sweat.'

Philip chuckled. He had been waiting for this chance. 'What you want, Llewellyn,' he said, 'is the kind of sun that grills a hunk of meat to a turn in a few minutes.'

Llewellyn's mouth opened, and then his brown face split in a grin of delight. 'Ah, you were listening, my lord,' he said. 'I used to tell you stories like that when you were a boy.'

'Yes, I remember, Llewellyn.' Philip smiled affectionately at him, remembering vividly a small boy perched in his favourite seat, high up in the watch tower of Blanche Garde, above the great gatehouse. The valley and the winding stream were spread out far below, and on a clear day you could see the blue streak of the sea at Ascalon, and the white speck of the castle of Montgizard, far to the north. He and Joscelin used to signal to each other.

Philip sighed. It was still painful to think about Joscelin. 'Well, look after Richard tonight,' he said, 'and see that he doesn't get into any trouble.'

They went back to the ladder-climbing practice. Philip was just in time to see young Richard ten feet up in the air, and climbing briskly.

'Richard!' he bellowed.

The boy stopped, and looked down. 'Yes, my lord?' he piped.

'What are you trying to do?' Philip demanded. 'Break your neck?'

'But I must learn how to climb a scaling-ladder, my lord,' Richard said in tones of great injury. 'I might have to climb the walls of Jerusalem when I go on Crusade. Llewellyn tells me they're the highest in the world.'

'Llewellyn has told you too much,' Philip said crossly. 'Now, come down immediately.'

Richard climbed down slowly and reluctantly. 'But can't I practise for tonight?' he asked.

'Tonight?'

'Yes, my lord. I'm your squire, so I must come with you.'

'You're my page, not my squire.' Philip ruffled the boy's red hair. 'Now, listen, Richard. You stay in Kidwelly tonight. If you don't, then you go home to Cardiff the next day. And you'll need a litter, because you'll be too sore to ride a horse by the time I have finished with you!'

Richard studied the stern face above him. But he did not see the faint twitch at the corner of Philip's mouth, so he nodded sadly.

'Yes, my lord,' he whispered, and wandered slowly away, head down and hands behind his back, the picture of abject misery.

Llewellyn had overheard the conversation. He coughed softly as the boy passed him. Richard looked up, saw Llewellyn's face crease in a swift wink, and stared in amazement and growing hope for a second. He grinned, and broke into a brisk trot, his small figure eventually disappearing through the gatehouse at high speed. Two minutes later he was trying on the tiny hauberk that his father had had cut down for him.

Satisfied at last with the practice, Philip ordered the ladders to be taken down. He found Sir Geoffrey by his side.

'Hopeless, my boy, hopeless,' Sir Geoffrey shook his head sadly. 'Still, you may have some luck. The main thing is to have a good meal before we start. Can't fight on an empty stomach, you know.'

The storming party assembled by torchlight in the inner ward of the castle. Philip had inspected his men earlier, and had carefully explained the plan to them, for his experience had taught him that men fought better when they knew what was in their commander's mind. So he did not bother to ride down the line now, and never saw the small figure on horse-back at the rear of the column.

Sir Geoffrey acted as guide. He might have had his doubts about the success of the attack, and he said so frequently during the march, but he led them without a fault or a check across the ford and to a wood about half a mile from the walls of Llanstephan. While the horses were being tethered and the ladders lashed together, Philip had a last word with Sir Geoffrey. The diversion in front of the gatehouse was not to start until sounds of fighting were heard from the west walls; after that, the more noise the Kidwelly party made, the better.

Sir Geoffrey rode away to take up his position, and Philip went forward cautiously to the front edge of the wood. The night was still very dark, and there was no sign of the moon. Black clouds were driving across the sky from the sea, and the tide must have been full in, for Philip heard the steady roar of the waves breaking on the cliffs beyond the castle.

He knelt down, and picked out the dark bulk of the walls against the lighter grey of the skyline. But there was no torch burning on the walls. Too early, Philip thought. But he could not wait for Gerwyn.

'Gilbert, Peter!' he called softly. 'Ladder parties ready? Right! Helms on.'

Inside the clumsy helm the night seemed darker still. Not for the first time, Philip thought irritably as he wrestled with the ponderous piece of metal, that it was high time someone designed a better type of helm than this.

Then he raised his hand, and stepped forward. To right and left he saw the ladder-carrying parties move slowly over the uneven turf. A faint jingle of mail was all that he heard, and the sound of the waves would drown that. The chief danger was not that of being heard, but of being seen.

'The torch, the torch!' a voice muttered behind him.

A spark of light flickered on the walls. Then the unsteady glow settled down into a reddish glare, proof that Gerwyn was keeping his word.

Twenty yards to go, Philip thought. Still the walls were silent. Surely the sentries had seen them? Or were Gerwyn and his friends distracting their attention?

Ten more yards, and the black walls loomed over his

head. They were frighteningly high in the darkness. Would the ladders be long enough?

A loud shout rang out from the walls, then another. The sentries had seen them at last. Philip rushed to the ditch.

'Ladders forward!' he bellowed. There was no point in silence now.

Gerwyn was right. The walls of the ditch had fallen in at that spot, and the ladder men scrambled down without any difficulty to the bottom. Philip saw the first slender ladder swing up into the air, pause, then bump against the wall.

With a shout of triumph he leapt for the bottom rungs. From above he heard a wild shriek, and instinctively he glanced upwards. A shapeless black bundle was hurtling down towards him. He jumped aside. With a thud a man's body smashed into the ground by his side.

Philip bent down. But there was no white armband around the man's elbow, the distinguishing sign the attackers and Gerwyn's friends had agreed to wear.

Philip heaved himself up the narrow rungs. The ladder swayed and bumped. Grimly Philip climbed upwards into the darkness. But it was slow work. His shield was pulling him to the left with its weight, and then he felt the ladder lift off the wall and begin to topple to that side.

Desperately he flung his weight to the right. For an agonizing second he swung to and fro like a pendulum, while the cold sweat poured down his face under the helm.

At last the ladder came to rest, and up he went again. A hand touched his shoulder, and a familiar voice shouted by the side of his helm.

'Up, my lord! Give me your hand.' It was Gerwyn.

Philip swung his leg over the parapet, Gerwyn heaved, and he sprawled in a heap on the battlement walk, panting loudly. Not for the richest fief in England, or the ransom of Saladin himself, he vowed, would he ever climb a scaling-ladder again.

He sprang to his feet and ripped out his sword. 'The stairs, Gerwyn?' he shouted.

'To the right, my lord.'

Philip raced along the narrow walk. Below him the great castle was being aroused into clamorous life. Trumpets were sounding and torches waving, while steel-shod feet tramped hurriedly over the stone courtyard in response to shouted orders.

He reached the stairs just in time. Three men were pounding upwards, heads down in their haste. Philip hacked down savagely at the first helmet. The man shouted, swayed to the left, and vanished into the darkness, for there was no side-rail.

The second fellow paused, staring up in horror at the sudden apparition in hauberk and helm that had appeared on the wall. The pause was fatal. Philip darted down two steps, and lunged for the throat. The wretched man wore no hauberk, and the hard driven point slid through his leather coat. With a screech of terror he collapsed, his limp body spread-eagled on the stairs, his head and shoulders dangling over the edge.

The third man-at-arms did not wait. He turned and clattered back down the stairs to the safety of the ward. Philip laughed exultantly. The stairs were blocked for the moment, and he could turn to see what was happening elsewhere.

He saw Gilbert's lanky figure, one long arm swinging up in the air, and bringing a sword down on an unseen enemy. Philip laughed again. The second set of stairs was blocked. Then he heard Peter's excited yelps farther to the left, and the deep tones of Gurth's old Saxon war cry: 'Out! Out!' All four stairs were guarded.

Sir Geoffrey heard the clamour from the walls. He charged out from the shelter of the wood, his men spreading out in long lines behind him. They waved torches and blew noisily on trumpets, while Sir Geoffrey bellowed orders to non-existent troops, and rode from one flank to the other.

Philip sent the next man up to guard his set of stairs. He longed to rush into the fight, but he knew that he must keep his head and blend the confused struggle into one controlled attack on the ward and the keep.

A small figure rolled over the parapet and fell at his feet. It was Richard de Clare.

'What are you doing here, you young fool!' Philip demanded furiously. Then he started to laugh.

'Ware right, ware right, my lord!' Gerwyn shouted.

Philip flung up his shield. He heard the twang of a bow and the hiss of the shaft. With his sword hand he crushed Richard to the ground. An arrow struck his shield with a loud *clock*, and another shaft screeched over his head.

'All right, my lord, I see them,' said a calm voice from behind.

Two deep twangs rang out, the note of the cross-bow. From the distance came a loud shout, and then a scream as an archer toppled down to the ward below.

Philip jumped up again. 'Jean, Gilles,' he ordered. 'Make your way along the wall. Watch the keep, and shoot down anyone on the mound as I told you this afternoon.'

The well trained men clattered along the wall, rewinding their bows as they went. 'Stay there, Richard!' Philip said, and leant over the wall, peering down into the ditch. The last man must be on the ladders, for he could see no one at the foot of the walls. Llewellyn scrambled over the parapet and joined him.

'All up, my lord,' he said.

'Good! Tell Sir Gilbert, Sir Peter and Gurth that when they hear your trumpet, they are to cut their way down the stairs to the ward. Sir Peter with the Kidwelly men will make for the gatehouse, and the others are to form up at the bottom with me, and charge for the keep. Come back here when you have told them.'

Llewellyn ran away instantly. Philip returned to his original stairs. Gerwyn reported that no one had tried to climb them. They crouched down, for arrows were whistling up from below. Philip held up his shield; Richard was lying just behind him with a tiny shield in front of his face.

'I'm not afraid!' he yelled excitedly, and ducked hastily as another arrow screamed over their heads.

Philip grinned at the boy. He was considering the position coolly. He had won the first round of the fight, and there was a temporary lull. But the crisis was approaching. He had control of the walls; de Braose was rallying his forces for a counter attack. The battle would be won or lost in the next few minutes, and whoever struck first would win.

'All ready!' Llewellyn's hoarse voice said.

'Then sound,' Philip said calmly.

Llewellyn raised the short horn that dangled from his neck. As the two blasts rang out Philip leapt down the stairs. He pushed the dead archer aside, and pelted down to the bottom.

A group of men were stationed there. Two were archers, and one of them raised his bow and drew the string back as he saw Philip. But they were too slow. Philip jumped the last four steps, and landed with a crash in the centre of the startled men. The archer went down with a thrust through his shoulder, and another doubled up with a howl as Llewellyn stabbed him in the chest. Then Gerwyn had joined them, and the Llanstephan men broke and ran.

The stairs were clear now. Gilbert had broken through, and the gigantic Gurth, wielding an axe, had just fought his way to the bottom of his flight of stairs. Farther along, Peter was already leading the better armed Kidwelly men towards the gatehouse.

Philip turned. The keep was the next objective. He raised his sword, and shouted to his men.

'To me, to me!' His clear voice rang out above the din.

In a flash the well trained men formed up behind in his favourite wedge formation. Facing them was a thin line of defenders.

Philip raised his sword as a signal to the cross-bows. 'Fire!'

At point-blank range a volley of bolts thudded into the enemy, and then Philip and Gilbert charged. But the Llanstephan men had had enough. They turned, and bolted frantically for the shelter of the keep.

A flight of shallow steps wound up the green mound to the great doors at the top. Men emerging from the keep met the panic stricken rush from below. The cross-bows posted by Philip on the walls poured in a steady and accurate fire, and a final volley came from the ward.

What should have been an orderly retreat inside the keep was transformed into a hopelessly jammed mass of shouting and struggling men. And into this mêlée Philip rushed with his experienced Crusaders.

There could have been only one result. But the fighting came to an abrupt end, and all heads turned as a tremendous hubbub broke out in the ward below.

From the dark tunnel of the gatehouse Sir Geoffrey

shot into view, crouching low in his saddle, and urging his horse to a gallop as he streaked across the courtyard for the foot of the mound.

Behind him and to his right was Peter with the fully armed men-at-arms from Kidwelly. Then the villeins, nearly a hundred of them, poured through the archway, and flooded over the whole of the inner ward, waving torches and weapons, and yelling like fiends. They reached the mound, and soon the slopes were covered with climbing figures. There was no more resistance. The Llanstephan men were herded inside the hall, pushed against the walls, and dropped their weapons.

Philip pulled off his helm and wiped his streaming face. Richard wriggled through the press and proudly took the heavy helm from him.

'There he is!' Sir Geoffrey exclaimed.

On the dais at the far end of the hall stood a solitary figure in hauberk, surcoat, and mail coif, shield on shoulder, and a naked sword in the right hand. A helm lay on the long table behind.

Followed by the three knights Philip walked slowly towards the dais, threading his way through the overturned tables and benches.

Chapter Nineteen

THE FIGHT ON THE DAIS

THE scene was a strange and picturesque one. A pile of burning logs in the fireplace threw out an angry glare on the rush-covered floor and flickered redly on the grey stone of the walls. The torches in their brackets, and those in the upheld hands of the Kidwelly men lit up the long hall from end to end, the tapestries on the dais, and the dark beams of the roof, catching shifting gleams from the steel of hauberk or helmet, and falling softly on the mass of white faces turned eagerly to watch the final act of the drama.

As Philip reached the foot of the dais he heard a series of loud clicks from behind. He raised his sword quickly.

'Don't shoot!' he cried, and the cross-bowmen reluctantly lowered their weapons.

'You had best surrender, de Braose,' he said to the tall
figure silhouetted against the candlelight of the high table.
'The castle is mine.'

'And if I do, your men will shoot me down?'

'No. You can leave unharmed. I give you my word.'

De Braose laughed shortly, and raised his sword. 'Afraid
to fight it out?' he asked.

'No,' Philip said, and leapt for the dais.

A roar went up from the hall. De Braose stepped
forward and slashed at the flying figure. Philip landed with
a clash of mail, and half on his knees, for the dais was three
feet or more above the floor level of the hall.

He threw up his shield to cover his head, and took the
blow there. But even though he braced himself for the
shock, the force of the blow made him stumble. He thrust
out with his sword. There was little strength in the lunge,
but it caught the centre of de Braose's shield, and gave
Philip a moment in which to recover.

Then he had jumped clear, and was on his feet. He
kicked aside a stool, and went for his man.

This would be a grim affair, as everyone in the hall realized. Neither man wore a helm. The mail coif over their
heads might ward off a glancing blow, but the first full
stroke flat on the skull would end the fight.

De Braose gave ground in face of Philip's furious attack.
But he was a good swordsman, and managed to parry the

stream of slashes and cuts with his shield or sword. And he had courage, too, for he rallied, and rushed in with a counterattack.

Philip stopped that with his favourite lunge. De Braose did not expect the swift point that darted at his throat. He threw his head back instinctively, shuffled his feet, and was off balance.

Philip leapt forward like a panther. A sweeping cut from right to left caught de Braose on the shield. He swayed, and then another slash from the other side rocked him towards the table. He bounced against the edge, and ducked as Philip hacked down viciously at him. The two swords screeched wickedly, but de Braose had saved his skull. Once more he backed away, and Philip followed up swiftly.

His foot slithered in the greasy rushes. He skidded forward, and lurched against the table, throwing out his right hand to keep his balance.

De Braose saw his chance. He cut at the top of Philip's exposed head. But his aim was hasty and inaccurate, and he was a fraction of a second too slow. Philip jumped back to clear the sweep of the sword. The back of his leg caught against the low stool. He swayed for a moment, and fell flat on his back. As he went, the edge of the table caught his wrist, and his sword dropped from his hand.

With a triumphant bellow De Braose swung his sword high in the air, poised himself for the kill, and then struck.

Philip saw the sword flashing down. He rolled sideways. A blow like that from a sledge hammer crashed on to his left shoulder. Desperately his fingers groped for his sword as he tried to struggle to his feet. He dared not take his eyes from de Braose. Then he felt the stool. With a flick of his wrist he sent it whizzing at de Braose. The man was poised for the final blow. Against all his instincts, his head jerked back automatically as the heavy little stool flew straight at his face. It missed him, but that did not matter.

Philip, on one knee, looked down, saw his sword, grabbed it, and was on his feet. His shoulder was numb, but he could still hold up his shield, and without a pause he rushed at de Braose.

Another deafening roar filled the hall. Gilbert was clutching young Richard's arm like a vice, and though there would be a large bruise there the next day, neither noticed it now as they watched the grim fight above their heads. Llan-stephan and Kidwelly men intermingled in a jostling mob as they pushed forward for a better view. Others jumped on to the tables, and held their torches high in the air.

De Braose backed away. He had used almost the last of his energy in that furious burst, and he had not Philip's superb fitness. He warded off two dangerous cuts at his head, but his guard was slower.

Philip felt that the fight was his now. Coolly he altered his aim, and brought his sword round in a wide, back-handed sweep that caught de Braose on the side of his head. As his man rocked to the left, Philip swung straight down for the top of the head. Wearily de Braose raised his sword to parry that deadly stroke. But his arm was aching with fatigue, and there was little strength left in his wrist. His sword was beaten down, and as his nerveless fingers opened, the heavy blade dropped to the floor. Philip laughed exultantly. There was no thought of mercy in his mind. For this duel could have but one ending, and he sprang forward to finish it. De Braose flung his shield away, and backed towards the table. That last flurry had brought them both to the corner of the dais, and de Braose's hands touched the huge chair that stood at the end of the high table.

Exhausted as he was, fear and desperation gave him sufficient strength to heave the clumsy piece of furniture up in the air with both hands. Gasping and swaying, he brought it down like a gigantic flail, the effort forcing the air from his lungs with a harsh grunt.

Philip tried to jump clear. But he had neither the time nor the room to move. Instead, he threw up sword and shield, and braced himself for the frightful impact. His sword was beaten from his hands, and the shield driven down with a crash on to his head. A leg of the chair caught his left shoulder, aching still from the previous blow.

An agonizing stab of pain shot through his shoulder and down his arm. For a moment a mist floated in front of his eyes, and the shouts of the eagerly watching spectators seemed to come from a great distance.

De Braose tried to lift the chair again, but he was too exhausted. Philip shook his head and slipped the heavy shield from his numbed arm. He saw de Braose pull out a knife from his belt, and come towards him once more.

Philip fumbled at the red sheath on his belt. He ripped out the knife that Jusuf had given him long ago, and the two men met in a last clash, each attempting to seize the other's wrist, and stabbing furiously at neck and chest. But the hauberks were too strong for the thin blades, and after a few seconds' struggle, they stepped apart, breathing heavily and stumbling unsteadily on their feet.

Philip lurched forward again and smashed his mailed fist into the other's face. He heard a cry of pain, and saw the blood gush from de Braose's nose. The effort had sent a warm spasm of pain through his injured shoulder, but clenching his teeth, Philip struck out again. The steel rings cut through the soft skin of the eyelids, and de Braose fell back against the table, dazed and half blinded by the flow of blood.

Philip made his final effort. He pounced on his man, and this time he caught the hand with the knife. Constant sword practice had given his wrists the strength of a vice, and as he wrenched and twisted, the knife fell from de Braose's hand.

The crowd had fallen silent during that last hand-to-hand struggle, and in the quiet they could all hear the tinkle as the knife hit the polished surface of the table, and bounced on a platter. Philip thrust de Braose down, arching his back over the table, and stabbed down savagely, grunting with each furious blow, hacking and ripping at the hauberk around the throat. And then he saw a gap, and the white of the bare skin. He paused, and struck for the last time.

De Braose lurched to one side, his body resting for a

brief second on the table, and then he slumped to the ground. Philip swayed on his feet as he stared down. Then he staggered away, bumped against the great chair, and collapsed into it, resting his head on his hands, breathing loudly like a man in the last stages of exhaustion.

'All right, Philip?' a quiet voice asked. Gilbert bent over him anxiously, and gently pulled away the hands. They were covered with blood. 'You're wounded,' he said.

Philip held out his hands, flexing the fingers wearily. 'No, that's de Braose's,' he muttered, and shuddered as Gilbert picked up a napkin from the table, and wiped the steel mittens.

'A drink, Gilbert,' Philip whispered, 'my throat is parched.'

'Here, my lord,' piped a treble voice, and little Richard held out a filled goblet.

Philip gulped down the heavy wine. Some strength seemed to flow back into his aching body, and he grinned at the boy.

'I owe you a good thrashing for disobeying me, young Richard.'

Richard grinned back impudently, the torchlight shining like dark gold on his hair. 'I wouldn't have missed that fight for three whippings, my lord,' he said.

Philip laughed, and felt the better for it. He saw Sir Geoffrey pick up a hunk of cold meat from the table, and gnaw at it greedily. He had eaten nothing for hours. The knight saw Philip watching him, and smiled broadly; the first sign of real pleasure that Philip had ever seen on that melancholy face. Sir Geoffrey waved the meat at him.

'Good meat they have here, Philip,' he said, and spat out a piece of fat. 'Well, you see, we did it. I always said we would!' And after that astonishing statement, he searched among the scattered platters on the table for more food.

Peter de Chaworth was prancing about excitedly. Seizing a goblet of wine, he jumped up on to the table. He raised the cup in the air, and shouted.

'To Sir Philip!' he bellowed. 'To Sir Philip d'Aubigny of Llanstephan!'

Swords shot into the air, and a wave of deep-voiced cheers rolled down the hall. Philip stood up unsteadily. 'Yes, I am no longer Philip d'Aubigny of Blanche Garde in Outremer,' his tired brain was thinking, 'but a d'Aubigny of Llanstephan, and a Lord Marcher of Wales.'

He looked down at the sea of faces shouting at him, and the waving torches that threw their flickering light on the stone walls of his keep.

But he saw none of that.

In front of his eyes was the sun-drenched courtyard of Blanche Garde, with Sir Hugo and Joscelin and Sir Fulk waiting for him on their horses, and the white strip of the road beyond as it climbed out of the valley and marched across the yellow mountains to Jerusalem.

Philip rubbed his throbbing forehead, and stepped to the edge of the dais. There was much to be done before he could sleep that night in his castle of Llanstephan.

Historical Note

You may be interested to know how much of this story is fact, and how much fiction.

The real Philip d'Aubigny was an English Crusader of the time of Henry III; he died in Jerusalem, and his tombstone can still be seen in the Church of the Holy Sepulchre. I have borrowed his name, and fitted his imaginary adventures into the actual events and battles of Outremer.

Many of the castles of Outremer mentioned in the story, including Blanche Garde, are still standing, though in various stages of ruin. Krak des Chevaliers has been largely restored by the French.

Raymond of Tripoli's remarks at Saffaria are historic, and so too are the incidents after the battle of Hattin, including the death of Reynaud de Chatillon. Usamah Ibn-Menquidh was a real person, and his memoirs have survived, and have been translated into English.

The sect of the Assassins flourished in the East for many years and the incident of the man jumping from the castle walls is supposed to be true. Conrad of Montferrat did die suddenly, and it was thought at the time that the Assassins were responsible.

The Crusaders never recovered the lands they lost at Hattin, though there were other Crusades, and the Latin Kingdom lingered on in name for over two hundred years. Krak finally surrendered to the Turks in 1271.

Jerusalem was not entered again by Christian soldiers until seven hundred years after Hattin. A British army captured the city from the Turks at the end of the First World War, and the commander of the army, Lord Allenby, entered on foot through the Jaffa Gate. He was followed by representatives of the French Army, whose ancestors had first captured the Holy City in the First Crusade of 1099.

About the Author

Ronald Welch (Ronald Oliver Felton) was born in Glamorgan and for much of his life was a teacher of history, and Headmaster of Okehampton Grammar School. He fought in the Welch Regiment during World War Two. He published a number of historical novels for children, including *Knight Crusader* in 1954, for which he won the Carnegie Medal. Ronald Welch died in 1982.